Also by J. M. Johnston:

Fiction:

Brainchild
Something For A Rainy Season

Non-Fiction:

First-Look Books: Computers

Biting the Wall

Biting the Wall

by

J. M. Johnston

Acme Press
Westminster, Maryland

This is a work of fiction. That means that the names, characters, places and events are purely imaginary, have never existed in any shape or form whatsoever, and any resemblance to reality is nothing short of a mind-blowing coincidence.

ISBN 0-9629880-8-1

Library of Congress Catalog Card Number 91-61880

First Acme Press printing January 1992

Acme Press
1116 East Deep Run Road
Westminster, Maryland 21158

Acknowledgments

The author gratefully acknowledges invaluable input from the following:

Bob Sapora—for the Old English
Howard Orenstein—for the Psychobabble
Richard Mitchell—for permission to use material from *The Underground Grammarian*
The Federal Energy Management Agency—for a tour of a real government communications relay station

and the hapless pianist—name and whereabouts unknown— at whose recital several decades ago in Bangkok the events in Chapter 15 are proported to have taken place. (So much for the disclaimer on the previous page.)

Prolog

Wilbur Moody College is spread out over 200 shady acres on the north side of a small rural east coast town. The campus includes all the standard academic trappings: a high arched gateway at the front entrance, done up in the school colors—brown and green, symbolizing the elements most likely to be found underfoot in the pastures and barnyards which dominate the countryside; a stadium surrounded by towering floodlights, with an indecipherable scoreboard at one end, and a concession stand with a single serving line and a pair of closet-size restrooms at the other; and a steepled chapel with clock and quarter-hour chimes, at least one note of which is conspicuously missing at any given interval.

The architecture features a comfortable amalgam of old and new, the oldest being the looming masonry and stone administration building, with its massive Georgian pillars flanking the three-tiered entrance steps, and its echoey halls, with odors of musty oak and floor polish; and the newest being a glass and steel student union, nearing completion and featuring a vast solarium dining room, guaranteed to overheat in the summer, freeze in the winter and leak the year round.

In spite of the ongoing construction efforts, the enrollment at the college has remained fairly stable for most if its hundred year history. It is small enough for informality, and large enough to offer a broad liberal arts curriculum, which includes enough areas of specialization to give the school some modicum of identity. This balance is maintained by means of a flexible admissions policy, and by setting the entrance requirements just high enough to discourage the incorrigibles, but low enough to keep the coffers in the black (and some would add, to assure perpetuation of the football team).

So while the college has never acquired a reputation for academic excellence, and no alumnus has yet achieved anything approaching immortality, it provides a well-balanced education for a reasonable cost. There are those who argue that the potential exists for Greater Things, but the philosophy of its current president, Horace Croup—a conservative administrator and self-proclaimed "good ol' country boy"—is that "if it ain't broke, don't let's fix it."

The one facility at Wilbur Moody which most assuredly has never needed fixing is the Computer Center. The tireless efforts of its small but capable crew had succeeded in getting nearly all faculty members to integrate the computer into their classroom or research, no matter how remote the subject matter. Thus:

A religion professor might be seen smiling beatifically as key New Testament words are compiled into concordance form;

An English Lit student, using a text analysis software package, proves conclusively that the works of Christopher Marlowe were actually penned by William Shakespeare;

An art professor squints as he diligently analyzes each brushstroke of a dramatic Turner landscape with a computerized digital scanner in search of the artist's elusive signature;

ROTC students, using war game simulation, cheer as they

devastate the enemy with enough firepower to destroy the world a dozen times over.

The administration's initial skepticism had eventually given way to reluctant approval. "Keeps 'em off the streets," President Croup was quoted as saying—although it was never clear whether he was referring to students or faculty.

Naturally, with all this demand, the computer resources had quickly reached saturation level, and the need for a new machine with expanded capabilities became apparent. There was, predictably, immediate resistance from the Administration, which always viewed any change in the status quo as a potential source of problems.

The computer users had persisted, however, and the resistance was short-lived. After all, the need was undeniable, the advantages considerable, and the cost bearable.

And since the replacement computer would simply be a bigger, faster and more powerful version of the old one, what possible problems could there be?

Wilbur Moody College was about to find out.

1

Van Ruedge thrust the flat prongs of the cork puller down into the neck of the chilled green bottle, twisted and drew the cork up and out. He extended the bottle across the rusty metal lawn table, cluttered with pruning shears, leather gloves and a pile of grapevine cuttings, and filled Llew's glass to the halfway point. "Last year's Riesling. The one you helped me bottle this winter."

Llew tilted the glass up at the hazy February sun, swirled its light gold contents gently, then brought the rim up under his nose. "Mmm. Peaches. . . and apples." He sipped the wine, holding it in his mouth while sucking in some air through his pursed lips. Then he swallowed it, and smiled. "Very pleasant."

Van shook his head, a tolerent grin on his face. "Never tell a winemaker that his wine is 'pleasant'. It's like telling an artist his painting is 'interesting'."

Llew thought a minute. "Okay. . . how's this: the wine is soft and mellow, but shows good acid. A hint of residual sugar enhances the fruit without masking the complexity. Full of promise."

"Better," Van nodded approval. "Except for the part about 'promise'. Could mean it's not very good right now."

"But it is," Llew insisted, and took another sip. "And I'll even let you refill my glass when I finish this one."

"You can take the rest of the bottle with you," Van said, pouring some for himself. "Lots more where this came from."

A chilly breeze ruffled the coarse white hair which curled over Van Ruedge's ears and down the back of his neck. His face was lean and his hands roughened by years of winter pruning. A former psychology professor at Wilbur Moody College, he had abandoned the comfortable groves of academia several years ago when the demands of his expanding vineyard had finally overwhelmed all other commitments and interests. What had begun as a weekend hobby with a few experimental vines had blossomed into a small scale commercial enterprise with nearly thirty acres of a dozen grape varieties, a barn full of tractors and spray equipment, and a winery crowded with crushers, destemmers, presses and rows of giant oak casks.

Van tugged his woolen scarf up from beneath the frayed collar of his denim jacket. "So how are things in my old stomping grounds?" he asked.

"A little unpredictable at the moment," Llew replied, leaning back in the webbed lawn chair and gazing out over the acres of bare grapevines which latticed the gently sloping hillside. "You know there's a new Vice-President for Business and Financial Affairs. . ."

"I heard. Hated to see old Wexler retire, but he was getting along in years."

"I miss him already," Llew sighed, "in more ways than one. This new guy—Hess, his name is—is something of an enigma. So far he's maintained a low profile, but there's an uneasy feeling around campus that he's about to make some sweeping changes—budgets will be slashed, funds redirected, some heads will probably roll."

Van nodded. "That always happens when somebody new comes on board. Once they feel confident enough, they start flexing their muscles."

"Well, it's a little unnerving. As Computer Services Director, I'm supposed to answer directly to him. But we've had almost no communication since he's been here. And I'm expecting delivery on our new computer system in a couple of weeks."

"You don't expect any problems there, do you?"

"I don't know what to expect," Llew admitted, rolling the glass gently between the palms of his hands. "That's what worries me. Everything was all set up before Hess arrived, but I've had no confirmation from him one way or the other. We need that computer—the old one has been running at saturation level for almost a year now, and my staff has worked minor miracles to keep our heads above water. But the users are starting to get impatient."

Van chuckled. "It's your own fault, Llew. Ever since you took that job, you've managed to get every department on campus itching to use the computer. No wonder your system is overloaded. How do you manage to do all that with a staff of. . .what is it, still three?"

"Plus myself. Well, we don't do everything ourselves. I try to get people in each department involved by running regular faculty training courses. So now they do most of their own programming, and some of them even teach their own programming courses. In my shop, Nina maintains the system, and Rama handles the operations. Winklejohn is my only support programmer, and he definitely is overworked. I've submitted a request for another body to help him, but it'll cost money, and Hess hasn't responded to that either."

Van refilled the glasses. "Will there be any problem transferring everybody's files over to the new computer?"

"Shouldn't be. It's just a bigger and faster version of the old computer, so all the software should run with almost no changes. Besides, Nina's a sharp systems programmer, and she's been boning up on all the new features. We'll start moving files as soon as it's up and running—campus users first, then outside users, including you."

"Good. I'm adding two more acres of Chardonnay this spring, so I'll need to expand my vineyard files a bit."

"I don't see any problem," Llew said, sipping from his glass. "You'll be notified when we're set up, and you can start entering the stuff you need from your terminal here."

Van picked up one of the grapevine cuttings and sliced into a dormant bud with a razor, then examined it with a pocket magnifier. "Do you think you'll have to raise your rates for outside users with the new system?"

"Not if I can help it. Again, a lot depends on what Hess has in mind. He's got the last word where funds are concerned."

"Well, I wouldn't worry. Everybody I've talked to thinks the Computer Center is the only department on campus that's really indispensible."

Llew grinned. "Depends on who you talk to. Most of the users seem happy enough. But then there are people like Harry Gross—"

Van snorted, reaching for another cutting. "Harry Gross is an ass."

"But he carries a lot of weight. He runs the Information Services Department, and that includes the Registrar's Office, Publicity, Development, Alumni. . . And if he had his way, *my* department would be a part of his little empire."

Van sliced a piece of Jarlsburg from a cheese plate on the table. "And then of course there's Stella Lukerella. . ."

Llew nodded. "Full professor now, and feistier than ever."

"It was when she first joined the Psychology Department that I began thinking seriously about leaving."

Llew rested his chin on a fist. "Are you sorry you did? I mean, do you ever wish you were back in the classroom, cultivating minds instead of vines?"

Van laughed and shook his head. "Everything you've been telling me makes me glad the only person I have to answer to is myself."

"Plus a lot of customers who buy your wine."

Van shrugged. "Nobody's complained so far."

Llew found that easy to understand. Van was good at everything he did, and his wines were no exception. Otherwise he would have been a fool to abandon a successful academic career to risk something as unpredictable as commercial winemaking—especially in the east, where the industry was still in its infancy.

But every time Llew visited Van in his vineyard to help him prune, harvest, crush or bottle, he felt some measure of the satisfaction he knew had prompted Van's decision. Especially when it came time to sample the goods. . .

"More?" Van indicated the half-empty bottle.

Llew shook his head reluctantly and got up from the chair. "Gotta get back. I just wanted to drop off those listings. I will, however, accept your offer to take the rest of the bottle."

Van removed the cork from the puller and plugged it back into the bottle neck. "Coming to the wine club meeting on Sunday?"

"I plan to. Who's doing the program?"

Van grimaced. "Bosley. Which means we'll probably be tasting some cheap imports from Albania or someplace. I may sit this one out."

"Spoken like a true wine snob." Llew patted Van on the shoulder. "Thanks again for the wine."

Van gathered the glasses from the table. "Careful going back. There's a new cop just inside the county line who tools around in unmarked vehicles."

"'Vehicles'?"

"Yeah. One day he's driving a jeep, the next day a sports car. Yesterday he was in a station wagon."

"Is that legal?"

"Must be—he's the law. I hear he's doing quite a business."

"I'll be careful. See you."

Cushlamochree—it's later than I thought, Llew realized as he drove back toward the college. And I've still got a half dozen people to see on campus. Wonder if I should give Hess another try. He hasn't returned any of my calls all week.

Never had that problem with Wexler. He and I got along great. And he was always on top of everything, knew that school like the proverbial back of his hand. Ought to—he was there nearly forty years before he retired.

And whose idea was it to replace him with this Hess character? President Croup? Now there's someone who really needs to be retired. Makes a lot of speeches, shakes a lot of hands, promises a lot of improvements, drinks a lot of bourbon, forgets a lot of promises. . .

There had to have been a search committee for the new V.P. Croup would have been on it, of course. And Harry Gross, who would have opted for anyone he thought might give me a hard time. Hoping I'll quit so he can swoop down from his limb and sink his talons into the administrative computer functions. Never understand how a terrific girl like Kay ever got involved with him.

Speaking of whom. . .I promised I'd drop over to her shop too this afternoon. Better hustle.

Llew stepped on the gas and turned the radio up a bit. The campus station was playing country and western so he moved the dial to the local PBS station and leaned back to the strains of a Mozart piano concerto.

Another radio, this one in the cab of a battered pickup truck parked alongside the road just ahead of Llew, remained fixed on country and western. The occupant of the cab tapped his thick stubby fingers on the back of the seat in time to the music as smoke from the cigaret dangling from his lower lip wafted lazily out the open window. The bill of a John Deere cap was pulled down over a pair of reflective sunglasses, through which two bloodshot eyes were fixed on the rear view mirror.

As Llew raced by, a wide grin spread slowly between the heavy jowls, and a sound like "Ih, ih" issued from behind the irregular rows of teeth. A pudgy hand with dirty fingernails removed the cap and replaced it with a county police hat which had concealed the flasher light on the dashboard. The hand then reached for the ignition key, and seconds later the truck was gaining on Llew's speeding Toyota.

A rapid flickering in his own rear view mirror caught Llew's attention, and he looked up to see the pickup bearing down on him with surprising speed. A truck? With a flasher? County road department, perhaps? Or a service vehicle? But they have yellow flashers, don't they? This one was red.

He slowed down, and so did the truck. Then he saw the patrolman's hat and a bulky arm with unbuttoned sleeves waving him over, and he remembered Van's warning.

I don't believe this, Llew thought, but flipped the turn signal and pulled off the road. When the car came to a stop, he retrieved the registration card from the glove compartment, got out of the car and walked back toward the truck.

The officer inside was writing in a notepad held against the steering wheel. Llew held up his registration card and drivers license. "Guess you'll need these?"

The man ignored him and continued to write in a slow, laboriously way. Llew began to feel a little awkward. Finally the officer said, without looking up, "Need your license and registration."

"They're right here," Llew told him.

The man looked up at him, and Llew could see a pair of puffy red eyes glowering at him above the rims of the sunglasses. He took the cards, studied them for a minute, then read, "Llew-el-lyn Mc-Quil-ly."

"McQuilla."

The man grunted, "Ih, ih," and copied some things down in his notepad. Llew shifted his weight from one foot to another. Finally, the officer looked again at the cards.

"Well, Mr Loo Ellen Mac Willy, you was doin' 65 in a 45 milenower zone."

"Yessir."

"You knowed that, eh?"

"Uh . . . I guess I wasn't paying attention. Won't happen again."

"Hope not," tearing off the speeding ticket and handing it to Llew. "This'll help ya remember. Them points add up fast."

"Yessir."

"Ih, ih."

Llew glanced at the ticket. Forty dollars. So much for getting a tune-up on my car this month, he thought.

The cop was looking at Llew's car, squinting. "What's at say?"

"Pardon?"

"Bumper sticker, on the back of your car."

"Oh. '*L'eau est pollute'—Buvez le vin.*' It's French. It means 'The water is polluted—drink wine'."

"How come it's in French?"

"Because I bought it in France."

"The car?"

"The bumper sticker."

The man thought about this for a minute, then handed Llew back his license and registration. "I'm a beer man myself. Ih, ih."

Llew pocketed the papers and walked back to his car. I really needed this, he thought, shifting the gears and easing back out onto the highway. In his rear view mirror he saw the truck make a U-turn and head back the other way.

2

The Wilbur Moody College Computer Center was situated, appropriately enough, in the exact center of the campus grounds, and occupied the entire basement of Chapman Hall, an ancient stone-facade structure with wide halls, heavy doors and high arched windows. Llew loved the place—it had character, it was convenient to everyone on campus, and there was plenty of room for expansion. Every so often, someone would suggest that a place with better climate control and improved wiring might be more in keeping with modern technology, but such notions were inevitably dismissed.

When Llew arrived back on campus the students were just changing classes. It was still early in the semester, and there was a care-free quality in their behavior that would eventually precipitate into tension at mid-term, and to downright panic as final exams approached a few months hence. But now they strolled in twos and threes, laughing and talking, seemingly without a care in the world.

He pulled up into his usual parking space beneath a tall oak which stood next to the rear Computer Center entrance. Rama's ancient one-speed bike with its huge balloon tires was chained, as usual, to the tree and secured with the biggest padlock Llew had ever seen. The lock was not completely closed, Rama having lost the key years ago, but from a distance nobody could tell anyway.

Llew's systems programmer, Arganina Vargenteen, was outside with Calhoun, her squat sturdy bull mastiff. They made an interesting pair, as Llew had observed on many occasions—Nina short and slight, her childlike face enveloped in an unruly mass of thick black hair, her elfish body hidden among the folds of a calico muumuu and a patchy fake-fur parka—and Calhoun, all head, jaws and shoulders, tapering off to insignificance at the other end.

Nina was teaching the dog to fetch. She threw a stick out onto the lawn, and Calhoun clambered after it, his stubby bow-legs moving like rusty pistons. The inertia of his bulk propelled him past the place where the stick landed, and his legs scrabbled furiously, shredding the grass as he tried to reverse direction. He scooped up the stick, along with a jawful of dirt and grass, and thundered back to Nina.

"G-O-O-D fetch!" Nina clapped her tiny hands and removed the stick from the dog's mouth. "Good fetch the stick!" Calhoun shook his massive head to expel the mouthful of soil and planted his twitching rear end on the ground, impatient for the next toss.

"Making some progress there, I see," Llew said, joining them. "What else can he do?"

"Lots of things," Nina insisted. "Watch. Calhoun . . . sit up!"

The dog hesitated, then raised himself precariously on his absurdly small backside, his hind feet shifting in all directions as he struggled to maintain balance. "G-O-O-D sit up, Calhoun!" Nina praised, grabbing at him just as gravity was claiming him from behind.

Llew scratched the dog's head appreciatively, in return for which Calhoun slobbered copiously all over his hand. "Good dog.

Yes, good wash hand." He wiped it on his trousers as Nina threw the stick again. "I don't suppose Hess called, by any chance?" he asked her.

"No, but Harry Gross did," she replied, clapping her hands to distract Calhoun's attention from a squirrel who had scampered across his path. "Twice, in fact. He insists you return his call immediately. Something about the changes he wanted made in the admissions file."

Llew groaned. "Wish that guy would get off my back. If we didn't have to spend so much time spoon-feeding him and listening to his gripes, we might get caught up on some more important work around here. Anything else?"

Calhoun had returned with the stick, but now stubbornly refused to relinquish it to Nina. "Well, your ectoplasmic friend was here a little while ago," she said, tugging at the stick in the dog's enormous mouth.

"Dahnu? What did he want?"

"He came over to open a new account for some project or other. Although what he needs a computer for is beyond me. He could just use telepathy."

"Dahnu uses the computer a lot," Llew told her. "He was in one of the programming courses I taught last spring. Besides, everybody's got some use for computers—you were majoring in art, as I recall, when you got involved."

"A major in art is one thing—a major in metaphysics, with a minor in alchemy, is another."

"Oh come on. Did you set an account up for him?"

"Account DAH355. Password 'SPOOK'."

"*Nina—*"

"Well, I can't help it. He makes me nervous."

"Nervous? Why?"

"I don't know. Something about the way his eyes always seem to be looking at you, even when he's facing the other way. And when he walks, his feet never seem to quite touch the floor."

"I'll admit he's—"

"And he never seems to go in or out of doors—he's just suddenly *there*, or suddenly *not* there. One time I was in the room when he made a phone call, and while he was talking it occurred to me that I hadn't seen him punch any numbers."

Llew grinned. "At least give him credit for resorting to the phone to make his calls in the first place."

"Anyway, when he got his account he went back to talk to Winklejohn about some programming support." She finally managed to wrest the stick from the dog's mouth and threw it back out onto the lawn. "Fetch, Calhoun!"

Llew looked at his watch. "Okay, I'll touch bases with the rest of the crew, then I've got some people to see on campus."

He went inside the building and down the hall to the computer room where Rama Pancajanya, the Computer Center's operator and dispatcher, was mounting a stack of reels onto the tape drives. A bulky beige turban encased his head, and he was bundled, as usual, in a heavy turtleneck sweater and baggy cordouroy trousers. He complained daily about the frigid temperatures required by the computer equipment, but Llew had never seen him wear anything but thong sandals on his feet.

"Has Gus Roddencroft been by to pick up his output?" Llew asked him.

Rama nodded. "Yez—he haz gome thiz noon to fetch it."

"Good. What are all those tapes?"

"Theze ones are brought by that Groze berson. He wishes me to run liztings for him."

"Harry Gross? I might have known."

Rama made a sour face. "I myzelf am not liking that one. Firzt he is telling me one thing, then another. I thing he iz the incomblete berson."

"Incomplete?"

"How you zay? He iz not all there."

"I agree with that. Besides, he's not supposed to be telling you to do anything except through me. Well, I've got to call him anyway . . ."

Llew returned to his office, picked up the phone and punched four digits. A moment later, Ginnie Schwartz, Harry's overworked and harrassed secretary, answered. "Information Services Department."

"Gross," Llew said.

"Yes he is," Ginnie sighed. "Just a second, Llew."

Llew waited as Ginnie put him on hold. Then a gruff voice said, "Gross."

"Harry? Llew here. Nina told me you called."

"Twice."

"No, she only told me once. What's up?"

"I meant—oh, never mind. Listen, those admission forms you turkeys printed up are a *mess.*"

Llew shut his eyes. Patience, he told himself. "What's wrong now, Harry?"

"What *isn't* wrong! The address fields aren't long enough for foreign students, the fields for fee payment are too long, and you've got some other columns labelled 'FLU'—what the hell does that mean? This isn't a medical form."

"Relax, Harry. FLU means 'For Later Use'. Winklejohn put those in so you wouldn't have to redesign the whole form the next time you needed to expand. And he made the field sizes variable—we can add columns or remove them. Besides, he was working from the specs you gave us. I've got them right here in front of me."

"Oh yeah? Well, does it say 30 columns for address?"

Llew counted. "Yep."

There was silence on the other end of the line. Then the sound of a throat clearing. "Okay. That dumb secretary of mine screwed up again. She gave you the wrong versions. I made some changes and told that bitch to throw away the old ones."

Llew seriously doubted that. "All right, Harry. Just send over whatever changes you want and I'll get Winklejohn back on it."

"I'm gonna fire her ass one of these days if she don't shape up."

Llew doubted that too. It was probably Ginnie's shape that prompted Harry to hire her in the first place. "You do that, Harry. And listen, one more thing. Rama said you gave him some stuff to do. In the future, anything you need done, give to me. I have to schedule his time."

"Suits me. I can't understand a word that Gunga Din says anyhow."

Llew hung up just as Winklejohn's massive frame imposed itself in the doorway. "That was Captain Sunshine," Llew told him, "calling to compliment you on your fine work on his admissions forms."

Winklejohn's metal crutches seemed to bend under the weight of his bulk as he maneuvered it over to a swivel chair next to the desk. "I suspected as much. Why you persist in indulging the iniquitous whims of that cretin is beyond my comprehension." He reached down to unlock the braces which encased each leg.

"Well, it's not as if I had much choice. Like it or not, we're mainly a service shop here."

Holding the crutches together for support, Winklejohn lowered himself into the chair, which squealed in protest. He leaned the crutches against the wall and removed a pipe and tobacco pouch from his jacket pocket. "I suppose I could muster some modicum of tolerance for the man if he didn't monopolize all my programming time. Several other tasks of greater exigency have been lingering in my in-basket for too long."

He placed the stem of the pipe between his teeth and prodded his pockets for matches. The milky color and long skinny stem of the Meerschaum contrasted starkly with the wide expanse of his coal-black face framed by a mass of dark bushy hair. Twin patches of white, one above each ear, made it look like he had been pelted by snowballs from both sides.

Llew opened the top drawer of his desk, found a book of matches and handed them to Winklejohn. "Nina says Dahnu was by to see you. What's he up to?"

Winklejohn leaned his head back and released a thin stream of smoke which curled into itself, looking for all the world like a tiny mushroom cloud. "His usual pursuit of Nirvana, I presume. This time he wants to use the computer to help him detect something called Zeta waves."

"What the hell are Zeta waves?"

"It's not clear, actually. He likens them to the Alpha waves produced by the brain when you sleep, or the Beta waves when you concentrate." He puffed his pipe and blinked his eyes slowly. "Dahnu believes the Zeta waves are potentially more powerful, but far more difficult to detect. So in typical augurous fashion he is fabricating a computer program to simulate a bio-feedback system."

"Why doesn't he just use one of those EEG devices? They've got several over in the Psychology department."

Winklejohn punched down the smoldering tobacco in his pipe and relit it. "Apparently because they don't measure the correct frequencies. Although just which frequencies are associated with Zeta waves is less than immediately obvious."

Llew sighed. "Okay. But whatever help you give him will have to be on your own time. We've got our hands full as it is. Which reminds me—how's the program for Professor Bede coming along?"

"The alliteration analysis of Beowulf? The output from the first part is ready, and I expect—"

The phone rang and Llew picked up the receiver. "McQuilla."

"*Hael! Eom Lareow Bede.*"

"Oh, yes, Professor Bede—we were just talking about you."

"*Thaet weorc thaet Winklejohn me fremeth—thaet gefliten sie?*"

"Yes, he has. The first part, anyway."

"*Thaet he hraedlic forthberen.*"

"Yes, I know. Things have been a little hectic around here. Tell you what—I'll send what we've got on over to you, and the rest as soon as Winklejohn can get on it. Okay?"

"*Swilc bith wundorful. Ic the helpe the thancword gife.*"

"No trouble at all. Take care."

"*Farath wel.*"

Llew hung up the phone. "Bede needs the first part now so he can proofread it." He looked at his watch. "I've got a few rounds to make—I can drop it by his office if it's ready to go."

Winklejohn retrieved his crutches and lifted himself from the chair, which emitted a groan of relief. "In my office. If you should chance upon Harry Gross in your meanderings, tell him I said—"

"I've already had one conversation with Harry today," Llew interrupted. "And that's about all I can take."

3

Leaving the Computer Center, Llew glanced at his checklist—Language department to deliver Professor Bede's material, Music Department to check with Gus Roddencroft about his magtape supply, Philosophy Department to see if he could invoke Dahnu and ask him about this brain wave thing . . .

And first stop, the Infirmary, to, uh . . . well, he'd think of a reason.

As he entered the campus Infirmary, the nurse at the reception desk recognized him and smiled—a little too knowingly, Llew felt. Going to have to start being more discreet, he told himself. "Hi," he said, trying to be casual. "Is Kay—" He winced, cursing himself—"I mean, Dr Gross in?" Off to a bad start.

"She's with a patient at the moment, Mr McQuilla," the nurse replied sweetly, and reached for the intercom. "I'll tell her you're here."

"Well, no . . . that's okay," he hurried, "I mean, I'll . . . uh, I can come back later."

"Don't be *silly*"—the sly smile again—"she'd never forgive you."

"Yeah, well . . . okay." He glanced around the small tile and linoleum room, where several students—waiting for a throat swab, a culture test or a prescription—sat looking passively at him. He feigned a cough and sat down at one end of a hard vinyl couch, trying to look casual.

A few minutes later, as Llew was about to attempt another escape, the door to the examining room opened and a student came out with a slip of paper which he handed to the nurse. "I believe you can go in now, Mr McQuilla," she called over to him.

He thanked her and, trying to ignore the annoyed looks of the students in the room who had arrived before him, went into the examination room and shut the door behind him.

Dr Kay Gross was seated at her desk, her shapely legs crossed beneath the secretarial chair. A silver stethoscope hung loosely around her neck, the earpieces disappearing beneath her long reddish-blond hair, the other end resting on the pronounced contours of her starched white vest. She was filling out a medical report on the student who had just left. "Just a second," she said without looking up. Llew leaned against the crisp paper-covered examination table and studied the muscle and circulation charts on the wall.

After a moment, Kay returned the medical form to its folder and got up, smiling at Llew. "Now then, sir . . ." putting her long arms around his neck, ". . . what can I do for you?"

His own arms went around her waist and pulled her closer. "Well . . . what have you got?"

"What haven't you had?" brushing her lips lightly against his.

He told her, and she promised to see what she could do about that. "When?" he asked.

"That's why I asked you to stop by," she smiled. "The night nurse called to say she can't get here till around ten, so I—oh, that feels *good*—so I told her I'd hold down the fort. Do that again."

Llew did it again, then asked, "What if a student comes in sick this evening?"

She nibbled his ear. "I'll leave two aspirin on the reception desk."

"What about Harry?"

"Harry doesn't need any aspirin," she murmured, running a hand under his jacket.

He squirmed. "That tickles . . . I mean what if—?"

She let her arms drop and made a face. "Do we have to talk about Harry?"

"Well . . ."

She smoothed the front of her smock, and Llew helped her. "It's his bowling night. Besides, I told him I'd be working late."

"Does he believe you when you tell him things like that?"

"He's too busy trying to cover up his own little escapades to suspect me of doing the same."

That aspect of Harry had always baffled Llew. Why did he find it necessary to fool around when he had a beautiful and intelligent wife like Kay?

All right, maybe not beautiful, in the Hollywood sense of the word—but she didn't miss by much. Her face was narrow and finely sculpted, with a firm mouth, high forehead, and exotically deep-set eyes. She was as tall as Llew, with a slim but well-proportioned body, the kind one expects to see on a golf course or tennis court.

And she was intelligent. She was an MD, in charge of the college infirmiry, and taught an occasional pre-med course. She was well-read, a stimulating conversationalist, and she played flute with a local chamber ensemble . . .

But she had also married Harry.

So, Llew thought, no one is perfect.

"He's been in a foul mood lately," Kay was saying. "Trying to break his own record for obnoxiousness."

"How come?"

"Lots of things. Frustration, mostly." She folded her arms and leaned against the desk. "He still dreams about taking over your department. But now he's worried about losing his own, with all the rumors of personnel changes in the making. And I guess I haven't been very nice to him either, lately." She looked at Llew with big, innocent eyes. "So I guess he's got *two* reasons to hate you."

"As long as he only knows about one of them. He doesn't take it out on you, does he?"

"You mean does he beat his wife? No, but I think I'd prefer that to being belched at, farted at and leered at. That man has all the charm of a stomach pump."

"Okay, I just wanted to make sure that—"

"Have you ever noticed how he glances around when he's talking to you? Like someone telling a dirty joke—'Didja hear the one about—?'"

Llew wished the subject of Harry hadn't come up in the first place. Once Kay got started it was hard to turn her off.

"He can turn anything into a dirty joke. The simplest word or remark becomes an innuendo."

Llew immediately thought of a way "innuendo" could be used in a dirty joke, but said nothing.

She was pacing the floor now, waving her arms. "Even when he sleeps. Most men just snore—he *snickers* in that lecherous, gutteral way that reminds you of somebody watching skin flicks at a smoky bachelor party."

Llew raised an eyebrow. "How do you know what goes on at a bachelor party?"

She smiled slyly at him. "No secrets are safe from a woman. Anyway, it wouldn't be so bad if I didn't have to put up with his behavior in public—but he seems determined to embarrass me in front of others. Do you know what he said to a neighbor, an old lady who told us her husband had just died? He said, 'You're *kidding!*'"

Llew winced.

"Anyway," she went on, "that's why we don't go out together much anymore. Although I suppose I'll have to make an exception for Byron Devilbiss's party next month."

"Right, I had forgotten about that," Llew said. Although not a frequent party-goer, he usually made an effort to attend this one. Byron Devilbiss was a flamboyant pianist, the *enfant terrible* of the Music Department, and his parties were as extravagent as his performances.

Byron was also a hopeless hypochondriac. "He was in here today for his usual supply of placebos," Kay said. "So far this month I've treated him for hemorrhoids, constipation, gas, heartburn and backaches."

"Maybe he just likes your bedside manner," Llew grinned.

Kay grew coquettish again, running a finger between the buttons of Llew's shirt. "And what is your opinion of my . . . bedside manner?"

"Ask me later tonight," he replied, "after you've refreshed my memory."

"Is that all that needs refreshing?" she asked, tracing new patterns with her finger.

"Now what were you saying about *Harry* turning every innocent remark into—"

"Are we back to him again?" she complained.

"Not for long," Llew replied, looking at his watch. "I've got to run. Have to catch Dahnu before he dematerializes for the day."

"Dahnu? What for?"

"He opened another account for some new project, and—"

"What on earth does he need a computer for?"

Llew looked at her oddly. "You know, that's exactly what Nina said. I suppose Dahnu makes *you* nervous too."

"Frankly, not as much as Nina does. Although I do hope he never comes in here for a physical—I'm not sure my nerves are ready for that. And speaking of examinations, I must have a waiting room full of ailing students. Kiss."

He did, or rather she did most of it, taking his breath away. "I hope you don't use that treatment on all your patients," he said as she drew back.

"No, but then I don't take all my fees out in trade, either. See you tonight."

He left, nodding to the nurse as he passed her desk. She nodded back, that knowing smile on her face again, reminding Llew of Kay's remark about women and secrets.

He dropped off Professor Bede's materials, then proceeded to Chandler Hall, which housed the English and Philosophy departments. The chairman of the English Department, Dr Madox F. Madox, was just stepping out of his office into the hall as Llew walked past. "Llew—I was going to give you a call."

Dr Madox was a large man with thinning hair brushed straight back. His head tilted back as well, as if someone had brushed too hard and driven the back of his neck into his spine. The real reason, however, was his heavy, drooping eyelids, which forced him to angle his head backward in order to see beneath them.

"Hello, Mad," Llew said. "How's the Henry James treatise coming along?"

"Exceedingly well, if I may say, with characteristic modesty, so, as it were, myself." He held up a thick bundle of papers. "The final, one hopes, draft, executed entirely using the phenomenal word processing capabilities of your computer. But not," he chuckled, "without some initial, if brief, measure of frustration, this being my first, but hardly, need I say, last, encounter with this facility."

"Computers take some getting used to," Llew admitted. "But ours is surprisingly user-friendly. And wait till you try the new one."

"Indeed . . ." A frown crossed what little Llew could see of Madox's brow. "That is, in point of fact, what I intended to ask you about. I have just returned from a meeting with President Croup, Vice-President Hess and several other department heads, regarding budgetary matters. Some references were made to impending changes in the Computer Center operations."

Llew didn't like the sound of that. "Changes? Like what?"

"I couldn't, with any assurance, due primarily to my lack of familiarity with the organization of your facility, as well as to the haste with which these references were made at the meeting, say. However, the implication, if I can trust my intuition, was that a major budgetary revision was, as they say, imminent."

Llew blanched. "But we're down to the bone now," he protested. "Our only major commitment is the new computer—and he can't renege on that. The old one is so overworked that terminal response runs at a snail's pace."

"I wish I could provide you with additional information," Madox said with a helpless shrug. "However," he added reassuringly, "it would appear, at least in my estimation, that Mr Hess, around whom this problem seems to center, is not entirely without experience in the field of computers. That he would intentionally take any action, the effect of which would be to undermine the effectiveness of the computer facility, seems, in light of the current trend toward expansion of such facilities, as well as the not inconsiderable amount of time and effort already expended toward achieving the present degree of excellence, unlikely . . . eh, to say the least."

"I wish I shared your optimism," Llew said. "But I have a very bad feeling about all this."

"Yes, well, I must run," Madox said, returning the manuscript to its folder. "I do hope, for your sake, as well, of course, as for all those, including myself, who have come to appreciate the benefits of the computer, that the situation will be resolved in a timely manner."

Llew thanked Madox for the information and left the building, his spirits at a new low ebb. I've got to get in to see Hess, he fumed, before he pulls the rug out from under my feet. It's already 3:30—Dahnu will have to wait.

As he was passing by the Music Department on his way to the Administration building, Llew stopped. Gus Roddencroft still remained on his list of people yet to see, to verify his request for additional mag tapes. As long as I'm right here, he figured, it should only take a second to run in and get it done.

Gustav Roddencroft was the head of the Music Department, a good friend of Llew's and an avid computer user. A composer as well as an administrator, he had written a number of works, most recently a song cycle for baritone and French horn with text from poems by Lee Iococca. He was currently working on his magnum opus, a large choral work based on patriotic and revolutionary songs of Liechtenstein, scored for orchestra and synthesized chorus—which is where Llew's computer came in.

As he walked down the halls of the music building, Llew could hear the muffled sounds of instrumental and vocal exercises emanating from behind the closed practice room doors, reminding him again of Byron's recital coming up in few weeks. Actually, it was unlikely that anyone could forget, as Byron had seen to it that dozens of Big-Brother-sized posters proclaiming the event were plastered up all over campus. The posters were devoted largely to a heroic rendering of Byron's Napoleonic profile, of course, even to the striking loden cape which he sported around campus.

Byron's recital programs were usually as ostentatious as was the artist himself. His repertoire was a little one-sided, however, consisting largely of fiendishly difficult and persistently ear-shattering works. He never failed to draw crowds, however, nor to give them their money's worth.

As Llew entered Gus Roddencroft's office, he found both Gus and Dahnu listening to a tape recording recently produced via the computer. Gus had written a program to produce the output on computer tape, which was then played through a device in his office which converted the digital information into sound.

Gus nodded to Llew and Dahnu smiled transcendentally. The music was too loud to get a word in, so Llew waited patiently. The sounds were typical of Gus's recent compositions—rhythmically irregular and extraordinarily complex. He categorized his works as neo-Ivesian, an offshoot from the recent school of maximalism in music.

The synthesized chorus produced a full, somewhat cavernous sound, but there was an odd metallic edge which appeared to be causing Gus to frown. He ran a tentative hand over his smooth head, then brought it down to scratch under the enormous shaggy beard which totally obscured the lower half of his face and most of his chest.

Dahnu's face bore little expression, which for him was normal. Although he was not oriental—or for that matter any nationality that you could quite put your finger on—his dark almond-shaped eyes and delicately-featured oval face reflected an inscrutability characteristic of the East. He had a slight, almost fragile build, and he wore tan trousers, a white silk shirt open at the collar, and a knit sleeveless vest of an intricate blend of strange dark colors. His fine, light brown hair fell forward, converging to a point over his high forehead.

Gus made a clucking sound beneath his beard, and reached over to turn off the tape player. "Still not right. Sounds too . . . mechanical. Dahnu?"

"I must agree," Dahnu said in his quiet, neutral voice. "I believe it detracts from the spiritual quality you are trying to achieve in this movement."

"Llew? Any opinions?"

"About the mechanical sound, yes. But I sort of liked it. Gave it a kind of other-worldly quality."

Gus shook his head. "More unearthly than other-worldly, I'm afraid. No, the chorus has to sound more human."

"Ever consider using humans?" Llew grinned.

"That's already been done," Gus replied gruffly. "Any *serious* suggestions?"

Llew thought a minute. "We might try increasing the bit-sampling rate—should give it a smoother response."

"Is that possible?"

"Not at the moment, actually, with the computer we've got now. But the new one will provide much faster response so we can increase the bit density without slowing down the action."

"When will you have the new computer, Llew?" Dahnu asked.

Llew breathed a sigh. "Good question. There's talk that our enigmatic new VP might pull the plug on the whole thing. I was on my way over to try and catch him this afternoon. I just needed to confirm your usage estimates—both of you, in fact. Gus?"

"About the same, I guess. I'd like to spend full time with this thing, but my contract requires me to perform an administrative function or two from time to time."

"Welcome to the club. Dahnu, what's this brain-wave thing you're doing?"

"It's rather . . . controversial, I'm afraid," Dahnu replied, almost apologetically. "It involves what I have labelled 'Zeta waves'. Unfortunately, I've been unable to convince many people of their existence. So I hope to use the computer to isolate and display some evidence of them."

"What do they do? The Zeta waves, I mean."

"Oh, they don't *do* anything—they're simply emitted when the mind is in a particular state of consciousness."

"What kind of state does the mind have to be in to produce these things?" Gus asked.

"That's where the controversy comes in," Dahnu admitted. "Zeta waves are produced when the brain consciously brings about physiological changes in the body—functions which are typically performed automatically."

Gus scowled. "Come again?"

"For example," Dahnu said, clasping his hands in front of him, "control of blood pressure or body temperature—both are normally automatic functions, regulated by the brain. But the yogis of India have developed the ability to control them at will—slowing the heartbeat, for instance, or raising the temperature in one hand while lowering it in the other. Others have achieved the same results using bio-feedback devices. And it is during this control process that Zeta waves are created."

"But how do you intend to use the computer to find these . . . Zeta waves?" Llew wanted to know.

"There are some pieces of equipment in the Biochemistry lab which I believe can be modified to detect the waves. But they are not sensitive enough to provide a clear trace. So I am hoping that by interfacing them with the computer, I can refine and enhance the data—in the same way, for example, that satellite imagery is enhanced to bring out detail."

At that moment the door to the studio banged open and Byron Devilbiss swept into the room, his loden cloak trailing cape-like from his shoulders. A dank, black cigar was clenched between his gleaming array of teeth.

"Rottencrotch!" he bellowed. "What were those *ghastly* sounds I heard from in here a few minutes ago? Sounded like a chorus of constipated robots!"

Gus grimaced. "Byron, just what is it you—"

"Dahnu, you old wraith! How are things in Elysium?" Byron flicked a core of cigar ashes at a waste basket, missing by several inches. "And Llew—where's that computer printout of all the coeds' vital statistics I asked you for?"

Llew grinned. "Byron, I suspect there's already more data about the women on campus in your head than in our computer."

Byron howled with glee, nodding and stomping the floor. Suddenly there was a rapid beeping sound from his watch—"Whoops! Pill time!" He reached under his cloak and withdrew a handful of plastic vials. "Let's see—it's four o'clock, so it must be *yellow*," he said, removing the cap from one of the containers and shaking two yellow pills out into his hand. He swallowed them, then poured a cup of coffee from Gus's thermos to wash them down.

"How's the recital shaping up?" Llew asked as Gus retrieved his thermos and stashed it away in a desk drawer.

"Stupendously!" Byron insisted, recapping the vial and putting them all back into his pocket. "Chopin, Prokofiev, Reger . . . and to bring down the house, Busoni's *Fantasia Contrapuntistica.*"

"Isn't that piece for *two* pianos?" Gus asked skeptically.

"Of course—I'm playing both parts!" He stuck the cigar back between his teeth. "And don't forget my party the week before the recital—a veritable bacchanal, worthy of—"

The phone rang, and Byron snatched it up before Gus could reach it.

"Rottencrotch's office—who's this?" Then he grinned. "Arganina! Does Llew know you're carrying on with Rottencrotch on company time? Sure, he's here—hold on." He handed the phone to Llew. "For you. Miss Tiny-tits. Something about her dog crapping in the disk drive."

Llew took the phone. "Nina? Yeah, of course that was Byron. Tell him to what? Okay, but I suspect that's a physical impossibility . . . even for Byron. Now, what is it you . . . ? He *did*? When? What time does he want me to be there?" He looked at his watch. "Okay, I'm on my way. Thanks."

He hung up. "Nina says Hess wants to see me in his office. I'd better get right over there before he changes his mind. May never get another chance."

"Good luck, Llew," Gus said. "Hope you can still salvage the new computer."

"If I can't," Llew replied on his way out the door, "you may *have* to use human voices."

4

Llew hurried across campus. In his mind he rehearsed all the reasons why the new computer was essential and why the Center's budget could not be cut. I'd feel better, he thought, if I had been able to talk to Hess a couple times before, so I'd have a better idea of what to expect. And how to deal with it.

As Llew reached the steps of the administration building he saw Harry Gross coming out the front entrance, a smug grin on his face. The long wirey strands of hair which he combed over the balding top of his head were blowing in the breeze, and his shirtfront was loose around his protruding gut. He hiked up his trousers and began whistling tunelessly as he trotted down the steps.

"Hello, Harry," Llew greeted cordially. "Off for the day?"

"Nope—too much to do," Harry replied, without stopping. "Gonna be *very busy* around here for a while, looks like." He chuckled, and resumed whistling. Llew was curious, but resolved not to give Harry the benefit of an inquiry, so he continued up the steps.

Inside, he made his way to Hess's office, where the secretary told him he was expected. He stepped into the room where he and Sam Wexler, Hess's predecessor, had met regularly and always under the most informal and relaxed conditions. This was the first time Llew had been asked here since Hess took over, and he felt anything but relaxed. He was determined, however, not to show it.

Hess sat behind the large desk at the far side of the room. He was a short, chubby man with a perfectly round head and the smallest mouth Llew had ever seen. His face was pinkish in color except for a pronounced blush in his cheeks, as if someone had tweaked them roguishly. He was dressed in a conservative grey suit, the coat of which was buttoned in front. Llew felt underdressed, and wished that he still carried an emergency tie in the pocket of his sports jacket like he used to.

"Sit down, Mr McQuilla," Hess gestured to a nearby chair. Llew noticed that the half-full coffee mug on Hess's desk had Sam Wexler's initials on it. Otherwise, except for a telephone, the desk was conspicuously bare.

Hess leaned back in his chair and brought his pudgy fingertips together under his chin. "Mr McQuilla, how long have you been the Computer Services Director here?"

"Going on five years," Llew replied.

"And you were responsible for acquiring the present computer system—a MAX-11, I believe—for both academic and administrative use?" His voice was high-pitched and had a nasal quality.

"That's right."

"And now, because of growing demand for computer resources throughout the college, you propose to replace it with a larger model of the same brand—a MAX-15."

What is he getting at? "It's already on order, and we expect delivery in a few weeks."

Hess pursed his thin lips, causing them to virtually disappear.

After a moment, he said, "Did you investigate other computer systems before committing to this one?"

"Of course. I put out RFPs to half a dozen different vendors, and arranged demos for each one that responded. None of them could hold a candle to the MAX, in terms of capability, ease of expansion, price, support, user-friendliness . . ."

"Was the Sultan 6000 one of the computers under consideration?"

Llew thought a minute. "That was one of the companies I queried, but they didn't reply to the RFP."

"Did you try a different vendor?"

"There aren't any other vendors in this area for Sultan, to my knowledge."

Hess nodded. "Well, for your information, Mr McQuilla, the Sultans are being distributed by a company called BrandeX, Inc. They service most of the east coast."

"BrandeX?" Llew searched his memory. "Never heard of them. And frankly, information on Sultans is scarce as well. What I've read suggests that most of the models are bigger and more expensive than we need. And the software doesn't seem—"

"Then you haven't done your homework thoroughly, Mr McQuilla," Hess interrupted. "Fortunately, I have. And my conclusion is that the Sultan 6000 is a significantly better choice for this institution."

Llew stared in bewilderment. "But . . . the choice was made by committee. I was on it, along with representatives from several other departments. Besides, the contract with the MAX vendor has already been signed, and delivery—"

"The committee only made a recommendation, based on the options open to them at the time. My predecessor, Dr Wexler, made the decision, apparently under some pressure from you. And I am effectively unmaking that decision."

"But—"

"In fact, I have already cancelled the contract with MAX and signed one with BrandeX for a Sultan 6000, delivery to be made at approximately the same time as the MAX was due."

Llew sat stunned. Hess rose from his chair and retrieved a folder of papers from a nearby table. "I am not exactly a stranger to computer systems, Mr McQuilla, and the Sultan 6000 in particular has always impressed me. When I discovered that it was not being considered as a replacement here, I requested a bid myself, which BrandeX was prompt to submit. I have studied it carefully, and find that it exceeds in every respect that of the MAX. And at a price competitive with what you were about to pay."

He returned to his desk and laid the folder next to the coffee cup. "I have made these facts known to the other members of your committee, as well as President Croup, and have received their support for this move."

Llew's mind raced. He *had* expressed a preference for the MAX, but no pressure was applied. And Wexler had agreed completely with his assessment. "What about conversion?" he asked, grasping at straws now. "The two systems won't be compatible, so most of the programs now in use will have to be modified to run on the new computer. With the MAX, it would mean only a simple upgrade in the operating system."

Hess shrugged. "I believe that's what your programming staff is for."

Llew felt his defenses rising. "My staff consists of only three people, one of whom is just an operator. And one is a systems programmer, who will have to learn a whole new operating system in a few short weeks. And the third is so overworked now that—"

"All appropriate documentation will be provided," Hess informed him. "And of course the MAX will continue to function in a backup capacity until such time as all the bugs have been ironed out. In addition, I have arranged with BrandeX for the services of a consultant to assist with systems matters during the transition."

Well, that's something, anyway, Llew thought—I've been trying to get money to hire a new body for over a year.

"There is . . . one other matter you need to be made aware of," Hess said, looking down at his desk. "As you must know, we have been doing some restructuring of personnel and budget allocations. In particular, I have been examining staff salaries with respect to the overall relevance of their positions. Frankly, Mr McQuilla, your salary is one of those which I consider far out of line."

He looked up, met Llew's widening eyes briefly, then swiveled his chair around to face the array of portraits of past campus dignitaries on the wall. "This has prompted me to examine the position itself, with regard to function, administration and efficiency. My conclusion is that the Computer Services directorship, as it is currently defined, is anachronistic and superfluous."

I'll wake up any minute, Llew thought. Nightmares can't go on forever.

"Therefore," Hess went on, "to bring matters into a more realistic perspective, and to partially finance the services of the new consultant, I am eliminating the position of Computer Services Director, effective immediately."

He swiveled back and shuffled some papers in front of him. "The members of your staff will not be affected. The academic functions of your position will be relegated to a committee of representatives from each department currently using the computer facilities, who will report directly to me. As for the administrative functions—"

Llew suddenly knew that the worst was yet to come . . . and why Harry Gross had been whistling.

" —will be absorbed by the Information Services Department under Mr Gross. As for you—"

Llew shut his eyes. Right, let's pick up the pieces . . .

"In view of your years of service to the college, it would hardly be appropriate to just let you go altogether. We would like to make continued use of your expertise in some alternate capacity. I've recommended that you be offered the position of Custodian of Institutional Archives. The salary, of course, would necessarily be significantly—"

Llew was searching for just the right words to tell Hess what he could do with his offer. But what came out, to his own surprise, was, "I'll take it."

Hess's little jaw dropped. "You will? I mean, eh . . . with your qualifications, a position in industry or—"

"I said I'll take it," Llew insisted, now increasingly confident that his abrupt choice was the correct one. "Anything else?"

"Er . . . no, not at the moment." Hess was frowning. "I will arrange for an office for you, and will expect you to transfer your belongings by the end of the week."

"Does that folder contain the specs for the Sultan?" Llew asked.

"The specs . . . ?" Hess looked down at the folder on his desk. "Yes, in addition to all the other pertinent information I have acquired in my negotiations with BrandeX."

"Would you mind if I had a look at it?" knowing what the answer would be.

Hess laid a defensive hand over the folder. "I don't believe that would be appropriate, as Computer Services materials no longer fall under your auspices." He rose from his chair. "And now if you have no further questions . . ."

Llew had plenty of questions, but his mind was in a turmoil. He felt like he was suffocating and needed air. He got up and walked quickly out of the office.

He left the building, trembling with rage and frustration. I've been fired, he said to himself, shuddering at the word. *Fired.* Hess didn't use that term, but that's what it amounts to.

But for what? People don't get fired without a reason. Just because he didn't agree with my choice of a computer? Because I wasn't wearing a tie?

What do I do now? Go back to the office and tell the crew?

Not yet. I've got to think. Go somewhere and *think* . . .

"I think . . . I'll have another carafe of this wine, Archie," Llew told the bartender at Duffy's Tavern.

"Don't you think you ought to eat something, Llew?" Archie asked, removing the empty container and glass and wiping the copper surface of the bar in front of Llew. "Not good to drink so much on an empty stomach. Need some kind of food."

"Wine *is* a food," Llew insisted. "Did you know that? One hundred percent product of the grape. Healthful and nutritious. 'Take a little wine for thy stomach's sake', it says somewhere."

Archie placed a bowl of popcorn on the bar. "How bout some snacks for yours?"

Llew nodded. "Snacks. Right. And another carafe to wash them down."

The bartender left, and Llew turned back to the thin, dark-haired girl in sweater and jeans sitting next to him at the bar. "Where were we?"

"Life is a sign wave, or something like that," the girl replied, a bit thickly.

"A sine wave, right. A sine wave represents a single frequency oscillation. Mainly, it goes up—" cupping his hand high over the bar "— and down," swooping down along the top of the bar, almost knocking over his wine glass. "Just like life, see? One minute you're up here . . . and the next minute—*pffi!*"

"*Pffthhh,*" she agreed, giggling and reaching for her glass, which Archie had refilled from Llew's replenished carafe.

"Up until today," Llew went on, "my life was in a steady state condition." He moved his hand in a straight line. "No ups or downs. Predictable and comfortable."

The girl suppressed a hiccup. "Yeah, well, you know what they say . . ."

Llew thought a minute, then looked over at her. "What do they say?"

She looked back at him with slightly glazed eyes. "Who?"

"Who indeed?" he replied, returning to his drink. "Who could have foreseen that in a few short, traumatic minutes, I would go from running the most efficient computer shop of any college in these parts to fighting cobwebs in some dusty archive vault?"

The girl shook her head. "Not me."

"The real question, however, is *why?* Why is he doing this to me? He's made me out to be some kind of *incompetent.* And now he wants to eliminate me altogether and undo everything I've done."

He turned back to the girl. "And the problem is, I don't know what to do about it. He's even got the president on his side—you can't fight city hall."

The girl was staring at the bowl of popcorn. "Did you know," she said, holding up a single, fluffy kernel, "that no two pieces of popcorn are exactly alike?"

Something was nagging in Llew's mind. Suddenly it clicked, and he looked at his watch. "Cushlamochree—it's nine-thirty! I was supposed to meet Kay at eight!"

His shoulders slumped. "It's too late now. She was supposed to leave at ten. But maybe I can still call her . . ."

He excused himself, slid off the stool and made his way through the crowded, noisy lounge to the wall phone. He punched Kay's office number, then used the finger to shut the noise out of his ear while the phone rang. Finally, a woman's voice answered, "Infirmary."

"Kay? Llew. Listen, I'm sorry. Something's happened—it's too complicated to explain, and besides I can't hear a thing in this place. But I've got to talk to you. Can we—"

"Excuse me," the voice interrupted. "If you're calling Dr Gross, she's already left. This is Ms Peterson, the night nurse. Can I take a message for Dr Gross?"

Oh good grief, Llew thought—this is all I needed. "Uh . . . no, that's okay. I'll call back."

He hung up and returned to the bar. Guess it's just as well I *didn't* go over to the infirmiry this evening. The night nurse must have gotten there early . . .

He squeezed back onto his stool and finished the wine in his glass. "Sorry," he said to the girl next to him, whose hand was in the popcorn bowl. "Where were we?"

The girl turned to face him. She had frosted hair, a square jaw and was wearing a two-piece suit. There was a briefcase in her lap. "I beg your pardon?" she said curtly.

"Sorry," Llew muttered again, and reached for the carafe.

By the time he had finished it, Archie had refilled the popcorn bowl twice. And sure enough, Llew had not found two pieces alike.

5

"The man has got to be *crazy!*" Nina stormed. "Who ever heard of a Computer Center with nobody running it?"

"It seems we are dealing with a person of limitless ineptitude," Winklejohn said, scowling and puffing on his Meerschaum.

"I thing thiz will gauze many broblems, izn't it?" Rama ventured, a worried look in his dark eyes.

Nina paced the floor of Llew's office, folding and unfolding her arms. "After all you've done for this place. Doesn't that count for *anything?!*"

Llew sat slumped in his chair, trying to ignore a slight hangover from the night before. He appreciated his friends' support, but wished that Nina would express it at a lower level of volume. Besides, there was nothing they could say that he hadn't already mulled over in his own mind a dozen times since yesterday.

"And what I *really* can't understand," Nina went on, "is how he got everybody on the committee to go along with it!"

Llew rubbed his temples. "I'd lay odds that 'everybody' consists of just President Croup and Harry Gross. Dr Fermat in the math department was on that committee, and he called me this morning to find out what the hell was going on."

He swiveled his chair around toward the window, squinting against the light. "He told me some very interesting things. Apparently, President Croup has given Hess virtually free rein. And he's using it. He's fired at least a dozen people, including the entire janitorial staff and the cafeteria food service crew, and replaced them with some outside contract service agencies."

"A veritable grim reaper," Winklejohn remarked.

Nina snatched a piece of paper from the desk top. "And then he has the *gall* to send Wink, Rama and me letters to assure us that *our* jobs are safe.

"'It is my hope'," she read, with exaggerated haughtiness, "'that we will be able to work together as we embark in a new and more productive direction.'" She crumpled the letter angrily and pitched it into the waste basket. Winklejohn sighed as he applied a match to his copy, while Rama reduced his to confetti with a huge pair of scissors.

"He's playing it smart," Llew said. "He realizes that guys like you are not as easy to replace as administrators and service people. And he can't afford to be caught short when it comes time to convert hundreds of programs over to the new system."

"More than likely," Winklejohn mused, "he realizes that the EOC and ACLU would have his head if he tried to fire a woman, an expatriate and a handicapped black from the same department."

"Juzt zo," Rama agreed. "I myzelf would zue him up inzide and down the other!"

"Then maybe we should all just up and quit," Nina suggested. "Leave the bastard high and dry."

Llew shook his head. "No, that would only make matters worse for the users who depend on the computer. And on us. That's one reason why I didn't resign on the spot—as I'm sure he was counting on."

"Fat lot of good it'll do us or the users if he's moving you out of here," Nina pointed out.

"That remains to be seen. At least I can keep an eye on the situation until I know what he's up to."

Winklejohn raised an eyebrow. "You suspect a *motif ulterieur* in this turn of events?"

"There has to be," Llew insisted. "I mean, the whole situation is insane. We've got a shop here that has been enormously successful . . . and popular. Suddenly we're accused of doing everything wrong, and I'm a waste of their money."

That, Llew realized bitterly, is the real kicker. It was not *his* salary that was out of line, as Hess had claimed, but those of his staff—and on the *low* end of the scale. During the last salary adjustment, he had found out that Nina, Winklejohn and Rama were only to receive half of the increments he had requested for them. So he had negotiated with Wexler to split his own raise among the three of them, to make up some of the difference. Only he and Wexler knew this, of course . . . and Hess, if he had examined the records as he said he did.

"Anyway," he said, "I'm not leaving until I know what's going on. Or until the whole thing blows up in his face."

"In which event," Winklejohn chortled, "we shall derive great pleasure in sweeping up the pieces."

"And what muzt we do in the meandime?" Rama asked.

"Just go along with whatever he asks," Llew replied, "while I do a little checking up—starting with this BrandeX company that's selling us the computer. Hess has all the specs in a folder in his office, but he wouldn't let me see it. I'll have to find the answers somewhere else."

He got up out of his chair. "Right now, though, I've got to start thinking about packing all the stuff in this office. I'll need some empty boxes—Rama, could you see what you can scrounge up from the supply room?"

"Just where are you being moved?" Nina asked.

"Someplace in Usher Hall. I haven't been over there yet to see the place."

"*That* dump? My god, that's way out on the edge of campus."

"It'z the middle of *nowhere,*" Rama added.

"That's about the way I feel just now," Llew said. "I suppose I should mosey on over there and check out the place."

Llew headed across campus in the direction of Usher Hall. He briefly considered stopping off to see Kay in the infirmary, but he wasn't up to the sly glances of the receptionist again so soon. He had phoned Kay earlier to explain about last night, but she had already guessed the reason. While he had been getting the shaft from Hess, Harry had gone right over to the infirmiry to regale Kay with the news.

"The hardest thing I ever had to do," she had told Llew over the phone, "was to pretend to be pleased when he told me about it—especially when he gloated about you getting what was coming to you. He even skipped his bowling to stay home and chart a new course for the administrative computer service."

Besides, the night nurse *had* shown up early last night, so it wouldn't have worked anyway. Llew felt an urgent need to see Kay alone, but it looked like things were going to be a little tricky for a while.

Usher Hall was one of the oldest buildings on campus, and had at one time housed the Chemistry and Biology departments. There were odors of formaldehyde and hydrogen sulfide in the dank halls, the walls and high ceilings were mottled, and the paint was peeling from the trim. Aside from an auditorium and a few oversized classrooms, the building was now used primarily for storage.

Llew's office was numbered 021, which meant the basement. The whole damned building looks like a basement, he thought as he made his way down the wide, unlit staircase. Through a set of heavy double doors, down another hall, last office on the left. And it was, of course, locked.

Cursing, Llew returned to the main floor, looking for some kind of central office. Finding none, he headed over to the Maintenance building, which fortunately was also situated on this remote end of campus.

The office of Paisley Braithwaite, maintenance supervisor, was empty, so Llew checked the adjacent rooms and halls, listening for the jingling sound which always signified Paisley's whereabouts. The man always carried dozens of keyrings in his oversized Harpo Marx utility coat, a single key for each lock on campus. "The wiy Oi see it," he would explain, his thick Aussie accent uncorrupted by twenty years in the States, "if one kiy fits several locks, then Oi've got to replice all those locks everytoime a kiy gets lost, see? This wiy, Oi've only got to replice one."

Following his ears, Llew found Paisley getting a soft drink from the Coke machine. Paisley was a hefty man with a waxed mustache, curled at the tips. "A kiy to 021? Oi think Oi can manage that," rummaging in his sagging coat and withdrawing a huge ring of keys. "Let's see, now . . . roight, this one 'ere ought to do it. Cem on, then."

Llew followed Paisley back to the dungeons of Usher. "Donno wot you want with this room, anywiy. Oin't bin used in years. And roight next to the plumbin' pipes, too, it is. The loo's just above—mikes a 'ell of a racket when somebody flushes."

Paisley unlocked and opened the door, and felt around the inside wall for a light switch. Miraculously, the light came on—a bare light bulb in the middle of the ceiling.

The room was small and empty, except for a metal desk with a slightly bent frame and a secretarial chair which leaned slightly to one side. Llew could see a spring emerging from beneath the Naugahyde seat cushion. The floor hadn't been swept in ages, and there was a moldy smell in the air.

As they stood looking, a rumble sounded from above their heads, followed by a crescendoing roar in the wall behind the desk.

Paisley nodded. "That would be the johnny upstairs, loike Oi told you."

Llew leaned against the wall, feeling his spirits sink and all his incentive being swept away along with the cascading water. Just quit right now, he told himself—forget it, get as far away from this place as possible and let it go to the dogs. The hell with it. I can't cope with this. And Hess knows it. He's driven the final nail.

So it's Hess 1, McQuilla 0? something deep inside him demanded. Is that the way you want to remember it the rest of your life? Admit defeat in one short 24-hour period? Crawl away on your knees, whimpering like a whupped dawg?

He took a deep breath—no way. "Do you know of any other rooms on campus that aren't being used?" he asked Paisley. "What about Higgens?"

"'Iggens?" Paisley rubbed his square chin. "'At's where the Post Office is. The rest of it is all classrooms, except for the bisement."

"What's in the basement?"

Paisley grinned and shook his head. "Well, Oi ain't roightly sipposed to siy. It's one o' them security things, if you tike moy meanin'."

Llew didn't. "I thought the campus security office was in the administrative building."

"Not *that* kind of security—*gov'ment* security, loike."

"Government? There aren't any government installations on this campus."

Paisley smirked. "'At's wot *yew* think, mite.' He glanced around. "All very top-secret. There's none that knows, 'cept them wot runs this plice."

"Then how do *you* know?"

Paisley raised his bushy eyebrows and tweeked the curled tip of his mustache. "Cause Oi service the plice. Look after the plumbin' and the 'eatin', don't Oi? And Oi'm sipposed not to talk about it, neither, so Oi'd best shut up while Oi still got me job." He took the key off the ring and handed it to Llew, "'Ere's your copy. Oi'll be off now. If you be needin' anythin' else, ring me up strightawiy."

"Right. Thanks." Llew pocketed the key and turned back to the room as Paisley left. What's it to be, then? he asked himself. The already claustrophobic room seemed to be steadily shrinking, like the oppressive cell in *Pit and the Pendulum*, along with Llew's determination.

The temptation to quit was overwhelming. With his experience, it wouldn't take long to find another job, as Hess had pointed out. He knew the position of Custodian of Institutional Archives was a token one, with only sporadic responsibilities. And the pay cut would drive him out eventually, anyway.

On the other hand, he couldn't shake the gnawing feeling that his dismissal—or "reassignment"—was more than a simple cost-cutting move. Hess had made him out to be some sort of incompetent, and nothing could be further from the truth. In the past five years he had built up a computer facility that was remarkably efficient and served an unusually wide spectrum of users. And done it on a shoestring budget.

So to just up and leave would effectively be admitting that Hess was right. Eventually, of course, the Computer Center expenses would skyrocket, and the walls would tumble down around Hess's ears—but then it would be too late to say I told you so. If he could just stick it out for a while, there might be some way to nip the whole thing in the bud before the situation became irreversible. And to get the answers to some questions at the same time.

He wished he had a cigaret. He had quit smoking years ago, but at times like this . . . *No,* he swore—Hess can take my job away, but I'll be damned if he's going to force me back into bad habits.

There was another muffled roar upstairs, so Llew quickly turned off the light, shut and locked the door and headed back to the stairs. I'll stick it out for the time being, he vowed, which will at least give me a paycheck while I check out some other jobs . . . and do a little snooping around here.

"You had a phone call," Nina told him when he returned to the Computer Center. "Somebody named . . . Ebbsedik?"

"Really? Mike Ebbsedik . . . I haven't heard from him in years. I used to work for him before I came here. Very sharp guy—completely immersed in computer technology. I think he runs his own consulting business now."

"He wants you to call him back. I left the number on your desk."

Llew returned to his office and picked up the phone. He punched the long distance number and waited while the phone rang on the other end. Then a voice said, "Ebbsedik."

"Mike? Llew."

"*Llew*—how ya been?"

"You don't want to know," Llew said.

"Figured. Lookin' to swap out?"

"How did you know that?

"Well, you gave my name out as a reference, so I figured—"

Llew blinked. "Wait a minute. I haven't sent out any applications for a job yet. If I had, I certainly would have checked with you before using your name."

"Yeah, that's what I thought, too. But somebody logged in a few weeks ago, said you had applied for a job. Needed some input on you."

"That's crazy. What was the name of the company?"

"Tell you the truth, I don't remember. Guy said it so fast it missed the buffer. Nobody I recognized, though. Thought I had everybody in this goddam business stored in my look-up table."

"What did he want to know?"

"Well, that's the other thing that didn't quite compute. Asked a lot of questions about your reliability and integrity . . . how dependable you were, whether you always followed orders, things like that. Figured it must be a security position of some kind . . . needed a clearance. Told him you were disgustingly honest, never known you to even get a *speeding* ticket, for chrissake."

Llew winced, recalling yesterday's episode with the county patrol cop in the pickup truck. My god, had that only been *yesterday*? So much had happened, he hadn't even thought about paying the ticket.

"Anyhow," Mike went on, "thought the whole thing was a little weird, so figured I'd better get on-line with you about it. If you *are* looking for a job, why not come back to work for me? Always use good people."

"To tell you the truth, Mike, the situation here is still pretty much up in the air. I appreciate the offer, and if things don't work out, I might take you up on it."

"Good enough. Anything else I can do in the meantime . . ."

Llew thought a minute. "Maybe there is. What do you know about Sultan computers?"

"Sultan? Spinoff from another mainframe—GenData, I think. Bit of a distribution problem, I hear."

"Ever hear of BrandeX, Inc?"

"Mmm. Rings a bell . . ."

"Think you could check it out for me?"

"Glad to. Don't like gaps in my database. What do you need to know?"

"Everything."

"Got it in the high-priority queue."

"I appreciate it, Mike. Call me if you get anything."

"Spool any output to you right away. Don't take any punched cards."

Llew hung up the phone and leaned back in his chair, puzzled. Why would anyone be requesting a reference for me? Mike said a few weeks ago . . . Makes no sense.

Well, I've got other things to worry about. Like packing. God, where to start? Five years accumulation of manuals, documents, files . . . It'll take at least a couple dozen boxes.

And where am I going to put it all in that tiny closet I've been relegated to? Going to have to do some severe sorting . . .

He looked wistfully around the room which had served as home to him almost as much as his own apartment. The double-hung windows that never quite closed all the way, the asbestos-lined pipes running along the ceiling, the stone walls which had been painted and repainted over the years, the dark green functional carpet on the floor, thread-bare in spots . . .

The prospect of moving depressed him, and thoughts of quitting were beginning to reassert themselves when Nina came back into the office, followed by Calhoun. "Sit down, Calhoun," she ordered. "That's a good dog. G-O-O-D sit down."

She went over to Llew's terminal and logged in. "The president's office called a few minutes ago while you were on the phone. I took it on the other line."

"Croup himself?"

"His secretary. She said Croup was furious."

"Good god—what have I done now?"

"It's not you this time." She entered a command on the keyboard. "You'll see."

Llew grinned. "Oh *ho*—bet I can guess. Another blast from The Campus Curmudgeon."

"You got it." She leaned back from the terminal as a page of text filled the screen. "This one is about a speech Croup made in town a week or so ago."

Llew rolled his chair up closer to the screen, his spirits already on the upswing. This was the third time a scathing criticism of one of the president's speeches, by someone calling himself "The Campus Curmudgeon", had appeared over the computer's Public Address network.

Llew had established the Public Address file to allow computer users to broadcast news, announcements and items of general interest to all the remote terminals on campus. After the first two of these tirades had appeared, the president had ordered Llew to screen all future entries. So now all messages went into a temporary buffer, and only persons with privileged accounts could release them to the Public Address network.

Which was fine, except that now The Curmudgeon had apparently figured out how to access the network directly. Every computer system has its whiz kids and hackers, and although they caused Llew frequent headaches, he couldn't help being impressed by their accomplishments. Besides, he had done his share of it in college.

Llew read:

> Well, our beloved college may finally be on the verge of entering the Twentieth Century. In a daring departure from his standard laissez-faire policy, President Horace "Keep-'Em-Guessing" Croup has told a group of local educators that "We maintain a commitment to creativity and innovation in all parts of our curriculum. For example, recognizing that traditional classrooms tend to perpetuate traditional approaches, the Communications Department proposes to establish an Ideal Classroom for the teaching of basic writing courses."
>
> He goes on: "This would involve bringing together in one room a large variety of audiovisual implements, creating a relaxed atmosphere by having the room carpeted, pictures on the walls, some easy chairs, and by having duplicating equipment and a variety of newspapers and magazines available. Both students' perceptions and teachers' approaches to the task of learning to write will be encouraged to be changed."

Now why haven't we thought of all this neat stuff before? Because we've been hung up perpetuating those traditional approaches—things like drill and practice, writing and rewriting, that's why. Even desks! When what we've really needed all this time is a dentist's waiting room redone by Radio Shack, magazines and Muzak, comfy chairs and a shiny new Xerox machine so the scholars won't have to fight over the latest issue of Popular Mechanics.

Notice the refreshing absence of flat, empty surfaces where a thoughtless student might accidently write words on a piece of paper and set the whole class back a century. Makes you wonder how anybody wrote anything before the advent of all those audiovisual "implements".

And is there any doubt that this very speech was produced in just such an innovative, relaxing setting? Just look at the daring departure from stodgy tradition in the structure of that last sentence, which goes the tired old passive at least one better. But lest we rush into anything without due consideration, the Prez assures us that such innovative approaches will require a Needs Assessment Task Force. "Goals should be set for some time in the future, and a definitive methodology established for evaluation and feedback." It takes some of the sharpest minds in academia to discover that plans are about the future, not the past, and to call for a "definitive methodology" when any simple-minded taxpayer would settle for a mere method.

What is required, he informs us, is "enterprise preassessment", which can only be achieved through "prefeasibility studies." We wonder what they'll do when they discover that some enterprise is indeed prefeasible. In this college, where the preposterous has always been prepossible, they'll doubtless appoint more Task Forces to preconsider the prefeasibility of

> preplanning. Then our preprofessional Communications students can break up into small groups in their Ideal Classrooms—beer, pretzels and 20-inch color implements at hand—and rap about preplanning their preassessment preprograms.

Llew nodded approvingly. "That's good stuff. Let's get a hard copy of it to file with the others. Still no idea who's doing this?"

"The secretary said Croup thinks it's you," Nina said, typing an instruction to spool the text to the printer.

"Naturally. I'm to blame for everything these days." The printer next to the terminal began chattering. "No, I could never turn out anything like this. Somebody's still breaking into the system, just when I thought I had it tamper-proof. You're the only one I know who's good at that sort of thing, but you already have a privileged account, so you wouldn't need to. And all due respect, this doesn't look like your work either."

"The user name is supposed to be recorded when somebody enters a file into Public Address," she reminded him.

"Only if it goes into the holding buffer first, like it's supposed to. But our mystery critic has bypassed that, so there's no record."

Nina removed the printed copy from the terminal. "My guess is that it's somebody in the administration. How else would they know what Croup says in every one of those speeches?"

Llew grinned. "Are you suggesting that there are signs of intelligent life among Croup's troops?"

"I guess that's a little farfetched," she sighed. "Anyway, Croup insists we get it off the system."

Llew shook his head. "Not just yet. Leave it for a while till everyone's had a chance to read it. If Croup calls again, tell him I'll get around to it as soon as I finish packing."

6

Llew maneuvered his car into the only parking place he could find which faced downhill. There were plenty of empty places across the street in front of the large campus auditorium, but they all faced *up*hill, which wouldn't do him any good as long as his car refused to start.

Several days after Llew's job as Computer Center Director had been terminated, the ignition switch in his car began acting up. It seemed to be playing Russian Roulette with him, cooperating most of the time, until he happened to be in a hurry or have important errands to run, at which point it simply refused to function. So he had taken to parking the car facing down on hills, just in case.

He got out of the car, making sure the parking brake was on tight—the hill was a long one, dizzyingly steep and treacherous in adverse weather conditions. Crossing the street, he noticed one of Byron Devilbiss's grandiose posters dominating the display board near the entrance to the auditorium, where the recital was to take place.

The auditorium was situated on the north end of campus, at the peak of the hill. Unfortunately, Llew's new office in Usher Hall was on the opposite side of campus, which meant having to pass by the Computer Center at least twice a day, a prospect which he found depressing.

At least today he would be spared that unpleasantness. After a week of procrastination, he decided he'd better get acquainted with the campus archives which he was expected to maintain in his new position. They were supposedly stored in the library—in the basement, no doubt. Lew resigned himself to spending the day there, determining what would be involved in creating a computerized index to the archive files.

The library was a drab three-story stucco building, constructed nearly fifty years ago and badly overcrowded for at least the last ten. Its chances for replacement in the forseeable future, however, were slim, owing to the severe belt-tightening measures imposed by Hess.

The library was fronted by a spacious grassy mall with sidewalks, flowerbeds and a fountain in the center. Across the mall were two relics of Wilbur Moody College's earliest days—Higgens Hall, a squat, rectangular building which currently housed the campus post office; and Dodgson House, a stately, ornate mansion bequeathed to the college by a wealthy alumnus several decades ago. Dodgson was once a private home, with three floors and countless rooms. The ground floor was currently being used for meetings and social functions, the upper floors for offices and guest quarters.

It was also the center of some recent controversy. Hess had been pushing for its sale to help fill the campus coffers, arguing that the upkeep for the ageing structure was a serious drain on resources. But his attempts to dispose of the house had met with stiff resistance from the more conservative factions in the administration. It gave Llew a measure of satisfaction to know that not all of Hess's efforts were going unchallenged.

As Llew passed by Dodgson House on his way to the library, the front door opened and Hess and another man came out onto the wide veranda. They proceeded down the steps and onto the mall, where they turned to look back at the house.

Hess was talking and the other man was nodding. Llew wasn't close enough to hear what was being said, and he intended to keep it that way.

The man with Hess was thin, square-shouldered and slightly pale, and wore a tight-fitting plaid jacket and narrow trousers. He had sharp, rather aquiline features, with small dark eyes and sunken cheeks. His nose curved down to a point, and a straight pencil-line mustache paralleled his thin lips, giving the impression of two mouths. A matchstick protruded from one corner of the lower one.

Hess was now pointing over toward the adjacent building, Higgens Hall, where students were filing in and out to check their mail. The other man nodded again, reaching up with boney fingers to move the matchstick to the other side of his mouth. After a minute, Hess looked at his watch, and the two men resumed walking across the mall.

He hasn't given up, Llew decided. He's determined to have his way with Dodgson House. And he may get it yet, especially if he succeeds in winning Roberta Turnbuckle, the formidable chairwoman of the college's Board of Trustees, over to his side. And rumor had it that the crusty old dowager was already becoming uncharacteristically cooperative with him.

As Llew started up the library steps, he noticed a tall, well-dressed young man with wire-rimmed glasses and a briefcase, studying a campus map. Lots of stange faces around here today, Llew thought, and walked over to him. "Can I help you find something?" he asked.

The young man looked up. He had a pleasant face, with a boyish, clean-cut look. "Well . . . yes, as a matter of fact. I was looking for the Computer Center."

Well well. "Okay, it's in the basement of Chapman Hall. You can see it from here." Llew pointed toward the center of campus. "That large reddish building just beyond the chapel."

The man nodded and smiled. "Much obliged," he said, and walked off in the direction Llew had pointed.

A few weeks ago, Llew thought as he continued up the library steps, I could have asked him *who* he was looking for, too. And it probably would have been me. Now it's none of my business. Hell of a note.

He stopped and looked back. I wonder if that could be the BrandeX consultant Hess was talking about, he thought. In which case I should have asked. Might have picked up some useful information. But on the other hand, I'd have a problem explaining why I wanted to know . . .

Llew went on up the steps and through the large glass doors. Inside, he walked past the check-out desk and over to the directory posted on the wall. There was no mention of an archive collection. Probably in some long-forgotten recess of the building, visited once a year by some hollow-eyed historian.

He returned to the desk, where a skinny girl consulted a printed map of the library resources and told him that the archives were located in a room at the far end of the basement. Llew nodded and thanked her. My god, he thought, I'm doomed to spend the rest of my days underground.

In the basement, he made his way down a series of narrow, dimly-lit corridors and past endless stacks of ancient bound volumes of periodicals—*U.S Geological Survey 1912 - , Smithsonian Reports 1890 - , Dr Chase's Last Receipt and Household Physician, Scribner's Monthly 1870 - , Littell's Living Age 1853 - , Congressional Record 1867 - . . .*

Eventually he came to a metal door beneath a burned out florescent light. He knew instinctively that the door would be locked, but tried it anyway.

After cursing at the unyielding doorknob, he retraced his steps back through the narrow aisles to the staircase. Now he would have to go to the head librarian to request the key . . . and he really wasn't ready for a barrage of Wally Webster's outrageous puns.

Wally wasn't a bad sort, really—chubby and twinkley-eyed, he had an infectious laugh which erupted at the slightest provocation, and he never seemed to take anything seriously. And in less serious times, Llew even enjoyed his company. In small doses, anyway.

Back upstairs, he spotted Wally standing outside his office talking with a tall, severely-dressed woman with short straight hair. As he started over, he saw that the woman was Stella Lukerella, the acerbic member of the Psychology Department whose name had drawn a shudder from Van Ruedge during Llew's last visit with him.

Stella was a fiercely independent woman, the only faculty member who had refused to attend any of the computer orientation sessions which Llew had established for users requiring computer accounts and programming support. Now, when her programs blew up—which was frequently—Llew politely but firmly refused support until she agreed to attend the next training session. This had earned Llew a prominent position on Stella's hate list.

He hesitated, and briefly considered traipsing all the way across campus to see if he could wangle an archives key out of Paisley. Then he decided to just grit and bear it, and headed over in their direction.

"Well, if it isn't the sailor who fell from grace," Stella said frigidly, arching a heavily stenciled eyebrow.

News travels fast, Llew observed. "Fine, thanks. Hi, Wally. How's library life these days?"

"Oh, stacking up," Wally replied with a chuckle, and Llew grinned in spite of himself.

"If you've come looking for a job," Stella said, filing the tip of an unfashionably long fingernail with an emery board, "the Psychology Department needs someone to clean out the mouse cages in the labs."

"Oh, I didn't know you'd been promoted," Llew replied. "Congratulations."

She ignored this. "I could see it all coming, Llew. You're always overcompensating because of all those basic inferiority feelings . . ."

Here it comes, Llew groaned.

"But then again, you don't see any congruence between yourself 'as it is' and your 'ideal self'," she lectured. "You tried to accomplish too much too fast, and finally stumbled over your own limitations. You got careless, made some bad decisions, and now you're paying the price."

Look who's talking about ambition, Llew thought. An intensely competitive person, Stella had clawed her way to the rank of full professor in record time, leaving a trail of bruised and scarred individuals who got in her way.

"It's the old castration syndrome," Stella went on. "In a desperate attempt to restore your ego-integrity you grab hold of any little thing to gratify your needs—like accepting a position with little or no responsibility, a job that won't pose any threat, where you can regain some measure of your former security." She put the finishing touches on her fingernail and held it up to the light.

"You and that emery board are two of a kind, Stella," Llew remarked, then turned to Wally. "I've just been down to the Archives section . . ."

"Ah, the Archives," Wally's eyes lit up. "Where a scholar can really feel at tome."

Llew winced. "Right. Well, anyway, the door is locked and I need to get in there."

"Gee," Wally frowned, "I haven't got the key. Harry Gross borrowed it when he was in charge of that material, and he never returned it. Actually, I don't think he ever used it—too enGrossed in other things, I guess." He giggled.

Great, Llew thought—now I'll have to go over there and get it from Harry. First Hess, then Stella, now Gross . . . and it isn't even noon.

"Let's leave the poor man to deal with his problems," Stella said to Wally, pulling at his arm. "I need you to find some books for me."

"Blow in my ear and I'll folio anywhere," Wally said, and snorted.

Llew smiled at Stella. "Thanks for the words of encouragement. I'll do the same for you when your turn comes."

He left the library and headed over to Harry's office. Maybe I'll be lucky and Harry won't be there, he thought. Maybe Ginnie can just find the key and I'll be out of there in a couple of minutes . . .

"He's on the phone," Ginnie told him. "Go on in."

Harry was sitting behind his big desk, his feet up on the cluttered surface. The phone was cradled between his shoulder and head, leaving his hands free to turn the pages of the National Enquirer. He didn't look up when Llew entered.

"The blonde? Sure I remember her," he was saying. "Real hot stuff. Yeah, right." He chortled gruffly, motioning Llew to a chair.

Llew remained standing and waited patiently. Harry flipped the pages of the newspaper. "What's that, Charlie? Oh, she finally went out with you, eh? How was it? D'ya get any?" He snickered. "Long as your old lady don't find out, what the hell. Remind me to give you some pointers on that score sometime."

Llew grimaced and shifted his weight. Was it worth repeating this conversation to Kay? Nothing she didn't already know. And it would only get her started again on Harry's indiscretions. He cleared his throat to get Harry's attention.

Harry said, "Hang on, Charlie," and covered the mouthpiece. "Whatcha need?" he asked Llew.

"Key to the archives. In the Library."

"Okay, be with you in a second. Charlie? Now, what were you saying about a job?"

Llew shifted his weight to the other foot.

Harry grinned into the phone. "What's the matter, Charlie—you get canned? Happens all the time." His eyes shifted briefly up at Llew. "Well . . . yeah, there have been some changes around here, too. Might be able to fix you up. Know anything about computers?"

Llew had had enough. "Harry, I need that key. If you could just—"

"Just a sec, Charlie." Harry leaned over toward the office door. "Hey Ginnie—get Llew that key to the little room in the basement of the library." He glanced over at Llew, then leaned back again. "Charlie? Still there?"

Llew left the office, his teeth clenched. Ginnie handed him the key. "If I'd known what you wanted, I could have spared you the agony," she told him.

"I should have asked," Llew replied, thanked her and left.

Harry's office was housed in the Administration building, which was not far from the Computer Center. As he started back toward the library, Llew noticed a large delivery van parked at the loading dock of the Center. Heavy wooden crates were being removed from the truck and carried into the building.

Nina was standing outside with Calhoun. Her ankle-length flower-print skirt was billowing in the breeze, and she kept one hand on top of her disarrayed hair. With her was the young man who had asked directions at the library. He was leaning over to pat Calhoun, who was sniffing his shoes. After a minute, he nodded to Nina and went inside the building.

Curiosity got the better of Llew, and he walked over to the loading dock. Two men were easing another crate onto a large dolly. "I take it the Sultan has arrived," Llew said to Nina.

"That's it."

"Who was that you were talking to?" he asked. "The guy from BrandeX that Hess arranged for?"

"Oh, no. That was Hen3ry."

"Henry?"

"Hen3ry—with a '3'." She sighed. "Isn't he beautiful?"

"With a what?"

"With a '3'. It's pronounced like 'Henry', though, because the '3' is silent. He says it wreaks havoc with computer files because they're never programmed to expect numbers in names."

Llew shut his eyes. "Nina, I haven't the vaguest idea what you're talking about."

"I'm talking about Hen3ry," she insisted. "He works for a consultant firm called DigiTech, somewhere over in New Jersey. Hess contracted them to help plan the physical layout for the new system. Hess was supposed to meet Hen3ry here about an hour ago, but he hasn't shown up. I told Hen3ry he could wait in my office."

"I thought BrandeX was going to supply its own consultant."

Nina wrinkled her tiny nose. "They did. A real sleeze named Slade. He's supposed to handle the installation and start-up of the Sultan, and do the initial maintenance."

Llew remembered Hess talking to someone in front of Dodgson House. "I may have seen him . . . 'Would you buy a used car from this man?'"

Nina nodded. "That's the one. He arrived a few days ago, and already he acts like he owns the place."

"He and Hess seem to get along okay."

"Yeah," she said, her eyes narrowing. "Like old friends."

"Did you show Henry . . . er, *Hen3ry*, around inside?"

"Just a quick tour. He didn't see any problem fitting the Sultan in. But he did say right off that we needed more safety features. He says the place is a fire trap."

Llew sighed. "He's right. I tried to get funding for a ceiling sprinkler a couple years ago, but the building is so old it would have cost a fortune to install it."

"And smoke detectors and more fire extinguishers. He says with all the boxes full of printer paper and trash bins full of scrap paper, the place could go up like a torch." She leaned over to help Calhoun, who was trying to sit up on his tiny haunches. "G-O-O-D sit up, Calhoun."

"Sounds like Hen3ry's got his act together. How long will he be staying?"

"Only for a day or two." She made a sour face. "Why couldn't it be *him* staying around to do Slade's job?"

Llew grinned. "Do I detect a note of, eh . . . interest?"

"Well he's *nice.* And Slade isn't. I mean they're complete opposites, like night and day . . ."

"*Yin* and *Yang,*" said a quiet voice behind Nina. She shrieked, and Calhoun fell over backwards. Llew turned to find Dahnu standing beside him.

"Dahnu!" Nina said in a shaky voice. "I wish you wouldn't *do* that!" Calhoun peered around from behind her skirt.

"My apologies," Dahnu said humbly. "I was just passing by, and couldn't help overhearing your comment about two people being opposites. In the Taoist religion, they would represent complementary entities, which are called *Yin* and *Yang.*"

"There's nothing complimentary about Slade," Nina insisted, regaining her composure.

Dahnu turned to Llew. "I also thought I heard some reference to 'fire' . . ."

"We were just discussing the need for better fire protection in the Computer Center," Llew told him.

"I see." A shadow of a frown crossed his normally placid face. "It's just that . . . I have recently had disturbing premonitions of situations involving fire. It's probably nothing . . ."

"Maybe something you ate," Nina suggested.

Dahnu's familiar smile returned. "I doubt if any items on my rather severe diet would permit such a reaction."

"There's Hess now," Nina said, indicating the small, rotund figure hurrying on short legs toward the upper entrance of Chapman Hall. "Probably just remembered his appointment with Hen3ry. I'd better go in and see that he finds him. Watch Calhoun for me?"

"Sure."

"*Stay,* Calhoun," she ordered, pushing down on the dog's rear end. "G-O-O-D stay." Then she hurried up the steps and into the side entrance of the building.

"How's the work going on the Zeta waves?" Llew asked Dahnu.

"I've made significant progress," Dahnu said. "I've been able to display brief images of the waves on the graphics terminal. Unfortunately, it's very intermittent, and the images tend to get confused with the other, stronger electrical signals given off by the brain."

"Who's the guinea pig?"

Dahnu smiled. "Myself, of course. Since Zeta waves are only produced when the brain consciously performs automatic functions, my choice of subjects is limited."

Llew looked skeptical. "You mean you can really do all those things with your insides, like make your heart beat slower and your temperature go up?"

"Anyone can," Dahnu assured him, "with patience and practice."

"But what's the point? If all these things happen automatically, why do you want to interfere?"

"Is it wrong to interfere with a headache? Or to lower dangerously high blood pressure? Not everything that happens in the body is necessarily to one's advantage."

"Can't argue with that. Any problems with the computer end of it?"

"The programs appear to be working as intended," Dahnu replied. "Winklejohn has been very helpful. However, to properly process the signals further, I need a higher degree of accuracy than the computer seems able to provide."

"Well, I hope the answer to your problems is in those boxes," indicating the wooden crates on the loading dock. "Not exactly what I had in mind, but . . ."

Nina rejoined them. "Hess didn't even apologize to Hen3ry for being late," she said. "But Hen3ry was courteous enough to thank me for letting him use my office."

"I don't suppose Hess asked for your input on any of the problems of installation or conversion," Llew ventured.

"Are you kidding? When Hen3ry told him I'd been very helpful, he just scowled and looked like he wished I'd leave. Then Slade came in, so I did."

"Well, the morning is shot, anyway," Llew said, looking at his watch. "How bout some lunch at Duffy's?"

"Fine with me . . ." She looked around, then put her fists on her hips. "He's done it *again.*"

"Who has? What?"

"Dahnu. He was standing right here not *two seconds* ago . . ."

The faint sounds of sirens in the distance made Llew look up from the table where he was working. He glanced at his watch—11:45—why do fires always seem to happen at night? he wondered.

He leaned back in the heavy straight-backed chair to stretch. Didn't realize it was so late. Time flies when you're having fun. But they'll be closing the library shortly . . .

Stacked on several tables in the small room were numerous volumes documenting the activities and functions of Wilbur Moody College over its hundred year history. Anything pertaining to physical expansion, personnel, athletics, publicity, and academic and social programs was included, along with several abortive attempts to catalog it all into some organized fashion.

Llew's intention was to essentially finish the indexing, categorizing all the materials for easy storage in computer files. It was tedious work, but he had made a good start.

Among the documents was the original set of architectural drawings for Higgens Hall. Not much imagination had gone into the design, which was strictly functional. But Llew's attention was drawn to the spacious basement, which Paisley Braithwaite had confided was currently housing some sort of government installation—apparently engaged in some sort of classified work, since Paisley seemed reluctant to talk about it. The plans gave no indication of the function of the basement, and the only detail shown was a set of stairs to the main floor. Llew seemed to remember an elevator in the building—must have been added later.

He had searched additional materials relating to the building, but although there were later references to repairs and modifications, including the elevator and the banks of post office boxes on the main floor, no further mention was made of the basement. Nor were there any records of transactions with any government agency—leases, contracts, purchase orders for services or equipment. Dead end.

The fire sirens sounded closer. Wherever it was, Llew was sure Byron Devilbiss would be there, or on his way. Byron's idea of entertainment was chasing fire engines and watching the action with all the rapt attention of a baseball fan at Yankee stadium. He won't miss this one—it must be close to campus . . .

Something caught his eye in the single small window high above his head. It was dark outside, but he could see faint light patterns flickering on the pane.

His curiosity aroused, he moved the chair around under the window and climbed up. Using his sleeve to rub off several years' accumulation of dust from the pane, he looked out into the darkness.

Cushlamochree! It's *Dodgson*! The whole damn place is on fire!

Llew nearly fell off the chair getting down. He grabbed his coat and ran out the door, switching off the lights and fumbling for the keys. He locked the door and dashed through the aisles and up the stairs.

On the main floor of the library, students and staff in a bustle of confusion were converging toward the front entrance. Llew hadn't realized how many people actually stayed at the library until closing time.

Outside, the fire trucks had arrived and more sirens sounded in the distance. The mall was a chaos of flashing lights and scurrying shadowy figures. Students were swarming onto the scene while police warned the crowds to stay back. A dozen firemen in heavy rubber coats were unrolling the thick, flat hoses from the trucks, while voices crackled from megaphones, barking orders over the excited clamor of the spectators.

The blaze was a big one. Clouds of black smoke swirled out of a dozen widening fissures in the walls of Dodgson House, and there were flames visible in almost every window. Llew made his way over as close as the police would allow, just as the hoses released their gushing streams of water. More fire trucks arrived on the scene, their heavy tires plowing huge ruts through flower beds and landscaped walks.

It was obvious that the fire was too well under way to save the building, and much of the effort was directed toward preventing it from spreading to the neighboring Higgens hall. Llew could feel the heat from where he stood in the cold early March chill, and the pungent smell of smoke filled the night air.

He saw some familiar faces in the crowd—including Byron, puffing fiercely on a cigar, his loden cloak flapping in the wind, the flames reflected in his wide eyes. Like a child watching a parade, Llew thought.

A police officer was returning to his patrol car from the direction of one of the fire engines. Llew went over and asked if anyone knew how the fire started.

The officer tipped up the bill of his cap and looked back at the fire. "They're saying it was faulty wiring—old place like that and all. But I donno. Seems like if that's what it was, most of the fire would be in one place. This one looks like it's coming from everywhere. Guess we'll never know."

"Was anyone inside when it started?"

"Couple people using the offices upstairs. Said they smelled smoke and called the fire department. No reports of anyone getting hurt."

The radio inside the car squawked, and the policeman leaned inside to reply to the call. Llew moved off to a different vantage point. The firemen seemed to be making progress, but there wouldn't be much left of the stately old mansion.

As he stood watching the fire take its toll, he remembered the conversation with Dahnu and Nina this afternoon. Dahnu had said something about a premonition of fire . . .

He had been right on target with this one. But then, Dahnu usually was.

7

The waiter brought the wine and held it out, label up, for Llew's approval. "You'll like this," Llew told Kay. "It's one of Van's—a blend of some of his better stuff." He nodded to the waiter, who busied himself with the cork.

"I haven't seen his wines in many restaurants around here," Kay remarked as a small amount was poured in Llew's glass. He sampled it, and nodded again to the waiter, who proceeded to fill Kay's glass.

"There are some places that carry them now," Llew told her. "This one does because it's near his vineyard. The owner recommends Van's wines, and Van recommends the restaurant to people who come out for winery tours."

She smiled. "You scratch my back and I'll scratch yours."

"Right. And speaking of doing nice things to each other . . ."

Kay reached over and took Llew's hand. Their table was situated in a remote corner of the dimly lit room, and the restaurant was far enough away from campus to assure privacy. Kay had exchanged her starched functional uniform for a silk print blouse and wraparound skirt, and her lustrous hair fell loose over her shoulders, softening the sculptured contours of her face.

"It *has* been a while, hasn't it?" she said wistfully.

"Three weeks, two days—"

"—Five hours and—" looking at her watch—"twenty-two minutes."

Llew held his own watch up to the light. "Either you're slow or I'm fast. According to my mine—"

Her smile tightened into resignation. "It's just that Harry has become so unpredictable these days. I never know when he's going to be home, or how long he's going to be out. It's difficult to make any plans of my own."

Llew gazed glumly into his wine glass. "I suppose he's ecstatic about his new responsibilities."

"Having a ball, especially now that he's got a couple more people to boss around."

"Winklejohn and Rama. At least he doesn't have any authority over Nina—not that that is likely to stop him."

"How are they taking all this?"

"As well as can be expected," he sighed. "Wink and Rama are pretty adaptable, although the strain is bound to show sooner or later. Nina's another matter, though. These past few weeks have been rough on her. She keeps threatening to quit."

"How is she going to manage a new computer system that she doesn't even know?"

"She'll pick it up. Although it would help if she had some documentation. Hess promised that BrandeX would supply a complete set, but so far she hasn't received squat."

"But didn't you say the new computer is supposed to start up today? How is she going to run it if—"

"She won't—at least for the time being. Hess arranged for BrandeX to supply a consultant familiar with the Sultan. He'll maintain the system until Nina can do it. In the meantime, she'll manage the old system, which they're keeping around for a while as a backup."

"I'm sure she loves that."

Llew leaned back in his chair. "She says the worst part is the BrandeX consultant, fellow named Slade. She refers to him as 'Slimey' Slade. Says he won't let her near the new system."

"Things really are bad, aren't they?"

"They've been better. And they'll probably get worse."

The waiter brought their lunches and Llew refilled both their wine glasses. He set the bottle on the table and sat gazing at the colorful label. "Maybe Van Ruedge had the right idea to get out of the business altogether."

"He got out because he found something he liked better," Kay reminded him. "At least you enjoy . . . *enjoyed* what you were doing."

"I don't enjoy what I'm doing now."

She nodded sympathetically. "How long are you going to stick it out?"

"I change my mind about that every ten minutes," he shrugged. "I guess the only thing that keeps me going is knowing that Hess expects me to quit sooner or later. And while he's waiting, he keeps dreaming up ways to speed up my departure. Did you know that I'm not allowed in the Computer Center any more?"

Kay looked shocked. "Why?"

"Something to do with those pieces by The Campus Curmudgeon that keep cropping up on the system. President Croup still thinks I'm responsible for them. So Hess sent me a terse note accusing me of 'irresponsible and unprofessional behavior'. He stopped just short of firing me—he still hopes I'll save him the trouble."

"You *aren't* writing those things, are you?"

"Of course not. And I don't have any idea who is. But Hess

doesn't really care—he'll go along with anything that serves to discredit me. I'm surprised he hasn't accused me of burning down Dodgson House."

"You probably would have been doing him a favor if you had. He wasn't having any luck getting the administration to sell the place. Now at least they'll get the insurance money for it."

"Insurance money?"

"Of course. It'll be a bundle, too."

"I never thought of that. All those antiques and paintings and—"

Kay shook her head. "Not that much actually got destroyed. I was told that most of the valuable items had been moved out of Dodgson over the past few months."

"Moved out? Where?"

She hesitated. "Most of them to one of the residences on Park Street owned by the college."

Llew stared at her. "Not the one—"

She nodded. "Right. The one Hess is living in."

He shut his eyes. "I don't believe this . . ."

"Some large oriental carpets, the pictures, that huge oak Chippendale hutch, lots of furniture . . ."

"Where did you hear all this?"

"I'm on the long-range planning committee, remember? Apparently it was done at the insistance of the chairman of the Board of Trustees."

"Roberta Turnbuckle."

"Herself. She claims that Hess is a 'connoisseur' of fine furniture, and felt that he should assume responsibility for them until the fate of Dodgson was resolved."

"Which, of course, it now has been."

"Right. And now that the insurance company is satisfied that faulty wiring was responsible for the fire, they'll pay up and the issue will be closed."

Llew sighed. "I ran into Paisley Braithwaite yesterday. According to him, there was nothing wrong with the wiring in the house. But apparently he's been outvoted. Hess has already accepted a bid for the rewiring of Higgens Hall, because it's even older than Dodgson."

Kay smiled. "Maybe they'll even get around to Usher one of these days."

"If it doesn't collapse first. Every time someone upstairs flushes the john, it sounds like the whole foundation is being swept away."

She grinned. "I hope you keep a life jacket in your office."

"There isn't room." He reached for the wine bottle. "How do you like the wine?"

"The what? Oh—this," holding up her glass. "I haven't been paying much attention to it, I'm afraid." She drank some and nodded her approval. "Nice. Harry, of course, wouldn't like it. He doesn't like any white wines."

"I thought he only drank beer and Scotch."

"These days that's about it. But he used to drink red wine. Fancied himself a real authority. Except that he mispronounced all the names. 'Beaujolais' came out 'Bollojay', and he said 'Merloo' for 'Merlot'. If you tried to correct him, he'd get mad and his tongue would stick. *Then* you ought to hear him try to pronounce—"

"Wait a minute—his *tongue* would stick?"

"To the roof of his mouth. Just the tip. So his words come out all garbled. It only happens when he gets drunk or angry—and of course that only makes him angrier."

Llew cocked his head. "Can I ask you a personal question?"

She smiled. "If *you* can't, nobody can. But I'll save you the trouble. I married him for the same reasons that every young, impressionable girl who wants to get away from home gets married."

"Because you were young, impressionable, and wanted—"

"—to get away from home. And your next question, why do I stay with him . . ."

"Why do you?"

She hesitated. "That's . . . harder to answer. But it has a lot to do with reasonable alternatives." She looked at her watch. "We've got to get back—my waiting room is probably getting crowded with students, giving each other germs."

They paid the bill and walked out to Kay's car. Llew's car was still experiencing starter problems, and had been left parked, as usual, facing downhill on the north side of campus.

It was raining lightly outside, and the air was nippy. The wine had warmed their insides, so they lingered in the front seat warming up the rest as well. After a few minutes, the windows began to fog up.

"Do you really have to go back right away?" Llew asked, his lips tracing familiar patterns over her flushed cheeks.

She sighed softly. "You know I—*mmmffff*—do. And so do you, so you can custode your archives."

"They'll wait," moving down to her neck. "I'm still researching yours. I seem to recall a couple of nice volumes around here somewhere . . ."

She giggled and pushed him away. "I think you need the proverbial cold shower, Mr McQuilla." Then she reached over and touched his cheek. "I guess we both do."

He took her hand. "You scratch my back . . ."

She smiled. "And speaking of 'back'—that's where we've got to get pretty quick or I'll be the next one to lose my job." She reached under the seat and produced a cloth. "Here—do something about the windows so I can see enough to drive."

Minutes later they were hissing along the wet highway toward campus. From time to time, the car would weave slightly as Llew persisted in his research efforts. Then Kay said, "What's that?"

"What's what?"

She was looking at the rear-view mirror. Llew turned and looked out the rear window to see a flashing red light through the rain. "Oh no," he groaned.

"Where did *he* come from?" Kay asked, slowing the car and turning on her right-turn blinker. "I haven't seen another car on the road except for that taxi we passed a minute ago."

Llew was nodding, his eyes closed, as Kay came to a stop off the side of the road. She turned around and looked back. "My god, it *is* the taxi! Llew, we've been pulled over by a *taxi cab!*"

"I meant to tell you . . ." he started.

Minutes later, a familiar stocky figure got out of the taxi and walked leisurely up to Kay's car, note pad in hand. He was not wearing a raincoat, but there was a plastic shower cap over his patrolman's hat, which was dripping around the brim.

Kay was digging in her pocketbook for her license and registration. Llew rested his arm over the seat back with his hand over the lower part of his face, hoping the patrolman wouldn't recognize him.

The man took the cards and examined them. "Well, Mizz Katherine Gross," he said, reading from the license, and pronouncing her name "Grahss", "you musta bin in a awful hurry when you passed me back there, 'cause I wuz doin' the legal fifty-five." He continued to study the identification, seemingly oblivious to the rain, which had become heavier. His uniform was drenched and sticking to him, and water was dripping onto his notepad. "And seemed to me you wuz weavin' a bit now and then. You, uh . . .been doin' some drinkin'?"

Llew squeezed his eyes shut and willed Kay to say "no", and hoped that the cop wouldn't persist.

"No," she said. "Of course not."

The cop nodded. "Well, I ain't gonna pursoo it—mainly cause I ain't got my breath tester. But the rest is gonna cost ya forty. Need yer signatoor," leaning over to hand her the sopping pad and a pen.

As he did so, he peered over his reflective sunglasses at Llew, and his mouth widened into a grin. “Well, looky who we got here! Mr Loo Ellen Mac Willy.”

Llew sighed in resignation. The cop brushed some dripping water from an earlobe. “Guess it’s true about birds of a feather stickin’ together. Gracious me, one of these days I’ll stop somebody else for speedin’, and there in the front seat along with the driver will be Mizz Grahss and Mr Mac Willy. Ih, ih.”

Kay handed back the notepad, her signature already all but blotted out by the rain. He tore off her copy and gave it to her. “Now you jest keep it under the limit and there won’t be no more of these. And, uh . . . don’t let Mr Mac Willy tell you no differnt. Ih, ih.” He gave a brief salute, flinging drops of water over his shower cap, and strolled back to his taxi.

Kay stuffed the ticket into the glove compartment. “Where on earth does he know you from?” she asked Llew as she started the motor.

He told her. “And I don’t think I ever paid the ticket, either. Any day now they’ll be coming with a warrant and drag me out of my nice new office.”

8

Back in his dungeon office, Llew squeezed around the desk and eased into his rickety chair, which Paisley had temporarily patched together until a replacement could be requisitioned. The new computer was supposed to be up and running by now, so it was time to see just what things looked like. He found himself secretly hoping that there would be problems, so that the first seeds of doubt about Hess's own competence would be sown.

Since he no longer had a personal direct line to the computer, Llew had gotten Paisley to run an extension from an unused phone jack upstairs, allowing him to dial into the computer via modem without interfering with his office telephone. He switched on the terminal, typed the auto-dial sequence, and waited.

When the connection was made, he took a breath and typed the log-in command. According to a recently circulated notice, the command would be the same as in the old system. A message on the screen then requested his user name and password, also to be kept unchanged. He entered these, and the screen announced:

```
S U L T A N OPERATING SYSTEM, VERSION 5A
PLEASE TYPE 'HELP' FOR USER INFORMATION
```

Llew typed HELP and the message read:

```
WELCOME TO THE SULTAN 6000.

FOR THE CONVENIENCE OF OUR USERS, AN
INTERFACE HAS BEEN PROVIDED TO ALLOW
MOST OF THE PREVIOUS COMMANDS FROM THE
MAX-11 SYSTEM TO BE UTILIZED.  ALL
FORMER FILES, PROGRAMS AND UTILITY
ROUTINES HAVE BEEN PRESERVED.  UNTIL
FURTHER NOTICE, USERS MAY CONTINUE TO
OPERATE AS BEFORE.
```

Llew leaned forward, resting his chin on a fist. I'm *impressed*, he thought to himself. Assuming, of course, that everything really does work.

He typed DIRECT to see if all the files in his own directory were still accounted for. The screen returned with:

```
USER MACQ150 - NO FILES IN DIRECTORY
```

No files? But there should be dozens. What have they done with all my files? Maybe they're in another directory area. . .

He chose the name of one of the missing files and typed SEARCH LLEW21.FIL.

The screen printed:

```
ERROR - PRIVILEGED COMMAND
```

Llew swore. SEARCH never *used* to be a privileged command. And obviously I no longer have a privileged account—which shouldn't surprise me. Let's see what else I'm not allowed to do . . .

He typed SYSTEM to check the system status:

```
ERROR - PRIVILEGED COMMAND
```

He tried DEVICE to see what peripheral units were on-line:.

```
ERROR - PRIVILEGED COMMAND
```

Growing more aggravated, he tried ACTIVE, then PARTITION, then TASK . . . all without success. He leaned back and rubbed his eyes. Okay, he told himself, let's just think this out. Either all these standard commands have now been made privileged, or else they aren't included in the interface between old and new systems. "MOST OF THE PREVIOUS COMMANDS HAVE BEEN PRESERVED", the message had read—but obviously none that provide any system information.

And that still doesn't account for why my directory is empty. The message had also said that all user files had been retained.

He took a deep breath and continued typing all the commands he could think of. It didn't take long to verify that all the system-related commands were now restricted. On the old MAX system, any user could display information on his terminal screen using these commands. No one could make system modifications, of course, except by those with a privileged account, which meant Llew and his staff.

Now, it appeared, the only information available to general users was the files in their own personal accounts. Almost as if someone didn't want them to know what the rest of the system was doing.

Llew searched his memory for the account names and passwords for some of the other campus users. He logged into Professor Bede's account and requested a directory listing, which was promptly displayed:

```
[ACCOUNT BEDE650]
FILENAME                SIZE

WYRD.DAT                  22
WIDSITH.TXT              113
HEOROT.HYG                55
CAEDMON.LST               98
    .                      .
    .                      .
    .                      .
```

Well, his account seems to be intact. Let's look at Dahnu's . . .

```
[ACCOUNT DAH355]
FILENAME                SIZE

KRISHNA.BAK               72
ATMA.YOG                 112
LAOTZU.TAO                14
    .                      .
    .                      .
    .                      .
```

Llew was beginning to feel decidedly discriminated against. He switched to the other account numbers he had used on the old system. All of them were empty. It was like being locked out of your own house . . . and none of the neighbors with spare keys were at home.

Well, in cases like this, having exhausted all legal means of entry—his eyes narrowed—one just has to break a window or two . . .

The phone rang on the other line as he was selecting the appropriate crowbar. It was Mike Ebbsedik.

"Llew? Sorry for the long turnaround time. Got multiplexed off onto some other channels right after we talked."

"No problem. Any luck with BrandeX?"

"Checked with the standard trade listings—not much luck. Doesn't necessarily mean anything, though. Could be new. Other thing is, there's no shop at the address listed—just a box at a private post office."

"That doesn't surprise me," Llew said. "I've tried calling them a dozen times, and someone keeps telling me they'll return my call. Which they never do."

"Tried that myself—same output. Haven't given up, though. How're things going there?"

"They aren't." Llew told him about the old system front-ending the new one.

"Have a problem getting that through the logic gate," Mike said skeptically. "What's the point? From what I've learned about the Sultan, the operating system is fairly user-friendly. Why go to all that trouble?"

"That's what I'm trying to figure out."

"Any support people there from BrandeX?"

"A fellow named Slade. Wylie Slade, I think."

"Hmm . . . doesn't parse."

"I haven't met him yet, myself. But I think it's about time I did."

"Might be worth the effort. I'll add him to my query list."

"Good. I appreciate all this, Mike."

"Hang in there."

Llew replaced the phone and sat back—carefully—in his creaky chair. Right, he thought—the first step is to meet this Slade fellow and see if I can get some useful information out of him. Might save me a lot of blind alleys. And maybe he isn't as bad a chap as Nina makes him out to be.

The only problem is, I'm not supposed to be in the Computer Center. But maybe Slade doesn't know that. Hell with it—let them throw me out.

Besides, there are all my missing files that need accounting for.

A muffled roar above Llew's head speeded his decision, and he grabbed his jacket, switched off his terminal and left.

Several minutes later, he approached the back entrance to the Center. Tied to the stately oak by a long rope, and looking woefully dejected, was Calhoun. When he saw Llew, his entire back half went into a fit of wagging.

Llew squatted down to pat the dog, who immediately tried to climb into his lap, almost upsetting them both. "No no, Calhoun— down, boy! That's right. Yes, you can lick my hand. G-O-O-D lick hand."

Leaving the dog straining on the rope, Llew trotted up the steps and into the entrance hallway, wondering why Nina had left Calhoun outside. She usually kept him in her office until she, Rama or Winklejohn could take him outside for exercise and other necessities.

Nina was hunched at her desk, busily typing on a terminal. Because of her diminuative size, her head was barely level with the screen and her fingers just under her chin as they flew across the keys. Her eyes squinted against the drift of smoke from the unfiltered cigaret in her pursed mouth. Her hair seemed even more disarrayed than usual.

"Looks like they're keeping you busy," Llew said. Nina responded with a blast of invective so fierce that Llew quickly shut the office door.

"I don't care *who* hears me!" she shouted. "If they don't like it they can all go—"

"Now calm down," Llew urged. "It can't be all that bad."

She glared at him. "What if I'd said that to you when you were given the boot?"

She had a point. "Okay, just how bad is it?" he asked. "You don't mean they've given *you* the boot . . ."

"Not yet," she steamed. "And at this rate I'm not going to give them the chance. Llew, I'm *this close* to telling them to stuff—"

"By 'them', you mean—"

"Slimey Slade, mainly." She emptied the ashtray into a wastebasket, replaced it on her desk and ground her cigaret in it. "But Hess comes over every day and adds his two cents."

"Really? Hess comes over *here* every day? What on earth for? I mean, vice-presidents usually have better things to do than—"

"Sometimes twice a day. He and The Slime shut themselves in with the new computer for hours at a time. God knows what they do in there—I keep listening for the sounds of whips and high-heeled shoes."

"Okay, okay. Have you been on the new system yet?"

"Been *on* it?" She waved her hand. "I haven't even *seen* it! I watched them unload the big boxes and haul them inside. There were a couple of guys here from BrandeX to assemble it, but Hess wouldn't let anyone else near it. Except Slade."

Llew eased himself into a chair. "I don't like this, Nina."

"*You* don't like it! Harry Gross has Winklejohn doing nothing but writing new administrative programs, and dumps all kinds of nitpicky work on poor Rama. And Slade has me purging the entire system of old files he says we don't need anymore, including everybody's backup files, files that haven't been accessed in six months, files that—"

"Wait a minute—you're not working for Slade."

"Wanna bet? Hess says he's in charge—'during the transition'."

"Then you *have* been on the system—I mean, if you're able to access all the directories . . ."

She shook her head. "Not all of them—just the ones that came from the old MAX. They've all been transfered into non-privileged accounts on a separate disk pack, and the protection code changed so I can delete. But I can't do a SYSTAT or even a directory listing on the rest of the system."

"Do you know what happened to my files, by any chance? All my directories are empty."

She lit another cigaret. "They're safe. I was told—listen to this, buddy-boy—I was told to delete everything in your accounts. So I just distributed your files around into other accounts and changed the names. I kept a record of where they are, so you can transfer them back a little at a time."

"Not without a privileged account I can't."

"It shouldn't be hard to get around that. I plan to do a little breaking-and-entering as soon as I get through with all this chicken—"

The door opened, and Slade walked into the room. He had a folder labelled "Sultan 6000—SYSTEM NOTES"in his hand. He looked suspiciously at Llew.

Llew nodded to him. "You must be Sli . . . uh, Slade."

"You must be McQuilla." Slade's voice had an edge to it, which befitted his sharp features. He still sported a matchstick in the corner of his mouth. "Something you need?"

Llew's first impulse—second, actually, the first being rather crudely physical in nature—was to demand an explanation of Slade's orders to delete all his files. But since Nina had assured him that they were safe, he moved on to number three. "I was curious about how you managed the interface to make the Sultan come out looking like the MAX. And why."

"Why what?"

"Why you felt it was necessary. Most of the users on campus are computer-literate enough to pick up new operating system commands without much trouble."

Slade shrugged. "Just minimizing the hassles. The software was available, so we used it."

"Did BrandeX supply it?"

Slade hesitated. "Yeah, that's right."

"How long do you expect to use it?"

"Use what?"

Was he being purposely vague? Llew wondered. "The interface. When do you plan to switch over to the new operating system?"

Slade shrugged again. "Donno yet. We'll see how it goes."

Llew was tempted to ask how *what* goes, but asked instead, "When can we see some Sultan documentation? I'm curious to see what some of the features are."

Slade's eyes shifted just a bit. "Don't have enough copies to go around right now."

That didn't answer the question. "Yeah, well okay—I can probably pick up a set from some of my friends in the business."

Slade's eyes shifted back, and Llew regretted this last remark. Better to just play harmless for the time being—it was going to be enough of an uphill battle as it was.

Slade maneuvered the matchstick to the other side of his mouth. Then he said to Nina, "See me when you're finished with that." He glanced back at Llew and walked out the door.

When he was gone, Nina cocked her head. "I can't remember—did he say 'please'?"

Llew frowned. "I don't think so . . . but I'm sure he meant to. He'll probably be back to apologize when he realizes he's forgotten." He walked to the door. "When he does, tell him I'm sorry I had to rush off. Maybe the three of us can get together for tea sometime."

"Anything else I can tell him for you?"

Llew thought a minute. "Yeah, but it'll keep for a while. By the way, I noticed Calhoun tied up outside. Whose idea was that?"

Nina's mouth tightened. "Guess."

Llew nodded. "Hang in there," he said, and left.

9

The monthly meeting of the college administrative staff was held, as usual, in the faculty dining room. Staff business lunches were not Llew's cup of tea, and he could remember attending only three or four during his tenure at the college. And besides, he wasn't even sure that his new position as Custodian of Institutional Archives entitled him to participate.

But the subject for discussion today was the fiscal year budget—an interim report by Vice-President Hess—and Llew's curiosity was aroused. Some reference to the Computer Center would have to be included, and any information about the new system at this point would be helpful.

It had been nearly three weeks since the new computer had gone into operation, and six months since C. Willard Hess had assumed the position of Vice-President for Financial Affairs. Llew had been keeping his ears open for local reaction to each, and so far the reviews had been mixed. Perhaps here he could get a feel for faculty response to the current situation.

Since his presence in the dining room might prove awkward, Llew opted for the small adjacent lounge. There was a heavy wingback chair next to the entrance where he could observe and hear without being seen.

President Horace Croup sat at the head of the front table. He was a tall, bulky man with thin wavy hair, a genial informal manner, and a loud voice which could be made even louder if one took his casual demeanor too literally. He hated controversy nearly as much as he hated criticism, and went to great lengths to avoid the former and pass the blame for the latter, since both tended to erode his air of relentless optimism.

Seated on his right was the Grande Dame herself, Roberta Turnbuckle, chairwoman of Wilbur Moody's Board of Trustees. She was a sturdy woman, as tall as most men at the meeting, which added to an already imposing mien of authority. Although well into middle age, she had taken recently to wearing her graying hair long and back over her shoulders, a style which was never currently in vogue at any appropriate stage of her life. A pair of ornate reading glasses, encrusted with tiny grape clusters on the frames, hung from a golden chain around her neck. She wore a number of large rings, the value of which were unlikely to ever be questioned. Nor was the power she wielded over the other members of the Board.

Next to her sat Hess, eating his soup in a slow, methodical way, in small sips so as not to pose too great a demand on his tiny mouth. From time to time, his eyes would briefly scan the other faces in the room, as if to identify possible sources of dissent.

Across the table, from Croup's left, were Ormand Otvos, Vice President for Academic Affairs and a strong supporter of computer services; Harry Gross, Head of Information Services—and now Coordinator of Administrative Computing; Kay Gross, Director of the College Infirmiry and Harry's wife; and Godfrey Daniels, manager of the campus post office, a pudgy individual with squinty eyes and a perpetually swollen nose, and reputedly one of Croup's favorite drinkin' buddies.

There were a half dozen other tables in the room, all occupied by members of the administrative staff who were finishing up the appetizers as student waiters served the main course. Llew had grabbed a quick bite before he came. He remembered that the meals here used to be pretty decent for campus food—until, as one of his economy moves, Hess had replaced the facility with a cheaper catering service. Since then, the soup had tasted straight from a can and the salad from a freezer.

No one at any of the tables seemed to be showing much interest in the main course, although Harry Gross seemed oblivious to this fact as he shoveled in the food while keeping up a one-sided conversation with Dr Otvos. Kay picked tentatively at her plate while replying politely and briefly to Godfrey Daniels's persistent attempts to engage her in conversation. She did not see Llew in the lounge, and would hardly have expected him to be at the meeting anyway.

Neither Roberta Turnbuckle or Willard Hess seemed to be eating much, and it was Roberta who was doing most of the talking. Hess apeared to be only half-listening, although he would smile his peculiar icy smile at her briefly from time to time.

After dessert—instant chocolate pudding with a vanilla wafer stuck in the top—President Croup lifted himself from his chair and cleared his throat. "Uh . . .I think maybe we ought to get started here, people. The purpose of today's meeting is, of course, to hear a financial report from our new Vice-President for Financial Affairs. Mr C. Willard Hess has been a mighty busy man since he joined us just a few short months ago, and we've already seen a lot of changes around the old place. And I reckon we're apt to see a lot more in the months to come.

"Before we get to that, though, I want to recognize a special guest at today's meeting—Mrs Roberta Turnbuckle, chairwoman of our illustrious Board of Trustees." He nodded in her direction—"Like to say a few words, Roberta?"

She smiled an acknowledgment at the scattered applause, and rose from her chair. "Thank you, Horace. I won't take much of your time, except to express my appreciation for being invited to attend your meeting." Her voice was husky, and had the rhetorical ring of someone at home behind a podium. "I just want to say how pleased I am with the reports of the fine job Willard . . . that is, Mr. *Hess*, has been doing."

"Hear, hear!" Harry Gross said, his mouth full of chocolate pudding. Llew wondered how many of those reports had originated from Harry's Publicity Department.

"And I would urge you all," Roberta went on, "to continue to give this fine gentleman your closest cooperation and support in his efforts to bring a greater measure of economic stability to this campus." She smiled over at Hess, who coughed and dabbed at his mouth with a napkin.

"Thanks, Roberta," Croup said, heaving himself back onto his feet. "We always welcome the valued members of the Board of Trustees to these business meetings—keeps us honest." He chuckled, and Harry Gross went *haw haw*; Kay kept her eyes down at the table, from which her untouched dessert had just been removed.

"And now, I think . . . uh, Willard, you want to go ahead?" Croup gestured toward Hess and sat down again.

"Yes. Thank you." Hess got up and put on a pair of rimless glasses. He seemed rather diminutive, particularly after the previous two speakers. "I'll go over the figures first, then answer any questions."

Llew listened while Hess rattled off numbers and statistics. Most of them had to do with savings that had been realized since his budget cutting measures—largely personnel reductions—had been implemented. A few items seemed suspect to Llew, but they would be difficult to assess without the printed figures.

Harry Gross was leaning back in his chair, smoking a cigar, oblivious to the annoyed looks of those seated nearby. Including Kay. Lew remembered her saying that a man who smokes cigars doesn't *have* to beat his wife. Unfortunately, Llew enjoyed an occasional cigar himself and had to remember not to indulge in Kay's presence.

Not that there had been all that many occasions lately for remembering. They had been able to meet only twice—briefly—since Llew had been targeted by Hess. Kay was finding life with Harry even more difficult now that his ego had been boosted several notches, and the subject of separation came up more frequently in her conversations with Llew. He wondered if she ever talked about it to Harry.

Llew's own feelings about the matter were ambivalent. He cared strongly for Kay and disliked Harry, and was reasonably sure that his feelings about one were not simply a reaction to the other. He also found the whole concept of "affairs" and clandestine relationships distasteful. One could never really be sure about one's true feelings in such unpredictable and pressured circumstances, where everything you said or did had to take into account an unsuspecting third party.

Maybe it would be better for Kay to leave Harry—at least it would put his own relationship to her into a better perspective, and probably resolve a lot of nagging questions in both their minds.

Hess was nearly finished with his report, and had yet to make any mention of computer services. Roberta Turnbuckle had not taken her eyes from him since he stood up, and the look on her face was a curiously reverent one. Llew was used to a sterner countenance on the woman, more fitting to her dominant—and dominating—position on the Board of Trustees.

He wondered why she was even here at this meeting in the first place. It was no secret that Hess had been Roberta's preferred choice to replace the retiring Wexler, and none of the other Trustees would think of arguing with her. Maybe she was just trying to verify that her choice had been justified. Except that Llew had the distinct feeling that her mind had been made up on that matter for a long while.

It nearly got by him, but Llew caught the word "computer" as Hess was summing up. "The transition is proceeding smoothly and will continue to be virtually transparent to the users, assuring everyone of uninterrupted service. This is due, in large measure, to the vastly improved capabilities of the new computer, and the fine support of the vendor." He looked up from his report. "Are there any questions? If not—"

"I've got one." Ormand Otvos's hand was up.

Llew leaned over closer to the door—Otvos was not one to mince words.

"This new computer," Otvos said, "which was abruptly substituted for the one our committee originally approved—for reasons that have never been clear to me—if it's such an all-fired improvement over the old one, when can we expect to see some evidence of it?"

Roberta Turnbuckle was glaring at Otvos, and Harry Gross was frowning as if he hadn't understood the question. Hess removed his glasses. "I have heard nothing to indicate any lack of satisfaction with the new system, Dr Otvos. Surely the fact that all of the previous software continues to operate flawlessly without any time-consuming conversion efforts attests to the excellent performance of the Sultan."

Harry nodded. "Piece of cake."

"I think you're missing my point," Otvos continued. "I'm not talking about continuity—I'm talking about *improvement.* In conversations with Llew McQuilla—whose departure from the Computer Center is equally mystifying to me—I was given to understand that file storage capacity would be greatly increased, response time would be faster, more sophisticated software would be available . . . I'm still waiting to see some evidence of any of this on our new system."

Couldn't have put it better myself, Llew thought. He had run numerous test programs, noting that the run-time specs were curiously identical to those achieved on the old MAX system. The only way to know for sure was to access the detailed system log file, but this required a privileged account. And so far, his efforts to break into the system had proved futile. But there were still a few tricks left to try . . .

Hess's mouth tightened into a tolerant smile. "I don't know what kinds of promises and assurances were made, but practical experience shows that claims of this nature must be approached cautiously and realistically. However, with regard to the items you mentioned, our detailed computer logs show that, in fact, overall efficiency has increased by a significant factor . . . and will continue to do so as upgrades are made to the operating system. And if I may say so, anyone promising overnight miracles is simply demonstrating his naivete'. . . and lack of credibility."

Llew saw Kay sit up stiffly. Don't say anything, sweetheart, he urged mentally. Let him talk. I need to find out all I can, and a brawl at this stage isn't going to help matters.

"And, of course, much depends on the applications to which the computer resources are directed," Hess continued. "Many users will notice dramatic improvements, while others will find that the differences are more . . . uh, subtle."

Otvos sat back and folded his arms. "Well, all the users I've talked to are apparently getting the 'subtle' treatment. It still takes Dr Fermat in the Math department just as long to solve a series of linear equations; Dr Graff in Statistics insists that the response time for his regression analysis program is no different than it was before . . . and even Professor Bede's chess program still loses forty percent of its games."

There was a ripple of laughter from the tables, and President Croup cleared his throat and stood up. "Hate to interrupt at this point, but I see we're about to run overtime. We'll have copies of the financial report distributed to everyone as soon as they've been printed. Now, if there is no further business . . ."

Llew slipped quickly out the door at the far end of the lounge and headed back toward his office. Dr Otvos's observations were intriguing, and he felt an even greater urgency to get past the computer's security system and see exactly what was going on.

Could Hess's crew be having problems and not telling anyone? Nina would surely suspect something if they were. Or was the MAX/Sultan system interface eating up so much of the resources that efficiency was being drastically compromised?

It was an unusually warm day for this time of year, and as Llew was shedding his jacket, he saw Winklejohn lumbering slowly along on his crutches toward the front entrance of the Computer Center. He ran to catch up with him.

"Ah, Llew—" Winklejohn greeted, wheezing from the exertion of transporting his prodigious bulk. "I've been trying to phone you at your office."

"I've been at a meeting listening to Hess wax eloquent about the new computer," Llew told him. "What's up?"

Winklejohn mopped his wide brow. "Distressing news, I'm afraid. Nina has thrown in the proverbial towel."

"She *what?* You mean she *quit?*"

"With a capital 'Q'. But oh, what an exit it was! To paraphrase the Immortal Bard, nothing became her job like the leaving of it."

Oh my god, Llew thought. "But why? Was it something Slade did, or what?"

Winklejohn shook his immense head. "There I'm afraid I can only conjecture. I was in my office, performing another in an interminable series of menial programming tasks for Heinous Harry, when—to paraphrase again—from out in the hall there arose such a clatter, that I sprang to my crutches to see what was the matter. As I stepped out the door, I was nearly decapitated by several disk platters, whizzing through the air like lethal frisbees."

Balancing precariously on one sagging crutch, Winklejohn waved the other one defensively in the air. "Next came a rapid volley of books, manuals, ash trays, a waste basket—" Llew reached out to steady the weaving form.

Winklejohn regained his balance and leaned heavily against the side of the building. "The target of this barrage was, as you have suggested, Slimey Slade. He was doing his utmost to ward off the obstacles directed at him—with little success, I am happy to report, as the sound of some of the heavier missiles making smart contact with vulnerable portions of his anatomy did reach my ears."

"Where is Nina now?" Llew asked him.

"That, unfortunately, is not clear. Everything she had not thrown out of her office she stuffed into boxes and deposited in her car, which she subsequently drove away. I tried to engage her in conversation, but any useful information was buried in a stream of profanity."

"When did all this happen?"

"Less than an hour ago. I felt it wise to find you and relate the circumstances as promptly as possible."

Llew ran a hand through his hair. "I'd better go and look for her. How bout you? Did you get any repercussions from all this?"

"None. Mr Slade was so thoroughly distracted during the interchange that even so prominent a presence as mine went unnoticed."

"I think you'd better stay out of his way for a while," Llew suggested. "Just in case."

Winklejohn didn't seem worried. "I believe it will be some time before Mr Slade recovers sufficiently to consider his options. One hopes that these events might prove devastating enough to induce him to abandon ship."

"Somehow I doubt that. Okay, I'll see if I can find Nina. Keep your ears open and let me know what happens when Hess finds out about this."

Llew hurried back across campus toward the steep hill where his car was parked. I hope she doesn't do anything rash, he thought. Anything *else,* that is. Too bad Hen3ry is gone—she could probably use someone to unload on right now. Guess it'll just have to be me.

I had a feeling it was building up to this. But I kept hoping she would be able to stick it out. She was my only real source of information about what was going on in there—such as it was. Well, let's solve her problems first, then get back to mine.

The ignition switch in his car, as usual, refused to cooperate. So Llew checked the road behind him for traffic, released the hand brake and let the car roll out into the street and down the hill. It was a steep hill, so it didn't take long to get up enough speed for the motor to start. As the engine chugged to life, Llew swore to take the damn thing into the shop before the week was out.

He drove the mile or so to Nina's apartment. There was no sign of her car in front, so he didn't bother stopping. Where would she be likely to go? he asked himself. Where would *I* go?

Where *did* I go when the ax fell?

He turned the car around and headed back toward Duffy's Tavern.

Nina's car was parked in the lot next to Duffy's. There were no hills nearby, so Llew parked his own car as close to the street as he could—if it refused to start when he was ready to leave, Maybe Archie the bartender or somebody could give him a push.

Inside, it took Llew a few moments to find Nina in the dimly lit lounge. She was sitting behind an overflowing ash tray at a table in a far corner. There was a bottle of Budweiser sitting where several others must have preceeded it, and a half-full glass next to it.

Llew sat down. "Welcome to the club," he said.

"Mmpf." She exhaled an aggressive stream of cigaret smoke.

The waitress, recognizing Llew, brought him a small carafe of white wine. He poured some into a glass. "Want to tell me what happened?"

Her mouth tightened. "I blew it, that's what happened. Played right into their hands."

"What do you mean?"

"I did just what they wanted me to do, which was quit. They knew if they got me mad enough, I would. So they did, and I did."

"How did it happen?"

She waved a hand. "I don't really remember. It just sort of accumulated. Slade said he wanted me to give Winklejohn a hand with some programming stuff he was doing for Gross, and I told him I was a systems programmer not an applications programmer and when was I going to get on the new system, and he said whenever they needed me for something and in the meantime just do as I was told or he'd give Rama my job and put me to mounting tapes, and I told him to kiss—"

"Slow down."

"So anyway, one thing led to another and the next thing I remember was throwing everything I could get my hands on at that son of—"

"Winklejohn told me about that part." Llew sipped his wine. "So you think they were trying to goad you into quitting."

"I *know* they were. Ever since you left they've been bending over backward to make life miserable for me there."

"What about Rama and Winklejohn?"

She shook her head. "They're safe—they don't pose any threat."

"Threat?"

Nina leaned forward and pointed a tiny finger at Llew. "Hess and Slade knew it was only a matter of time before I broke into their system and figured out what was going on. Wink and Rama don't know enough about systems to do that. And they wouldn't know what they were looking at if they did."

"What *do* you think is going on?" Llew asked.

She leaned back again. "As Paisley would say, 'Aven't the foggiest'. But they're up to something, Llew, that's for sure."

Llew sighed and refilled his glass. "Probably. And I haven't made much headway with getting into the system myself."

Nina grinned smugly. "Not to worry. I have."

"You *have*?" Llew's eyes lit up. "You mean you've found a way to crack the system?"

"Better believe it. Wink and I were working late last night, and I started playing around. Next thing I know, I'm getting all these privileged directories and SYSTATs."

Now we're getting somewhere, Llew thought. "Could you tell anything from what you saw?"

"Not much. Mostly device designations and partition specs. I'd have to fool around with it some more. But it was getting late . . ."

"I want to see for myself," he insisted. "Let's go back to my office and you can show me how you got in."

She frowned. "What time is it?"

Llew squinted in the darkness at his watch. "Uh . . . nearly two."

"I haven't had anything to eat all day, and I'm starving. Can you wait till I nosh something?"

"Sure. No problem. I'll tell you what. I was going to go by and see Gus Roddencroft this afternoon—why don't I do that and meet you back at my office?"

"Give me about an hour," she said, flagging down the waitress. "I have to go and check on Calhoun."

"Where is he?"

"I dropped him off at my place before I came here. Poor thing—he doesn't know what to make of all this."

"Neither do I." Llew quaffed the rest of his wine. "Maybe now we can find out."

Llew left Nina and returned to the parking lot. To his relief, the car started without difficulty. He pulled out into the street and headed back toward campus.

At least Nina didn't seem as despondent now as when he had found her. The prospect of finally getting into the guts of the Sultan was exciting, and would be the shot in the arm they both needed.

Llew found a parking place on the steep hill across from the auditorium. As he was crossing the street, he noticed Gus Roddencroft's car in front and heard the sounds of a piano inside. He trotted up the steps, hoping to postpone another trek across campus.

Byron and Gus were on the stage, standing next to the large concert grand. The piano tuner, Giuseppe Oppernocketti, was making adjustments to some mechanism behind the keyboard. Stenciled on the side of his tuner's kit were the words OPPERNOCKETTI ONLY TUNES ONCE, beneath which someone had scrawled "Except for Byron Devilbiss".

When he had finished, Oppernocketti wiped his hands on a cloth and stood back as Byron seated himself at the keyboard and hammered out several rapid passages from the Prokofiev 7th. A moment later, he stopped abruptly and shook his head.

"The action still isn't right, Op. It's the goddam humidity, I tell you. Plus the fact that this piece of junk should have been retired years ago." He retrieved a half-smoked cigar from the corner of the piano and stuck it in his mouth.

"It's the best of the lot, Byron," Gus said wearily. "The others are in even worse shape. You'll just have to make do with it—unless you want to donate your own to the cause."

"*What*? Subject my Bozendorfer Imperial Concert Grand to these primitive conditions? Come on, Rottencrotch—two hours in this steambath and it would shrink to the size of an upright."

Gus shrugged. "Well, I suppose we could hold the concert in your living room . . ."

"At least it's air-conditioned and humidity controlled, unlike this tropical rain forest you call a recital hall." Byron relit his cigar and pounded out a few bars of Scriabin. "You can hear the soundboard creak every time I—" He stopped suddenly, his head jerking around.

"What's wrong now?"

"Listen!" His eyes grew big and a broad smile spread across his face.

Gus shut his eyes. "Oh, no . . ."

"Fire sirens!"

In the distance, they could hear the unmistakable howl of sirens, punctuated by the bleating sound of fire trucks.

"Three alarm!" Byron jumped from the stool, snatched his cigar and his loden cloak, and was out the door before anyone could protest.

Gus was leaning against the piano, his hand over his eyes. "Give me strength . . ."

"Do you ever wonder what he would do if this happened during one of his performances?" Llew asked.

"I have nightmares about that," Gus admitted. "Maybe I could shackle him to one leg of the piano."

"Just make sure he's got a supply of yellow pills, green pills and blue pills within reach."

Gus scowled. "You think that's funny—I worry as much about Byron showing up in the first place as I do about him dashing out at the first siren." He looked at his watch. "I've got to get back to the office. Give you a lift anywhere?"

Llew didn't feel like pushing his luck with the ignition in his car, so he accepted a ride as far as the Music Department. It would only be a short walk from there to his new office where he was to meet Nina.

They left Oppernocketti to his hopeless task and walked out to Gus's car. "I don't hear the sirens anymore," Llew said. "At least this one wasn't here on campus."

"Off to the north somewhere, I think. Byron is probably just catching up with them." Gus started his car and pulled out into the street. "At least he'll be more open-minded about the piano when he gets back—chasing fire engines always seems to improve his mood."

"Is the piano really in that bad a shape?"

"Everything Byron complained about is true," Gus admitted. "It *is* old, and the keys stick. And the humidity doesn't help. I just hope the weather cooperates on the day of his recital."

"I thought you planned to get the college to have the auditorium air-conditioned."

"We planned a lot of things—including a new grand and a fleet of practice pianos. That was before our budget was shredded by your friend Hess."

Llew nodded. "I told you the Computer Center wouldn't be the only department to suffer the proverbial slings and arrows. Which reminds me—are you still getting your tapes processed okay?"

"So far. I run the programs from my own terminal, and Rama sends the tapes over as soon as they're finished."

"Any problems using the new system?"

"Not so far—the programs and everything work just like on the old system. Except that I had hoped for faster response time to improve the sound quality, like we talked about. But I haven't noticed any difference."

"That's got a lot of people puzzled, including myself," Llew admitted. "This machine has a larger word size, virtual memory, multiple buffering . . . all the things that should be making the user's life a lot easier. But it hasn't happened, and I can't figure out why."

"Actually, there was one other problem," Gus said. "The output from the tape I got back this morning came out all garbled."

"Garbled?"

"Well, nothing I recognized, anyway. I figure Rama must have sent me the wrong tape—I was going to take it back to him."

Llew frowned. "That isn't like Rama. I've never known him to make careless mistakes. Although with things in such a mess over there . . . Why don't you come by my office later and we'll dump whatever's on the tape onto my terminal printer, just to make sure."

Gus thought about it, then nodded. "If you're sure it's no trouble—I might have slipped up in one of the latest changes I made."

"No trouble at all," Llew assured him as Gus pulled his car into the music department lot. "Go ahead and drop the tape off to Rama. He can mount it on one of the Computer Center drives when we get ready to do the dump. Then come on over and we'll give it a try."

"Fine. It'll have to be tomorrow, though. Right now I've got to go by Harry Gross's office and straighten out another mess."

"Oh? What's Harry done this time?"

"The Campus Events Calendar they put out— the announcement about Byron's recital next week was left out."

"I wouldn't worry—I doubt if there's anyone on campus that doesn't know about it."

"Yeah, but that's no excuse for leaving it out."

"Agreed. Give him hell."

Nina was waiting for Llew in the dark hallway outside his office. "I was beginning to get nervous," she said. "It's like a tomb down here."

"You get used to it," he lied, unlocking the door and snapping on the light. They squeezed in around the desk and Llew switched on the terminal. He logged in, turned on the modem and typed the auto-dial instruction to connect his terminal over phone lines to the Computer Center. Moments later, a message on his screen welcomed them to the Sultan system.

He slid the keyboard across the desk to Nina. "Go."

Nina went through the steps she had found to bypass the computer's security system. "It's really simple, and I discovered it purely by accident. One of the user information displays initiates a command file which is stored in a privileged account. If you hit the ESCAPE key while it's being accessed, the file doesn't close properly, and leaves you in a privileged mode. From there you can go anywhere you want."

Llew leaned forward and watched the prompt symbol change to signify that they now had privileged status. "So I see. Somebody goofed in setting it up."

"They'll probably catch it sooner or later. So what we'll do is set up our own entry point. There are apparently a number of unused terminal ports that have been assigned to privileged accounts—the trick is to make the computer think you're attached to one of them. To do that, we'll add your account name to the device assignment table." She typed a series of commands.

"What if someone recognizes the name?"

"They probably will. So I'm creating a new account with a different name which will contain just a single, short program—a command file to assign privilege status to your regular account and then transfer control over to it. The command file will be automatically initiated each time you log into the new account. So you just sort of get in by the back door." She finished typing and logged off. "Okay, try it."

Llew logged in using the new account name and password, and a moment later a message reported that the command file Nina had created was being executed. Then the standard log-in messages appeared, indicating that Llew was in his own now-privileged account.

"Now we should be able to display the system files," Nina said. "Let's give it a shot."

Llew typed a command to display the Device Table, which shows the current status of disk and tape drives, terminals and printers:

DEVICE NAME	STATUS	ERROR COUNT	DEVICE LABEL	FREE BLOCKS
DISK0:	mounted	0	SYSTEM0	1423700
DISK1:	mounted	0	USER1	1771500
DISK2:	mounted	0	USER2	855314
DISK3:	mounted	0	TEMP3	500120
MAGTP0:	mounted	0	TAPE0	
MAGTP1:	mounted	0	TAPE1	
MAGTP2:	mounted	0	TAPE2	
.	.	.	.	
.	.	.	.	
.	.	.	.	

Llew scratched his head. "Does this look familiar to you, Nina?"

She was frowning. "Yeah. Looks just like the Device Table on the MAX. Let's try the SYSTAT display . . ."

The System Status Display showed names and ID numbers of jobs requiring system resources and the current status and priority of each job:

JOB ID	JOB NAME	STATUS	PRIORITY
00080	NULL COM		0
00081	SWAPPER	HIB	16
00082	ERRORFMT	HIB	8
00083	OPCOM LEF		8
00088	MCQUIL	CUR	4
.	.	.	.
.	.	.	.
.	.	.	.

Llew and Nina exchanged glances. "This *is* the Sultan, isn't it?" Lew asked. "The job numbers, names, priorities . . . all exactly the way they were on the MAX."

For the next half hour, they stepped through the rest of the internal tables, one by one. They examined the system management files to check accounting information, privileges and allowable resources for selected jobs; they displayed the system startup file, the system LOG-IN file, the queue manager file and the memory allocation file; they looked at selected utilities such as system backup, accounting and error logging.

Finally Llew sat back and folded his arms. "This is unbelievable. Everything is *exactly* the same as on the old MAX. Every bit of it, except that the device table shows one additional tape drive and disk drive. All the rest of the devices are the same, and all the system programs and utilities are the same. It doesn't make any sense."

Nina lit a cigaret and sat pondering. Then she said slowly, "There's one way it *would* make sense."

"I think I know what you're thinking. Well, there's a way to find out . . ."

Llew typed a command on the keyboard and the screen displayed a directory of system utility programs. He pointed to one of the items listed. "Remember LDUMP? The memory dump program I wrote for the MAX? It displays the contents of any specified location in memory."

She nodded. "And of course it's system-dependent—it will only work for MAX memories."

"Right. So what's it doing in the Sultan?"

He entered another sequence of commands. "Let's see what happens when I try to run it."

The screen began scrolling a continuous array of hexadecimal numbers. "Look at that!" Llew pointed. "LDUMP is *working.* Nina, we're talking to our old *MAX.*"

"And Hess has been telling everyone it's the Sultan 6000." She sat back. "No wonder their 'transition' went so smoothly."

"And no wonder the Sultan was able to simulate the MAX so well—it *is* the MAX. All that nonsense about an 'interface' between the two . . ."

"But *why*? Why this elaborate hoax?"

Llew nibbled at a fingernail. "No idea. Maybe they found out the conversion was more complicated than they expected, and they're trying to save face. But I have a feeling there's more to it than that."

"Are we going to blow the whistle on them?"

Llew shook his head. "Not yet. Not till we know what they're really up to."

"How are we going to do that?"

He thought a minute. "Well . . . we know the Sultan exists. We saw it being delivered and we presume it was installed. And we were *told* it was up and running. So it might make sense to get in there and see exactly what it *is* doing."

"Get in where?"

"Into the computer room. Where they're keeping it."

"But they won't let anybody even near the place."

He gave her a sly smile. "Then, my dear Arganina, we just won't tell them we're coming."

"You mean break in? Like at night?" She squealed in delight.

"Well," Llew said, "we broke into the system, thus setting us on the irreversible path of crime. Might as well be hung for a sheep as a chicken."

"Goat."

"Whatever."

Nina bounced up and down in her chair. "I'm ready! When do we go?"

Llew held up a cautioning hand. "Not so fast—this is going to take some planning . . ."

10

While Gus watched, Llew logged into his new privileged account and waited while Nina's command file shunted him around the security checks. He glanced at his watch. "I asked Rama to mount your data tape at the Computer Center at 11:00, so we should be about ready."

"Appreciate your going to all this trouble," Gus said. "I'm sure that he just got the wrong tape, though."

"Well, if the stuff on this data tape isn't yours, then it probably got dumped to the wrong drive and ended up on your tape instead. If that's what happened, we might at least be able to determine who it belongs to. Anyway, we'll see here in a minute..."

Llew typed MOUNT, and the screen displayed a list of tape drives currently assigned. "Drive 3—that should be it. I'll dump a couple of blocks to my printer here so we can look at it."

A moment later, the printer began to chatter as successive records were transferred from tape. Gus leaned forward, tugging on his heavy beard.

When the printer stopped, he shook his head. "That can't be my stuff. My output is always strictly numeric—this has alphabetic characters and all kinds of weird punctuation."

"It *is* weird," Llew admitted. "Almost like a binary dump. But that usually causes the line printer to go crazy and start spewing out paper. This seems to have some pattern to it."

"The Sultan system language, maybe?"

Not bloody likely, Llew thought, since this *isn't* the Sultan. But no point in getting anyone else involved at this stage. "I doubt it. And it doesn't look like any programming language I know. So it must be data. But whose, I'm not sure."

Gus leaned back. "At least it isn't mine. So maybe I didn't screw up my code after all."

"I would just rerun the whole thing if I were you," Llew suggested. "It's not likely to happen again."

"What about the tape?"

"It was obviously intended for someone else. I'll ask Rama to hang onto it for a while in case anybody comes asking for it."

"Fine. Well," easing himself off the sharp edge of the desk, "appreciate your help. Want to join me for a sawdust burger at the cafeteria?"

"Thanks—I promised to meet Nina at noon." Llew had arranged to meet her at Duffy's for lunch to plan Operation Computergate.

"What's she going to do, now that she's joined the ranks of the shafted brigade?"

"Do?" Llew hesitated. "Well . . . we've sort of been toying with the idea of going into business for ourselves."

"Yeah? You mean like consulting?"

"More like, er . . . troubleshooting."

Gus squeezed around to the door. "Well, say hello for me. See you Friday night at Byron's party, if not before."

"Tell me something," Llew said. "Why does Byron always hold

his parties *before* his recitals, instead of afterward like everybody else?"

"Probably for exactly that reason—because everyone else does. "However," he smirked, "his official reason is that after one of his performances, even the greatest party in the world would be an anticlimax. So the party comes first."

"I'll buy that. Although Byron's parties are a tough act to follow. By the way—how did he enjoy the fire yesterday?"

Gus chuckled. "He never got there. He was stopped for speeding. Some cop in an unmarked car, made up to look like a Driver Education car."

Llew laughed too, until he suddenly remembered the unpaid ticket in his glove compartment.

"So he turned around and came right back to campus," Gus told him. "Was he *mad!* The only time I've seem him that frustrated was when he went to a fire at a lumber yard, dragging me along. Biggest blaze you ever saw . . . and he couldn't find a match to light his cigar. Well, I'm off."

After Gus left, Llew looked back at the printed output from the tape. Queer looking stuff, he thought, studying the arrays of characters on the page. Somehow, though, it looks familiar. Where have I seen this before?

Getting close to noon. He turned off the terminal and printer, folded up the listings and stuffed them in his coat pocket. I'll show this output to Nina, he decided—maybe she can make some sense out of it.

Nina was sitting at the same table where Llew had found her after her bout with Slade. There was a carafe of white wine on the table and two glasses, one of which had wine in it.

"Thought I'd try it," Nina told him. "See what all the fuss is about."

Llew pulled up the chair opposite her. "And?"

She shrugged. "Think I'll stick with Bud. No offense—I know you wine snobs don't drink anything else."

"Don't kid yourself. Several of the members of our wine club are home brewers as well. And one member goes home after each tasting and drinks Scotch."

The waitress took their orders and Nina ordered a beer. Llew poured some wine into his glass. "Okay. Down to business. First, let's review the facts.

"One: a new computer system has been delivered and presumably installed in the Computer Center. Two: everyone has been told that the new system is operational. Three: the new system behaves suspiciously like the old system. And Four—"

"—It *is* the old system."

"Well, that's what it looks like. Which raises all sorts of interesting questions. One: *why* are we still running under the old system? Two: why are we being told it's the *new* system? Three: exactly what *is* being done with the new system? And Four: how do we get into the Computer Center to find out? Do you still have your key to the building?"

"The only key I have is to my office. They changed all the locks after you left and never got around to giving me a new key to the building. I told you they were trying to get rid of me."

"What about Winklejohn, or Rama?"

Nina shook her head. "Slade is always there to let them in, and locks up after everyone leaves. He keeps promising keys, but nobody's got one yet. Like the Sultan manuals he said everyone would get."

Llew took some paper from his pocket and drew a sketch of the Computer Center. "The windows all have bars . . ."

"And the only other entrance is the door to the stairway, which the security guard locks at dark."

"What about the air conditioner shafts?"

Nina rolled her eyes. "Come *on*, Llew—they only do that sort of thing in the movies."

He scratched his head. "Yeah. I guess that's a bit much." He doodled on the sketch he had made.

Nina looked at the paper he was using. "What's that stuff printed there?"

"This? Oh, it's a listing of some tape output." He unfolded it onto the table top. "It's supposed to be Gus's synthetic music output, but something else got on there by mistake. I thought it looked familiar, so I was going to ask you if you recognized it."

Nina studied it for a minute. "Sure, I know what it is."

"You do? Great—what is it?"

She picked up the listing from the table. "At least it *looks* like it. Don't you remember that book of *codes* somebody brought in once? I forget who. But he wanted to use the computer to generate coded messages. And also to decode them."

Llew snapped his fingers. "You're right—that was Tully Dunkle, in the Political Science department. He's an amateur . . . uh, what do you call it, when you work with codes and cyphers and stuff like that?"

"Cryptologist?"

"Sounds right. Anyway, there was some software for that on the market, so I ordered a few programs for him. He was gloriously happy. And after a while he was writing his own."

"Do you think this is any of his stuff?"

"Must be. I don't know of anyone else around campus who does this sort of thing. I'll run by his office this afternoon and show him this listing. If it's his, he can get the tape from Rama." Llew finished his glass of wine and poured another. "Now, where were we?"

"Still outside the Computer Center, looking for a way in."

"Mmm. Got any ideas?"

Nina pondered. "If we could get into the building before Slade locks up, we could hide somewhere . . ."

"I don't think there's any place to hide. And I don't think we'd be able to get in without being seen."

She nodded. "Yeah. And besides, the new locks work with a key on *both* sides on the door—how would we get out?"

"Right." His mouth tightened. "This is beginning to look hopeless. If we only—" He stopped abruptly as he recognized a familiar face across the room.

"What is it?" Nina asked.

"Over there, near the window. Isn't that Paisley?"

Nina squinted through the darkness. "I think so."

"He's by himself, and there's a whole pitcher of beer in front of him. Correction—a half-empty pitcher."

"That's odd. I know he comes here a lot at night, but I've never seen him here drinking during working hours."

"Why don't we invite him over? We're not making much progress at the moment."

Llew waved his hand to catch Paisley's attention, and motioned for him to join them. Paisley nodded, rose slowly from his table and brought his pitcher and glass across the room. Llew noticed that he was not wearing his coat of many pockets.

He set his pitcher and glass down next to Llew's and Nina's and pulled back an empty chair. "'Ow's loife, mites?"

"As well as can be expected for a couple of expatriates," Llew replied. "You?"

He sighed. "Well, for one who 'as just joined your ranks, Oi sippose Oi'm about the sime."

"Joined our ranks? You don't mean—?"

"Bloody oath Oi do." He refilled his glass from the pitcher and took a long quaff.

"When did this happen?"

"This mornin'. Called me into 'is fancy office, 'e did. Told me Oi 'ad two weeks."

"Who? Hess?"

Paisley nodded, wiping the foam from his mustache. "'At's the sod."

"But why? What reason did he give?"

"*Rison*? Since when does 'e need a rison? Wot rison did 'e give you?"

"He called it an efficiency move. To save money."

Paisley nodded. "Roight. So now 'e's got to piy some twit to do your job. Jolly efficient." He covered his mouth with a fist to suppress a burp.

"But who's going to do your job?" Nina asked.

"Oh, 'e's found some contract aigency to do it. Cost 'im a bundle, it will, especially 'avin' to chainge all the locks on all the doors all over campus."

"Change all the locks . . . ?"

"Roight. Oi've got all the kiys to them wot's on there now, so just to mike sure Oi don't get no funny ideas, they've got to go and get all new ones, don't they?"

Llew sat back and stared at Paisley. "You *do* have keys to all the doors, don't you?"

"The 'ole lot," he replied, pouring a fresh glass.

Llew and Nina looked at each other, then back at Paisley. He sipped from the glass, then looked up to see the two of them grinning at him.

He cocked his head. "Wot's up, mites . . . ?"

11

"What time is it?"

Llew pressed the light button on his watch. "Two A.M. The security guard should have been here by now."

Nina's car was parked between two empty ones at the edge of a faculty parking lot near the Computer Center. They could see the rear entrance next to the tall oak where Llew used to park his car in less troubled times. The office windows on either side of the door were dark, but Llew could see the hall lights through the heavy glass partition in the entrance door.

"He always showed up about this time whenever I worked late," Llew said. "But with all the changes that have taken place since Hess arrived—"

"There—" Nina pointed, extinguishing her cigaret in the ash tray. "That must be him."

Through the darkness they could see a figure with a flashlight strolling slowly along the path beneath the yellowish sodium vapor lights toward the Computer Center. The intermittent rasp of a walkie-talkie confirmed that he was the campus security guard.

When he reached the Computer Center entrance, he mounted the steps, checked the door, then flashed his light up at each window. Satisfied, he ambled off toward the next cluster of buildings.

"Let's give him a few minutes," Llew suggested.

"Doesn't he ever check inside?"

"He usually does that on his earlier rounds, before midnight." Llew glanced out the window into the darkness. "Have you got the keys?"

"You mean do I *still* have them? That's the third time you've asked me. Don't tell me you're nervous?"

"Who, me?" Llew feigned indignation. "Just because I'm about to risk thirty years of spotless reputation by commiting a felony?" He remembered Mike Ebbsedik's remark about his being disgustingly honest, and wondered what he would think of this little stunt. Actually, he'd probably love it.

"It's not a felony unless you break in," Nina insisted, dangling the keys in front of him. "We're just unlocking some doors."

Llew frowned. "I'm not sure that would hold up in court."

"Paisley didn't seem bothered when he loaned them to us. If we get caught, he'd be an accessory."

"When we told him what we intended to do, he practically shoved the keys at us. Besides, he could always say the keys were stolen."

"Which *would* be a felony." She put the keys back in her pocket. "Why do you think Hess fired him?"

"Beats me. Paisley has always done a good job. But Hess has been indirectly blaming him for the Dodgson House fire—says he should have known about the faulty wiring. Of course, Paisley still insists there was no problem with the wiring."

"Sounds like Hess was just looking for an excuse to get rid of him. Like some others I know."

"Does, doesn't it?" Llew looked at his watch again. "I guess we should get started."

They got out of the car and walked in the direction of the

Computer Center. Llew put his arm around Nina's waist. She looked up in surprise. "Why, Mr McQuilla . . ."

"Don't get all worked up," he grinned. "Less suspicious if anyone sees us."

"I get it," she sighed, hooking her thumb over the back of his belt. "Story of my life . . ."

When they reached the shadow of the tree next to the entrance, Nina gave Llew the set of keys. "Ready?" he asked.

She drew a breath. "As I'll ever be, I guess. I just hope Paisley's right about there not being any alarms."

"He would have known if there were any new ones. And *you* would have seen them being put in. Okay, keep out of sight till I check things inside."

Llew took a last glance around, then trotted up the steps to the door. He unlocked and opened it quickly but cautiously, checking the dimly lit hallway just inside. Then he slipped in and closed the door behind him.

He stood listening for a few seconds, then moved quietly down the hall toward the door to the computer room. To his left, his old office—now being used by Slade—was locked and dark, as were Nina's and Winklejohn's to the right. He could see traces of light under the door of the computer room, but it was always left on. He put his ear to the door and listened again, then cautiously tried the doorknob.

As expected, it was locked. He found the right key, and as quietly as possible inserted it into the lock. He turned it until he heard a click, then slowly pushed the door open a few inches and looked in.

The room was brightly lit, and the hum of the air conditioners was the only sound he heard. He opened the door a few more inches until he could put his head through enough to see the whole interior.

No sign of anyone. He left the door standing partially open

and made his way back to the entrance, where he signaled for Nina to join him. Seconds later she was inside, and he shut and relocked the door.

They returned to the computer room and shut the door behind them, then stood looking around. "Remember not to move anything," Llew warned. "We don't want to leave any traces of our visit."

The room was completely interior to the basement of the building, and as such had no windows, so there was no danger of being seen. There were two other doors—one into the office, and the other into the storeroom.

They circled the room slowly, inspecting each piece of equipment. There were four tape drives along the far wall, five disk drives along an adjacent wall, and three terminals—two with screens and one with hard-copy printer—opposite them. To the right of the entrance were two line printers, and to the left two tables with stacks of printer listings, hard-copy output and a rack of manuals.

In the corner between the disk drives and the terminals stood several tall red and silver cabinets containing the central processsing unit and asssociated memory units, all labelled "Sultan 6000". There was no sign of the MAX system.

"They're still using all the same peripherals," Nina observed, "which is exactly what the device file showed. Plus one new disk drive, which it *didn't* show."

Most of the connecting cables ran under the raised floor, so it was difficult to tell what was connected to what. A few of them, however, were strung out on top of the floor and seemed to be attached to the Sultan, causing Llew to frown. "That's not a good sign. I had expected to see all this stuff hooked right into the MAX. And I don't even *see* the MAX."

Nina pointed to a bundle of cables running across the floor and into the storeroom. "Those were never there before."

Llew walked over and opened the storeroom door. The light

was on inside, and crowded in among boxes of line printer paper, spare disk packs, backup tapes and supply cabinets, was the familiar MAX central processing unit.

"Aha! And it's up and running, too." Llew grabbed a chair and wheeled it in next to the MAX console terminal. "You watch—we'll get the Sultan log-in message, and it'll show the same devices and status we saw in my office. I *knew* it had to be the old MAX that we were—" He stopped typing and stared at the message on the screen.

"What's the matter?"

He retyped the log-in command. "Won't accept my account name."

"Which one are you using?"

"The new one. The one you set up for me."

She looked over his shoulder. "Try your old one."

He tried it, and the terminal requested PASSWORD. "Hmm. That one works. Why would one work but not the other?"

He typed in his old password. It was accepted, and a message welcomed him to the MAX system.

"*MAX*?" Llew sat back and rubbed his neck. "It's supposed to say *Sultan*. This makes no sense."

He requested a device list, and the screen showed only the system disk and one terminal—the console terminal he was using. A SYSTAT showed no jobs active except his own. And no users connected except Llew.

"The system's idle," Nina said, frowning. "Just what you'd expect if it were only being used as a backup."

"Dammit! I was so *sure*."

"Wait a minute . . ." Nina was looking at the SYSTAT. "Why are all these spoolers still listed if the line printer and terminals have been moved over to the Sultan?" She pointed to the utilities which transferred data from the computer to the output devices.

"Probably they just forgot to delete them. If we tried to queue something to the printer from here, it should just give us an error message." He typed a command to print a system file . . . and immediately the line printer in the computer room began to chatter.

Llew and Nina exchanged puzzled looks. "That's impossible," Llew insisted. "The line printer must be still attached to the MAX, but it doesn't show up in the device list."

"There are two CRT terminals in the other room," Nina said. "Try sending some output to one of them."

As Llew typed, she went back into the computer room in time to see the message appear in the screen of one of the terminals. "This one's attached, too—and *it* doesn't appear on the device list, either. Try the other one."

Llew directed the same messsage to the second terminal, but its screen remained blank. "No luck on this one," she called back. "Try accessing one of the other disk drives—one that the device list says isn't there."

Llew did, and it was. He displayed its master file directory. "All the accounts and files are here—Dahnu's, Gus's . . . even mine."

Nina came back into the storeroom. "Then all those devices *are* still connected to the MAX, like we thought. But why doesn't the SYSTAT and device list show any of them?"

Llew got up from the chair. "Here—you know as much about the guts of this thing as I do. Use my LDUMP program to look at memory and find out what's really there. I want to check out those two terminals in the other room."

Nina took over at the keyboard as Llew returned to the computer room. He pulled a chair up to the terminal which displayed the message he had sent from the MAX terminal. He tried logging in, using his MAX account name, and the system obligingly requested PASSWORD.

That's interesting, he thought. He did not respond to the request, and after a fixed time the log-in timed out. Then he started over, this time using the new privileged account name which Nina had set up for him. This one worked as well, as did the password. The message welcomed him to the Sultan system.

Same response as I get on my office terminal, he observed. Apparently whoever uses this terminal is also supposed to think he's on the Sultan, like all the rest of the users on campus. Rama, maybe?

The device list, SYSTAT and other system commands showed him the same information as the terminal in his office. He rolled his chair over to the second terminal.

This time *neither* account name worked. He tried a few others, without success. Curiouser and curiouser, he muttered, returning to the first terminal and checking the device list carefully. He found no entry for the other terminal.

He was puzzling over this when Nina rejoined him. "Learning anything?" she asked.

He shook his head. "The MAX console terminal in the storeroom welcomes me to the MAX system, and tells me nothing is running and only one disk drive and one console terminal are connected. But it lets me access other devices out here in this room. *This* terminal welcomes me to the *Sultan* system and shows me all sorts of information that I know come from the MAX. And *that* terminal won't talk to me at all." He sighed. "Hope you had better luck."

"I dumped most of the MAX system tables in memory," she told him. "Everything that was there before is still there. It's definitely the MAX which is still servicing everyone on campus, and making them think it's a Sultan. And it's using all these peripherals here in this room. There are even some users logged in at this time of night . . . including Dahnu, which doesn't surprise me. I don't think he ever—"

"Did you find out why none of it shows up in the MAX system status display?"

"Yeah—but it *only* happens on that one terminal. Since it's the system console terminal, it can be configured to do all kinds of things the others can't. So somebody's rigged it to display false information. Anybody using it, like we just did, would think he was on a stripped MAX computer. The system would appear to be idle—which is what it's supposed to be, now that it's been . . . ahem, 'replaced' by the Sultan."

"Makes sense. I guess."

"Also, it apparently won't recognize any new accounts, which is why you couldn't log in at first."

"These people can sure play some strange games," Llew mused. "And we still don't have a clue as to why. Or what the Sultan is really doing all this time."

"There are two other things in those dumps that bothered me," Nina said.

"Like what?"

"There's a new communications port that was never there before. I can't tell what it's for. It looks like the kind you find in a distributed processing system."

"Hmm. Maybe we can trace it. What was the other thing?"

"The log-in message—'Welcome to the Sultan 6000'—did it come up on this terminal here when you logged on?"

"Sure. Just like it did on the terminal in my office. They want everyone to think—"

"Yeah, but I checked the message display file on the MAX, and it's not there."

"Are you sure?" Llew typed a command to access the file in which all the initialization messages were stored. "You're right. It's not."

"Yet the message is displayed every time you log in. Where's it coming from?"

Llew searched a few other files, then shook his head. "That's impossible. Unless . . ." A thought suddenly took shape in his mind.

"Unless?"

Llew looked over at the Sultan mainframe. "Unless we really *are* talking to the Sultan."

Nina groaned. "I thought we'd settled all that. Llew, all those files and programs are definitely being processed by the MAX."

"*Processed*, sure—but only after being *pre*-processed by the Sultan." His voice grew excited. "Listen, it makes sense now. All the user terminals are hooked up to the Sultan, not the MAX. But the MAX is *also* hooked up to the Sultan—that's what that extra communication line is doing there."

He got up and went back to the open door to the storeroom. "What we've got is a distributed processing system. The MAX portion is handling all the user tasks, doing everything it used to do. Except that someone's made it look like it's not doing *anything*, except serving as a backup."

Nina's eyes widened. "Then it's exactly the reverse of what we've been lead to believe. The Sultan is acting as a front end to the MAX, not the other way around."

"Exactly—the Sultan is processing log-ins and then shunting all the users over to the MAX."

"But Llew, that can't be *all* it's doing—what's the point?"

"We'll only find out if we can access the Sultan directly." He rolled his chair back to the second terminal and reached for the Sultan systems manual on the adjacent table. "That must be why I couldn't log in with this terminal. It's on a direct line to the Sultan."

He paged through the manual, looking for system access information. "Standard log-in procedure—system account name followed by password. And it's already rejected all the account names I know."

"Try SYSMANAGER," Nina suggested.

"Huh? Where did you come up with that?"

She was standing behind the hard-copy terminal, looking

through the folded sheaves of printed output. "Somebody used this terminal, and the whole log-in is printed here."

"Great." He typed the account name. "And it *works.* But I still need a password."

She shook her head. "Nothing here. But passwords are never printed anyway. Try just hitting the RETURN key—maybe they never bothered to assign one."

He did, and the Sultan welcome message appeared on the screen. But this time it was followed by an elaborate sequence of technical information relating to the current version of the operating system.

Nina clapped her hands. "All *right!*"

"Now we're getting somewhere," Llew gloated, and began typing rapidly. "We're finally on the real Sultan. Let's look at devices . . ."

Moments later, a complex system configuration was displayed schematically on the screen. One portion showed the Sultan CPU linked to a single disk drive and tape drive, a communications line, one CRT and one hard copy terminal, and several other designations which Llew did not recognize. A second portion represented the MAX system, attached to the Sultan via the communications line and linked to all the campus terminals and all the peripheral devices in the computer room.

"Okay, the disk drive shown here is that new one next to the four old ones," Llew noted, pointing to the diagram on the screen, "and the CRT terminal is the one I'm using. But where's the other tape drive? And these other things—what the hell is a 'VSN'? Or an 'MTR'?"

Nina paged through the systems manual. "I don't find them listed under Standard Devices . . . and there's nothing under Special Purpose Peripherals either."

"Whatever they are, the SYSTAT shows them as up and running."

Nina went over and examined the Sultan cabinets. "CPU, multiplexor, cartridge disk drive . . . nothing non-standard here."

"Check in the back."

She walked around behind the unit. "Just the cable bank for the terminal ports. Hmmm . . ."

"Something?"

"Did you ever have cables going into your office?"

Llew got up and joined her. "Just for my terminal. What have you found?"

"A humongous bundle of cables where there used to be just one little one," she pointed. Several cables of different thicknesses were plugged into the back of the Sultan, wound together, and disappeared through the base of the wall into Llew's old office.

Llew tried the office door and found it locked. Searching through Paisley's keys, he found one that worked. He stepped inside and turned on the lights.

"Hey—don't do that!" Nina whispered, reaching over and snapping them back off. "Remember there's an outside window in here."

"Forgot."

"I brought a flashlight," she said. "But we'll have to keep it pointed away from the window—it could still be seen."

"We could pull the blinds."

"Better not—the security guy may remember them being open, if he comes back this way."

Llew grinned. "You know, you're in the wrong business. You should have been a detective. Or a mystery writer."

"Or a criminal . . . which is what I feel like right now. Let's hustle."

She scanned the room with the flashlight. It had been completely rearranged since Llew's departure. One end of the room was given over to several large metal cabinets, all of which had panel lights which indicated that they contained electronic equipment, and that the units were on and functioning.

"There's our extra tape drive," Llew pointed to one of the units. "Why would they have it back here instead of out with the others?"

Nina shook her head. "Unless they're trying to hide it."

"Do you recognize any of this other stuff?" Llew asked.

"Nope. But everything's connected together, including the tape drive. And all the cables go back out to the computer. Except this one . . ." She indicated a wire from one of the units, and traced it over to the wall near the desk. "It's connected to one of the phone jacks."

"*One* of the phone jacks? How many are there?"

"Two."

Llew frowned. "That's strange . . . there used to be only one."

"Maybe this equipment gets input over phone lines."

"It's a possibility." He thought a minute. "I can check that out."

"How?"

"The campus phone switching system is computerized. I helped with the installation a couple years ago. It's a separate computer system from the one here, of course, but since all the remote terminals use the phone lines it should be possible to break in and trace the connections."

In the distance they heard the campus chimes strike 3 AM. "We've got to move. Let's just take a quick look at this equipment and see if there's anything that would tell us what it is."

Nina shined the flashlight carefully over the surface of each unit, but there were no descriptive labels or manufacturer's names. "There's something here near the bottom," Llew said, running his hand along the base of the largest cabinet. "Put the light down here."

"Looks like a serial number or something stamped into the metal. Can you make it out?"

Llew took out his pocket notebook. "I think so. Maybe we can trace it from this."

As he was copying the number, Nina suddenly snapped off the flashlight and clutched his arm. "*Shhh* . . . !"

"What — ?"

She pointed at the window. A light was flickering across the pane from outside.

"The security guard," he whispered. "Keep your head down."

"Why did he come back? Do you think we somehow set off an alarm?"

Llew moved to the window as the light vanished, and carefully looked out. The guard was moving up the steps to the door and rummaging through his keys.

"He's coming in. Did we lock the door to the computer room?"

"I didn't—you have the keys."

Llew moved quickly back into the computer room and across to the door. Fumbling through Paisley's keys, he found the right one, shoved it into the lock and turned it, hoping the guard wasn't close enough to hear the *click.*

A moment later the heavy footsteps paused outside the door. Llew stepped back and held his breath.

The doorknob jiggled slightly. Llew waited for the sound of a key in the lock.

It didn't come, and seconds later the footsteps moved off toward the stairs at the other end of the hall. There was a faint squawking sound from the guard's walkie-talkie, then silence.

Llew and Nina breathed sighs of relief. "Let's get out of here," Nina urged.

"He'll go out upstairs," Llew assured her. "There's one thing more we need to do."

He returned to shut and lock the office door. "I've got to be able to access the Sultan from the terminal in my new office. All we've done so far is raise more questions—if we can do a little discreet monitoring we might come up with a few answers."

Nina sat down at the terminal and paged through the systems manual. "That shouldn't be hard, assuming it's done the same way as on the MAX. Let's see . . ."

She typed a command to display all terminals currently on-line to the Sultan; there were only two—the hard-copy terminal, and the CRT she was using—but there were plenty of spare ports. "Okay, what we'll do is take your terminal ID out of the table of MAX devices and redirect it over to this system. Then when you log in, you'll be attached to the Sultan instead of being shunted over to the MAX."

"What if I need to get back on the MAX? All my files are there."

"Once you're on the Sultan, you'll have access to the Device Assignment Table. You can do a temporary re-assign, which will put you back on the MAX until you log off." She smiled. "Want me to write all this down?"

"Please."

She scribbled on a pad of paper. "You'll have to be careful—if they do a SYSTAT while you're logged onto the Sultan, it'll show up."

"And it'll also appear in the permanent log file, if they check it later."

"I'm sure they do from time to time. But we might be able to wipe that out somehow." She flipped some pages in the manual. "Command files . . . here we go. Okay, we can add a short sequence to your log-off file that will automatically be executed every time you sign off. It'll delete the entries containing your connect time, your file storage charges and processing time."

Several minutes later, she sat back in the chair. "That's it. Let's hope it works. Now can we please get the hell out of here?"

"Okay. Let's make sure we leave everything the way it was when we got here . . ."

They retraced their activities as best they could remember, then locked the door to the computer room and the outer door, and slipped into the darkness.

"I suggest we run over to your office and log in again from there," Nina said when they were safely away from the building.

"Can't it wait till morning?"

She shook her head. "Don't forget, we have to wipe out tonight's session from the log file. Since that wasn't your terminal we were using in there, I couldn't modify the log-off file to do it automatically. They'd see right away that somebody had been tampering. Besides, I want to make sure we can still get back into this system from the terminal in your office."

As they walked across campus to Llew's office, Nina whispered, "Aren't you forgetting something?"

"Forget . . . ? Don't tell me we left something behind in the computer room?"

She grinned. "No, dummy. I mean about what happens if someone sees us strolling around out here."

Llew grinned back. "Oh . . . I see." And his arm went around her waist.

12

"Just thought you'd like to know," Van Reudge said, tightening the wires on the support post at the end of the row of vines. "Even though I realize that you're hardly in a position to do anything about it."

"Except feel like hell," Llew said. "Especially since I'm the one who talked you into putting your vineyard files on the college computer in the first place."

Van dismissed the notion with a wave of his hand. "No regrets—it worked fine and the price was right. But what they want to charge me now is out of the question. Especially if what you say is true, that they're still using the same old computer. And it seems to be running slower all the time."

"That's the increase in demand, from dozens of users who thought they'd be able to do more on the new machine. So now you're being asked to pay more for less."

"Not a chance . . . it's just not cost effective." He gave one more turn on the wrench. "How's the tension now?"

Llew tugged at the heavy wire over the still dormant vines. "Feels good."

"That's the last one," Van said, pocketing the wrench. "Reckon we can quit now."

Llew removed his heavy gloves and looked down the parallel rows of posts, strung together with strong wire like so many midget telephone poles. It would be another month before the buds on the well-pruned vines began to swell, and at least three before the emerging shoots would have any need of the supporting trellises. But by then the demands of spraying and training would leave little time for structural repairs. "How do things look so far?" he asked Van.

"Too early to tell. The winter was a mild one, and there seems to be little bud damage, if any. But one thing you learn in this business—every year brings new surprises. Some good, and some bad. As we've just seen."

Llew nodded. "At least you can get rid of most of your problems with the right sprays and careful cultivation."

"Preventive maintenance is the best solution," Van said. "Once the viruses and fungus diseases get hold, it's usually too late. Then the best you can do is be more careful next year."

The mention of virus and fungus brought Hess and Slade to Llew's mind. "Unfortunately, there was no way I could have forseen any of this mess at the college. And unless I can do something pretty soon, I won't have a next year to be careful about."

They loaded the tools and rolls of wire into Van's truck and drove back toward the house. "So why don't you just tell everyone what you found out?" Van asked as they bumped along the dirt road.

"Well, for one thing, I'd have to admit *how* I found out—and breaking and entering is still a crime, even for a worthy cause. And then there's always the possibility that Hess would come up with some perfectly reasonable explanation that never occurred to me—

whether it was true or not. Then my credibility would be totally wiped out . . . along with my access to the system."

"And probably your job."

"Such as it is. At least right now I'm able to get more information than I could before, and it all convinces me that Hess is playing some sort of devious game. The only solution I can see is to find out as much as possible before they catch me, and then hope that it's enough to expose them."

When they reached the house, Van pulled his truck up behind Llew's car. As they got out, Van said, "Appreciate you giving me a hand. Why not stay for supper? I'll tell Rose to set another place."

"I'll have to take a rain check this time," Llew said. "I'm going back and see that all your files get copied off onto a tape, and have Rama keep it someplace safe. If you're going to give up your account, they may just wipe out everything without telling you."

Van walked with him over to his car. "What happens next?"

"Next I think you ought to start looking into a small computer of your own. The prices have come way down, and you can do just about anything on one these days. In the long run, it'll cost a lot less—even if Hess hadn't raised the prices."

"I guess that's the way to go," Van admitted. "Most of my neighbors around here already have their own computers now. You used to see *Farmer's Journal* and *Cattleman's Monthly* around their homes—now it's *PC World* and *Byte Magazine*."

"Face it, Van," Llew grinned. "Technology has finally caught up with you, even out here in the boonies."

"Suppose I'll just have to give in to it, then. Can you help me pick out one that'll do the job?"

"Of course. And the right software, too. Then we'll transfer your files to it and you'll be back in business."

Van nodded his approval. "Sounds simple enough."

"It will be, "Llew assured him. "I just wish my problems were as easy to solve. Nobody's marketed any software to deal with this kind of situation."

Llew got into his car, held his breath and turned the key. The engine started up, and he relaxed. "Another little problem I've got to deal with one of these days . . ."

As he drove back to campus, Llew wondered why Hess had raised the rates so stiffly for outside users. He was sure they were quietly hurting for money, but this would only amount to a drop in the bucket.

More than likely, Hess was beginning to realize that the increasing demand for computer services was taking its toll on the performance of the MAX, and was hoping that by raising rates the paying customers would take their business elsewhere, thus easing the demand. But how long did he think he could keep this up? Eventually the whole system would grind to a halt, and the campus users would be demanding an explanation.

Llew glanced at his speedometer. Better slow it down a bit, he thought—I don't want another hassle with our friendly unmarked cop.

He watched for likely disguised vehicles. That tow truck over there? Or that sports car? What about that power company van? My god, it could be any of them. Visions of being pursued by a huge yellow school bus, its angry red lights flashing at him . . .

The car in front of him looked perfectly ordinary, and was dawdling along at well below the speed limit. A glance at his watch told Llew that it was getting late, and he still had many things to do before Byron's party tonight. There was one car approaching from the opposite direction, then it would be clear to pass.

Then Llew saw that the approaching car was a police cruiser, and as it passed, the driver in the car in front waved a chubby hand out the window. The man in the police car returned the greeting.

My god, that must be our cop ahead of me, Llew thought. And I almost passed him.

He dropped back into place and tried to see the driver through the back window, but the late afternoon sun was in his eyes. He could tell that the person was rather short and stocky, and wearing a hat of some sort. On the dashboard was something bulky that could be a flasher light, but it was hard to tell.

He's going irritatingly slow, Llew observed, as if he were . . . well, cruising. But I'd have to exceed the speed limit to pass. And if that is him, you can bet your boots he'll pull me over.

Llew finally decided not to risk it, and resigned himself to following at a safe distance for the remaining miles into town. There were several other cars behind him now, and he wished one of them would pass them both. Then one way or another he'd know for sure.

But no one did, and when the road finally widened, Llew eased into the left lane and accelerated carefully. As he passed the car in front, the driver—whom Llew had never seen before—smiled politely and gave him a brief wave. The object on the dashboard was a stuffed animal of some sort. Llew cursed and stepped on the gas.

He parked his car in the usual place on top of the hill. It was Friday, and too late to take the car into the shop to get the ignition switch looked at. Next week for sure, he vowed.

While trekking across campus, he glanced over at the Computer Center and felt a wave of relief that last night's venture had gone so smoothly. There had been a desperate moment there, with the security officer just a few feet away on the other side of the door, when matters could have turned out a lot worse. He hoped his luck would hold until he could figure out what Hess was up to.

Rama's bike was chained to the tree next to the rear entrance. Llew scribbled a note asking Rama to stop by and see him in his office before leaving for the day, and fastened it conspicuously to the handlebars.

From there he went to Tully Dunkle's office in the Political

Science department. He had taken the listing of Gus's tape by the day before; Tully had not been in, so Llew had left the listing with his secretary and asked her to show it to him.

"He just left for the day," his secretary said. "I did give him the material you dropped off yesterday, though."

"Good. Was it his?"

"He didn't say, but he didn't seem to recognize it. It must have been interesting, though, because he spent the rest of the day with it. And most of the day today. He tried to call you a couple of times, but got no answer."

"Hmm. Now he's got me curious. I suppose I can call him at home."

"I believe he said something about going to Byron Devilbiss's party tonight. If you're going, you can probably catch him there."

"I'll do that. Thanks." Llew left and went back to his office to wait for Rama, wondering what Tully could have found that intrigued him so.

When he arrived, he gave Nina a call to see if she wanted to go out to Duffy's for supper. There was no answer. Maybe she's still in the sack, he thought. Before calling it quits at 5 AM, they had checked out all the modifications to Llew's account from his own terminal, and wiped out all traces of their activities from the Sultan log file. They were both exhausted by then, and he could only hope that they hadn't overlooked anything.

After a few restless hours sleep, he had returned to his office and spent the rest of the morning playing hit-and-run with the Sultan—checking active tasks, dumping files, and especially monitoring any transfers of data. The sessions were necessarily brief, because he couldn't risk interfering with currently active tasks. And when the SYSTAT showed that another user—presumably Slade—had logged on, he quickly logged off.

So far he had learned very little, but his proficiency with the Sultan operating system was increasing with each session. This made it easier to do what he needed as quickly and efficiently as possible.

If I managed to prove that Hess is really up to something illegal, he pondered, I wonder if it would get me my job back? I wonder if I would *take* it back?

There was a quiet knock at his door, and he leaned over from his desk to open it. Rama came in and looked around.

"Goodnezz, you don't have mudge zpace in here, izn't it?"

Llew grinned. "Well, if office size is any indication of the responsibility of the job, I've got more than I need."

Rama perched on the free edge of the desk. "To tell you the truth, I am not really underzdanding what iz this new job they are giving you."

"To tell *you* the truth, Rama, neither do I. I spend most of my time trying to figure out what Hess and Slade are doing with that computer system over there."

Rama nodded. "Zo I alzo. I do all what I am told, but nobody ever exblain anything."

"So how do you like working on the Sultan?"

Rama waved a casual hand. "Oh, it is veddy zimple. Most of the time I forget it iz not the MAX."

Llew wished he could tell Rama the truth, but the less he knew at this point the safer he would be. "Do you always use the same terminal?"

"Oh devinitely," Rama replied. "There iz another one, which Mizter Zlade uses, but I am not allowed to touch it."

That explains why there are two, Llew thought—so that Rama can do his operations tasks without interfering with the Sultan. He *thinks* it's the Sultan, of course, just like all the other users on campus. "Do you ever see the MAX?"

"Zometimes. They are geeping it in the ztoreroom. One time I log in to zee what iz going on, but it iz not running any tasks now."

That's what they want you to believe, Llew thought. "Okay, I need to ask another favor. Can you dump all of Van Reudge's stuff onto a tape, and keep it somewhere for a while?"

"No broblem. I can do it firzt thing tomorrow."

"Good. And speaking of tapes, do you still have the one that Gus returned the other day?"

Rama shook his head. "No, they are taking it from me."

"They? Who?"

"Mizter Zlade. He axed me if zomeone haz gedding the wrong tape, and I am showing him that one. Then he iz becoming veddy angry, but I am thinging he iz glad to get it back."

Aha, Llew thought—so it was *Slade's* data on that tape. Or Hess's, or both. Something they generated on the Sultan got written off onto the wrong tape. I wonder what was on it that made him so angry? "You didn't tell them I listed the contents, did you?"

"Mozt devinitely not! I am not liking to talk to them unlezz they ax me a question."

"Good. And don't tell them about backing up Van's files either."

Rama agreed. "Well, I muzz go now. It is gedding veddy hungry."

"Thanks, Rama. I'll repay the favors one of these days."

Rama left, and Llew turned back to his terminal. One more short session, he decided, and then I'll get a bite to eat myself. Rama's right, it *is* getting hungry . . .

First, let's check out that new phone connection we found. All that equipment in my old office seems to be hooked up to it, so we can see where it goes.

All the phone lines on campus were shunted through a separate, dedicated computer system, like the spokes of a wheel. One spoke accessed the computer itself, so that those who maintained the system could punch the base number and enter the necessary modifications, such as adding new extensions or changing existing ones. Having served as consultant when the system was being installed, Llew knew the magic number and typed a command to access it over his modem.

A few seconds later, a menu was displayed which listed the options available for examination or modification. Llew chose a table containing all 4-digit extensions on campus.

The table was displayed on the screen. The extensions were listed in numerical sequence, along with codes indicating their location:

```
EXTENSION     LOCATION

1001            04 01
1002            04 02
1010            04 03
  .               .
  .               .
  .               .
```

The first two digits of the location code identified the building, and the last two specified the individual phone within that building. The Computer Center was in the basement of Chapman Hall, so Llew scrolled the display until the numbers for that building appeared.

He recognized the eight extensions which were allocated to the Computer Center—one for each of the offices, one for the computer room, and four multi-user lines for computer dial-in.

But now, he noticed, there was a ninth.

Unless another phone has been installed somewhere else in the building, he concluded, that's got to be the new line we found in my office.

But this only confirms that there is a new line—it doesn't tell me where it goes, or who can access it. Since there was no phone attached, maybe it's a single-access line, which means it should be in one of the other tables . . .

He returned to the main menu and selected another option. A moment later a short table of paired numbers was displayed, showing fixed sources and destinations, such as direct two-way lines from administration to security, and from grounds maintenance to shipping and receiving.

Llew found the new extension in the list, wrote down the corresponding number from the second column, and returned to the main menu. He again selected the original table showing the locations of each extension, and stepped down the sequence until he came to the number he had written.

The location code for that extension was given as 99 01, which meant Building 99, phone 01.

"99"? That's an odd one, Llew thought, remembering that the building code sequence had previously gone up to only 40 or so. Why the big gap? Well, let's find out just what "99" is . . .

He called up yet another list showing the location codes and their corresponding building names. He moved down the list to "99".

The entry in the "name" column was blank.

Blank? Why would the building name entry be blank?

He checked another table listing the location codes first, followed by their current phone extensions. There was no "99" entry.

He scanned each of the other tables listed in the menu, but found no more references to the new extension or to the location code "99". Maybe the line was just installed in anticipation of future expansion, he thought—although in places where money is tight, like college campuses, things don't usually get done until long *after* they're needed.

Impulsively, he picked up his other phone and punched the extension corresponding to "99". After a few seconds, a busy signal sounded.

He hung up, thought a minute, then typed a network access code on his keyboard, followed by the 4-digit extension. His priority status on the telephone system computer permitted him to tap directly into any network extension, presumably to test new lines and identify problems.

This time there was a loud, high-pitched chattering sound on the line when the connection was made. What the hell is *that*? he wondered, jerking the receiver away from his ear. Sounds like some of that electronic stuff Gus writes.

He hung up the phone. Electrical interference, probably. Most likely a faulty line. Dead end, he concluded with a sigh. The only thing I can can do at this point is try the number from time to time to see if the interference problem goes away—if that really is the problem—or wait till someone gets around to filling in the name of the building in the location table.

In the meantime, let's see what the Sultan is up to this evening . . .

The SYSTAT showed no other users currently on-line, so Llew stepped through the task list looking for signs of activity, particularly among the devices with those strange designations. He hoped to find anything that looked familiar, but the task names were cryptic and gave no clue as to their purpose. And they were all idle at the moment anyway.

Suddenly, one of the tasks went to active status, grabbing a sizeable chunk of memory and initiating a number of other tasks which had previously been idle.

Looks like we've got something here, he thought—one of those devices must be doing something. He quickly checked to see if anyone else had logged on.

He was still the only user, so he typed a command requesting that his terminal be entered as an output device for the active task. But a message promptly informed him that the data being processed was not in displayable form. Must be generating strictly binary code, he figured.

Then another of the devices became active. Maybe this one is converting the data to a readable form, he thought, and quickly attached to the second device.

This time his screen filled with a rapidly scrolling stream of symbols. He halted the display, quickly created a dummy file, and redirected the output over to it instead of his screen. Then he sat back and waited.

After a minute or so, he checked the SYSTAT again. Oh oh—I've got company, he realized. The list now showed two users.

He quickly closed the dummy file and typed in a command to dump what there was of it to his printer, with an auto-delete when printing was complete. Then he logged off.

The printer began to list the contents of the file. As Llew watched the flood of characters and numbers fill page after page, he frowned. Then his eyes grew wide and he leaned forward.

When the printing finally stopped, he removed the stream of paper and stared at it. The arrays of characters which filled each page were utterly meaningless to him . . .

But the format was identical to the tape output he had delivered to Tully Dunkle.

Nina had said it looked like code. Tully had reportedly found it fascinating. And Slade had been furious when he found the tape was missing.

And now here was more of the same, generated by this new computer whose real purpose was a tightly guarded secret.

Llew sat back and rubbed his stiff neck. I'll get to the bottom of this somehow, he vowed . . .

But I don't think I'm going to like what I find.

13

"Beer makes me sleepy and burp," Godfrey Daniels declared in his pinched wheeze, as the tuxedoed bartender refilled his glass with Wild Turkey for the nth time that evening. "Which is why I choose to limit my intake of spirits to a single breed. I refer, of course, to the patriotic product of the fruited plain."

He dispatched a generous portion of the bourbon into the orifice beneath his polyp nose, then squinted at the elongated goblet in Llew's hand. "And, eh . . . you, Mr McQuilla—what essence dignifies the inside of your glass?"

"Plain old fruit of the vine," Llew replied. "Champagne." He finished off the remaining portion and held out the empty glass to the bartender, a short wiry Italian who spoke little English but who mixed drinks with spastic energy and flourish.

"Champagne . . . of course, of course," Daniels nodded his approval. "The highest achievement of the noble Cabernet grape."

"Chardonnay," Llew corrected offhandedly, instantly regretting it. Fortunately, his reply was obliterated by a series of thundering chords from Byron's piano across the room, and he quickly changed the subject. "So how are things in the Post Office these days?"

"The Post Office . . . yes-s-s . . ." Godfrey Daniels frowned, as if trying to recall the significance of the Post Office. His lengthy tenure as campus postmaster had, to the surprise of many, remained intact during the recent siege of firings and "reassignments" instigated by Hess. Whether this was due to the fact that the position was partially a government appointment, or because he was an intimate of President Croup, was a matter of conjecture.

"Fraught with difficulty," he sighed, after another hefty quaff brought the subject back into focus. "Oh, we manage to keep the missives moving, mind you. In spite of the inconveniences rudely imposed upon us."

"Inconveniences?"

But Godfrey's attention was again distracted, this time by a slim dark-haired girl who walked by, weaving just a bit. Llew thought she looked familiar but couldn't place her.

"Handsome lass," Godfrey observed. "Vision of loveliness. Eh . . . what was I saying?"

"Something about inconveniences at the Post Office."

"Ah, yes-s-s . . . I was referring to the chaos created by the extensive re-wiring of our once sedate domicile. For weeks, we have had to tolerate the din of hammers and drills, and risk becoming entangled in loops of cables with each step, or running into electricians or telephone men at every turn . . ." He shook his head and took another long sip.

The rewiring operation in Higgens Hall had begun immediately after the Dodgson fire, presumably to prevent a possible recurrence of that event. Llew had noted with some curiosity that the contract for the job had gone to an out-of-state firm—the official reason given had been their immediate availability.

Llew remembered the enigmatic government installation supposedly occupying the basement of Higgens, and wondered how they were faring with all the activity. He also wondered if Godfrey knew about the installation, and briefly considered asking him about it. But he decided against it, in case the inquiry should find its way back to Hess.

"Fortunately," Godfrey said, holding his glass out unsteadily for the bartender to refill, "they seem to have wreaked all the havoc they could muster for the time being, and have at last vacated the premises."

"But don't you feel more secure, now that all the old wiring has been replaced?" Llew asked.

"A needless expense, sir," Godfrey insisted. "The old stuff was fine. The whole building is in a remarkable state of preservation."

At this point, his squinty eyes fastened on a buxom woman at the other end of the bar getting her own glass refilled. "And speaking of well-preserved . . . Fine figure of a woman, yes-s-s . . ." and he moved off in her direction, adjusting his tie.

Llew drifted back into the crowd, looking around to see if Tully had shown up. This evening's going to be a bust if I don't get to talk to him, he thought. I'll spend the whole time fretting about that stupid code.

Another absent face was Nina's. She hadn't answered her phone all day, which made Llew a little uneasy. Maybe he should have stopped by her place on the way to the party, but it was already getting late when he had finished up at his terminal. He had even skipped dinner, knowing there would be plenty of food at the party.

Most of the other faces in the room were familiar. President Croup, another bourbon devotee, was laughing heartily at someone's dirty joke, and was now launching into one of his own, in a booming voice which grew louder with each refill of his glass. In another part of the spacious room, Roberta Turnbuckle was talking to Willard Hess, whose mind seemed to be elsewhere in spite of his companion's animated discourse. At least Slade didn't seem to be here, for which Llew was grateful.

Byron's house was of sufficient size to contain the whole menagerie. A three-story Victorian mansion with pointed gables and vaulting parapets, it stood on the outskirts of the college, which it predated by a good half-century. Byron had come into possession of it years ago by means best left to speculation.

The cavernous living room, with its cathedral ceiling and tall narrow windows flanked by heavy velvet curtains, was filled with an abundance of musicalia, literaria and esoteria, all reflecting the tastes and whims of its owner. Shelves from floor to ceiling sagged under the weight of countless volumes of books, phonograph records and musical scores, interspersed with busts of composers and photographs of famous musicians, many autographed or inscribed with personal messages.

The furniture was antique but plush, the carpeting oriental over an oak floor, and a multi-faceted chandelier glittered from the center of the ceiling. A tall lemonwood secretary, inlaid with ivory, occupied one corner of the room, and a full-size polished suit of armor, the gauntleted hand of which wielded a double-edged ax, stood next to the ornate, gracefully curving stairway banister.

The most immediately imposing sight for arriving guests, however, was the seven-foot doorman, stationed just inside the entrance foyer. His facial features were Slavic, with narrow, piercing eyes, high prominent cheekbones and an oval hairless head. A thick handlebar mustache separated a wide nose from a massive jaw. A silk ruffled shirt beneath his formal tuxedo jacket was stretched tight over a barrel chest and broad shoulders. His striped trousers ended an inch or so above his enormous feet, which were bare.

His name was Otto, and although his origin was uncertain, he had served as Byron's valet and chauffeur for several years. Byron insisted that he had come with the house. Tonight, in his role as doorman, he spoke to no one, but gestured toward an adjacent anteroom for those with coats to deposit.

Llew made his way over to the far side of the room, where the thundering chords of Rachmaninoff's *Etudes Tableaux* emanated from Byron's gargantuan concert grand, making it necessary for those guests who insisted on talking to shout to make themselves heard. The host himself, resplendent in midnight blue tuxedo, attacked the keyboard with vehemence, his long dark-blond hair whipping around his face. His jaw clenched in concentration, he executed the final fortissimo triple-chords, flinging his mane backwards and rising to acknowledge the applause from the array of admirers—mostly female—who surrounded the piano.

Llew moved on over to one of the food tables, ladened with fruit, cheeses, raw vegetables and assorted dips. In the center was a huge iced bowl of giant shrimp surrounded by a moat of spicy red sauce. The dark-haired girl whom Godfrey had admired was dipping strawberries into her glass of Champagne. She looked up at Llew. "Hello again," she said.

Llew had thought she looked familiar, but still couldn't place her. "How's it going?" he replied.

"I'm okay. How bout you? Are you still going up and down the sign waves?"

Now he remembered. The girl at the bar in Duffy's, just after he'd been removed from his job. Her eyes had the same unfocused look as they had then.

"Much better," he lied, vaguely regretting having dumped on a total stranger. He tried to remember their conversation, but all he could recall was something about popcorn. "Enjoying yourself?"

"I always enjoy myself at parties," she replied, nibbling at the strawberry. "I like places with lots of people."

"Are you a student here?"

"Off and on. I find that going to classes interferes with my writing."

"Writing? What, uh . . . sorts of things do you write?"

"Different things. You might say I specialize in diversity."

"Oh. Has any of your work been published?"

She blinked. "Of course. What good is writing if nobody gets to read it?"

"That's a point." Llew helped himself to a handful of mixed nuts from the table.

"My first work was called *Petals in the Milk.* It was a collection of poems from my Romantic period."

Llew frowned. "I don't think I've, uh . . ."

"I'm not surprised," she sighed. "The publisher was a flake, and I don't think it got much circulation. They don't even answer my calls anymore."

She sipped from her glass. There were strawberry seeds floating around inside. "So now I just concentrate on the small magazines—the intellectual ones, like *The Quiverly Quarterly* and the *Okeefenokee Review.* And I'm working on a book . . ."

"A novel?"

"It started out to be. But I kept putting in more and more characters, and pretty soon I began to lose interest in the plot. So I decided to leave it out and just keep the people.

"Then there got to be so many people I started forgetting who was who, and what they were there for. So I finally just kept their names and left everything else out."

Llew frowned. "How can you have a book with only names and nothing else?"

She nodded. "That bothered me for a while, to tell the truth. Until I came up with the idea of making it into a telephone directory. All I had to do was put all the names in alphabetical order and add a seven digit number after each one."

"But there's already a telephone directory," Llew pointed out. "Lots of them, in fact."

"But they're all *real.* Mine is the first *fiction* one. And that makes it more interesting to read."

"Fiction?"

"Yeah. The names are just made up."

"Oh. So you don't use real people?"

"Only if I change their names. Like in novels, where they have to say 'all the characters in this book are fictitious'. To keep from getting sued and things."

Llew's glass was empty, and he was beginning to feel a urgent need for a refill. "How many names are you going to have in your telephone book?"

"About a thousand, I guess. I've got over 600 already, and it's just a first draft."

"Do you make up the numbers, too?"

"I did at first. But it got to be a bit of a drag. So then I found out that you can get the computer to do it."

"The computer . . . you mean the one here at the college?"

"Yeah. There's a program that just prints out numbers—all different. As many as you want, any size."

He nodded. "Random number generator." He remembered Nina mentioning some user who spent inordinate amounts of time using this facility.

"Right. So I make up the first three digits—that's the exchange, and there are only a handful of those—and let the computer do the last four."

"Clever."

"Of course, I'll have to give credit to the computer in the acknowledgement section of the book."

"Only fair."

"Well," she said, "my glass is empty. Guess I'd better get a refill."

"Good luck with the book. I hope it sells."

"Me too. It'll give me something to live on while I work on the next one."

"A sequel?"

"Sort of. The Yellow Pages." She weaved back toward the bar.

Llew decided to wait a few discrete minutes before returning to the bar himself, so he turned back to the buffet table. Near the other end, nibbling on a piece of cauliflower, was Madox F.

Madox, so Llew went over to join him.

"Ah, good evening, Llew," Madox greeted, his head tilting back an extra degree, as if to bring Llew into better focus. "How's life, to use a common cliche, with you?"

"Rather dull, I'm afraid," Llew replied, helping himself to some lobster bits. "Generating a computer index of archival documents is slow work."

"Doubtless a tedious and, at least immediately, unrewarding effort," Madox agreed, "not unlike, if I may conjecture, those of my own in cataloging the entire output, as it currently exists, of Henry James, with whom I seem to become, as fate would have it, more deeply involved, for better or for worse, with each passing, which they seem to do with disquieting haste, day."

"So I gather. Any, uh . . . particular problems with the computer part of your research?"

Madox frowned. "None that I didn't have, if memory serves, before, which were largely, if not entirely, of my own making, and which, curiously, seem to persist on the new system, whose processing capabilities, I have been repeatedly assured, should have minimized, if not eliminated entirely, them. It may, of course, have to do with the rumors, possibly exaggerated, of sabotage attempts on the computer facilities . . ."

Llew's eyes opened wide. "*Sabotage*? On the *computer*?"

"I assumed you had heard, associated as you are . . . or, I should say, were . . ."

"I hear very little any more. What happened?"

Madox rubbed his chin. "It's not, for the most part, entirely clear . . . but there reportedly is evidence that someone, assumedly unauthorized, succeeded in gaining entry into the computer building, and, while doing no harm, as far as can be determined by cursory examination, to the physical equipment, did apparently obtain access to the records and files, the consequences of which would, doubtless, be much more difficult, if not impossible, to—"

"When was this supposed to have taken place?" Llew asked, knowing full well what the answer would be.

"Just, I'm told, yesterday."

"Any, uh . . . suspects?"

"None, to my knowledge. But then again, as we are dealing with mere rumor, it is difficult to ascertain, with any degree of reliability, what might or might not, as the case might be—"

He was interrupted by a hearty greeting of "*Seo is god beormeting!*"

"Ah, Professor Bede!" Madox said. "Yes, marvelous party. Have you tried this delicious shrimp?"

The professor held up an ornate goblet. "*Tothsum! Ond hie meda gode gewrixleth!*"

"Yes, I imagine they do go marvelously with mead."

Llew chatted politely for a few minutes, then excused himself and made his way back into the crowd in order to think. Somehow, Slade—or Hess, or both—had discovered that their system had been infiltrated. Llew had tried to be careful, but there were dozens of ways to slip up, especially in a system that was largely unfamiliar to him.

The real question was, did they know *who* had broken into the system? It wouldn't be hard for them to guess. Nina's command file patch should have covered his traces, but there was no way to be absolutely sure.

At any rate, Slade would now doubtless take additional measures to insure that such an incursion would not happen again. Time was running out—another session after the party might be a good idea . . .

Llew noticed that Harry Gross had joined the joke-telling session with Croup. His gutteral snickering made an excellent counterpoint to Croup's loud guffawing and Godfrey Daniels' high-pitched giggling. Llew looked around for Kay, but didn't see her anywhere.

He did, however, observe that Byron was hustling a shapely blonde in a low-cut red dress up the stairs. That was at least the second time this evening—the girl on the previous occasion had been a brunette in tight-fitting slacks. He sighed, and headed back to the bar.

As his glass was being refilled, a voice close to his ear whispered, "Maybe he has more than one bedroom up there."

He turned, grinning. "What if Harry runs out of jokes before we get back?"

"Harry never runs out of dirty jokes," Kay replied, sipping her champagne.

"Maybe I should start spending more time with him. The last time someone told me a dirty joke, I couldn't think of one to tell in return."

"It's not Harry you need to spend more time with, my friend."

"I know. Any suggestions?"

"I'm working on it. Just, uh . . . don't do anything impulsive before then."

"Impulsive? Like what?"

She raised an eyebrow at him. "Haven't you been listening to all the rumors?"

His heart skipped a beat. "Rumors? You mean about us?"

"No, dummy—I mean about the Computer Center break-in."

"Oh, that." He breathed a sigh of relief. "What's that got to do with—?"

"You mean you weren't involved? Harry insists it was you."

"Me? What gave him that idea?"

"Who else is there? Nina—but she's not exactly the type to go breaking into places like that."

Not alone, anyway, Llew thought. But she's right—naturally I'm the logical suspect. "But why would I want to do anything like that?"

"Sour grapes, Harry says. So, did you or didn't you?"

Llew hesitated, and Kay nodded. "I thought so. Llew, you're going to get yourself in one big—"

"Kay, listen. I didn't go in there to wreck anything. And I didn't change anybody's files or screw up the system."

Kay looked skeptical. "So what *did* you—"

Llew took her arm and moved away from the table. "Something weird's going on. I found out that they're still running on the old computer system—the one I managed. But Hess has been telling everyone it's the *new* system, the one he brought in. You were there at the meeting last week—you heard him defending it."

"That's true." Her eyes widened. "And I also remember Dr Otvos saying that some users couldn't see any real difference between running on the old one and the new one. You mean . . .?"

"Not just some users, Kay—*all* of them. Except for people like Harry, who'll believe anything Hess tells them."

"But . . . why? What do you think he's up to?"

"I haven't the faintest idea. That's why we—*I* had to break into the place—to see if I could find out something."

"So Nina went with you, eh?"

Llew detected a sour note in her voice. He grinned. "Does that bother you?"

"Not rationally. It's just that you end up spending more time with her than with me . . ."

"I always did—she was working for me."

". . . and now you're even spending *nights* with her . . ."

"All in the line of duty. Look, if you knew as much about computer systems as Nina does, and had been pressured into quitting your job, you would have been there with me instead of her."

"I know that. I'm just frustrated and blowing off steam. What are you going to do about Hess?"

"Nothing, until I know what he's up to."

"But if he can prove you broke into the Center, he could fire you. Or even have you arrested."

"I'm gambling that he doesn't and won't. He has no idea what I found out in there, so I'm counting on a stalemate, at least until I can—"

She cleared her throat. "Harry's coming over this way."

Llew quickly changed gears and laughed heartily. "Did he *really*? Well, you never know about people like that . . . Oh, hello, Harry. Kay was just telling me about that student who faked appendicitis in order to get a medical excuse for missing a final."

Harry glared at him. "Yeah. Hard to know who to trust these days, ain't it?" To Kay he said, "C'mon, I wanna talk to you."

"Have a nice day," Llew muttered as Harry hustled Kay off, doubtless to chastise her for socializing with saboteurs. He sighed, turning back to the bar for another refill. Better take it easy on this stuff, he told himself, if I expect to get some computer time in after the party.

The joke telling session had apparently broken up, and President Croup was now talking with Hess and Roberta Turnbuckle. Croup was listening intently and frowning at whatever Hess was saying. Roberta's eyes fell on Llew over her grape-encrusted eyeglasses, and he saw her lean over and whisper to Hess. Then both Hess and Croup looked over at him.

Cushlamochree, Llew thought—have things really gotten this bad? Maybe I should just get out of here before I'm cornered into some sort of confrontation.

He started to move away and immediately collided with someone standing next to him, spilling both their drinks. "I'm sorry," he apologized, then saw that the person was Tully Dunkle.

"Llew—I was just looking for you," Tully said, wiping his glass with a napkin. "Did any get on you?"

"Don't think so—how bout you?" Llew hoped Croup and Hess hadn't seen his performance just now. Guilty persons always behave erratically.

"I wanted to get back to you about that tape dump you sent over," Tully said.

"Right—I was hoping you'd be here tonight." Llew began to regain his composure. "Were you able to make any sense out of it?"

"Not entirely." Tully looked around the room, then lowered his voice. "Llew, where the hell did that stuff come from?"

Oh oh, Llew thought—is it that bad? "It got onto one of Gus Roddencroft's tapes by mistake. I thought it was yours."

"Well, all I can tell you is that it's definitely code. And I'd be willing to bet my shirt that it's high-level security stuff."

Llew swallowed. "High-level security . . . ?"

"*Government* security, Llew. It's too complex for me to break with my limited resources, but I recognized enough of the structure and patterns to know that it's the same type used by government security agencies."

Llew shook his head. It's impossible. Hess couldn't be working for the *government* . . . could he? And Slade? If they are, he swore, I'm going to defect. "Tully, are you sure it isn't just some outdated code that's been declassified? Maybe someone else on campus is doing just what you're doing—playing around with cryptology for the fun of it."

"That's possible—but I think I know everyone who's involved with that sort of thing. We've got a club, just like your wine group. Besides, it would take a more powerful computer than the one on campus to handle a code this complex."

A more powerful computer. The thought struck Llew like a thunderbolt. In his mind, he saw the Sultan, locked out of sight, applying its greater power and speed to some mysterious application, supported by a batch of unidentified peripheral devices, while the MAX continued to service all the campus users. Is *this* what the Sultan is being used for—processing secret government code?

"And that's what puzzles me," Tully went on. "That new computer doesn't seem to have significantly more processing power than the old one—so it's hard for me to believe that this code originated on it."

Llew thought fast. Best to get Tully out of the picture, he decided, at least until I can think this thing out. "Yeah, you're right. Well . . . what might have happened is, a lot of the tapes we buy are 'scratch' tapes from other facilities. It was probably generated somewhere else and sold to us without being zeroed, and Rama accidently sent it over to Gus." Forgive me, Rama. "Things like that happen all the time."

Tully thought it over, then nodded. "Well, I guess that could explain it."

"So what I'll do is ask Rama to check the records and find out where the tape came from, and I'll contact them and clear the matter up."

Tully agreed. "I wouldn't wait, though. You don't want to fool around with things involving government security—you'll have the CIA snooping around before you know it."

That's all I need, Llew thought. "I'll get to it first thing tomorrow."

Tully disappeared into the crowd as Llew pondered the implications of what Tully had said. It just doesn't make sense, he thought. If Hess is doing some kind of secret government work, why did he fire me? My record is clean. I even had government security clearance a few years ago when I worked for Mike Ebbsedik. And if he's *not* doing government work, then what the hell *is* he—?

His train of thought was broken by an eruption of chords from the piano. My god, Byron's back downstairs already, Llew noted. He certainly doesn't waste any time. There was no sign of the blond in the red dress.

And where does he get all the energy? It was the Liszt *Spanish Rhapsody* this time, with all those ferocious octave passages. Next he'll do the Schumann *Toccata*, and the Balakirev *Oriental Fantasy* . . . Llew felt himself growing exhausted just thinking about it, and headed back to the bar for something to revive his spirits.

It was close to midnight, and Croup, Hess, and Roberta Turnbuckle had apparently left. The party was still going strong, however, and probably would continue for several hours. Llew spotted Kay standing with the people clustered around Byron's piano. He debated briefly whether to join her, but decided to leave well enough alone.

As he approached the bar, Llew saw Harry Gross arguing with the bartender. Harry was drunk, and yelling something the bartender didn't seem to understand. His words were garbled, and Llew remembered Kay saying something about this happening when Harry got drunk or angry. Right now he was both.

"Gollammit!" Harry shouted. "Whaffamagger wif you! I shleg gimme anoffer grazha Schrofsh! Cank you ungelschlam pwain Engwilsch?!"

The terrified bartender, his tiny mustache quivering, could only stammer apologies in his own broken English. Finally, in frustration, Harry snatched a bottle of Scotch from the table and poured a huge glassful. "Gef my owm grazha Schrofsh, by golm . . ."

He took a healthy swig from the glass, then fumbled around in his coat pockets. "Wherszh my shligarzh? Who shtole my shligargzh?"

Llew changed his mind about another drink, and headed back toward the piano to suggest that Kay get Harry home while he was still on his feet. The music had stopped again, and Llew saw that Byron was talking—at close quarters—to another girl. He had his hand on her arm, and any minute, Llew knew, they would head toward the stairs. Then Llew saw that the girl was Kay.

He hesitated, wondering what to do. Byron was pouring on the charm, but Kay's expression was one of polite tolerance. Then she smiled, shaking her head, and Llew saw Byron's shoulders slump. Can't win 'em all, Devilbiss, Llew thought.

Byron nodded and was lighting a cigar when Harry stumbled up to them, tripping on the piano leg and spilling most of his drink. "Whaszh goin on?" he demanded. "*Hey*—where dzhlu geck lak shligarg?"

Kay's mouth tightened, and Byron stared at Harry with mild disgust. Harry pointed an unsteady finger at Byron's cigar. "Izhat my shligarg you're schmolging?" He turned on Kay. "Dlig you glivim wunga my shligarzh?"

Llew felt a slight tremor, and an instant later Otto, the giant barefooted doorman, strode past and over to where Byron stood with folded arms. Harry looked up at the chiseled face glaring down at him and took an unsteady step backwards.

Kay took his arm. "Time to go, Harry. Thank Byron for the nice party and say goodnight."

Harry mumbled something incoherent, and allowed himself to be led away. Llew's eyes met Kay's briefly, and then she and Harry were gone.

Byron deposited his cigar into an ash tray next to the piano, and sat down at the keyboard. With a dramatic flourish, he hiked up his sleeves and launched into the Chopin *Revolutionary Etude.*

As the guests reassembled around the piano, Llew looked at his watch and set his empty glass down on a table. Fun is fun, he thought, but duty calls. The quiet intimacy of his closet office, a friendly terminal for companionship, the CIA prowling around outside . . . what better way to polish off an evening?

14

"Hey—no fair!"

"Hmmf? What?"

"You were dozing. I don't think you've heard a word I said."

Llew fluffed the pillow up against the headboard and pulled himself to a half-sitting position. "Sorry. I haven't had much sleep in the past couple of days."

"Well, I haven't had much of *you* in the past couple of *months*, Kay complained. "You'll just have to postpone these minor activities like sleeping till some other time."

Llew yawned, and said "Sorry" again. "I heard every word you said. Really. You were telling me how Harry uses his fork to pick food from his teeth at meals . . ."

"Llew, I told you that *months* ago!"

"Hmmm . . . ?" He feigned a snore.

Kay shoved him. "Llew!"

"Just kidding, just kidding." He turned over toward her and buried his face in her neck. Her arms went around his head.

"That's better," she said, running her long fingers lightly through his hair. "Do you still like that? You used to say it made chills run up and down your spine."

Llew snored.

"*Llew!!* All right, buster . . ." Her hand shot under the covers, and Llew let out a yelp and jerked his knees up to his chest.

"Serves you right," Kay said, reaching for a pack of cigarets on the night table. She lit one and held the pack out to Llew. "Want one?"

"Gave it up," he grumped, rearranging the rumpled sheets.

"I know that. But you used to share one with me after we made love."

"I finally started worrying that you'd get addicted."

She smiled slyly. "To smoking or making love?"

"Besides," he said, "people in the medical profession shouldn't smoke. Sets a bad example."

"I only used to do it in bed."

"Smoking or making love?"

"Actually, both activities have been curtailed rather severely in the past month or so." She dragged heavily on the cigaret.

"Well, whose fault is that?"

"Nobody's. I'm just being bitchy. I've missed you."

Llew put his arm behind her and she leaned her head against his. "And now I'm being selfish," she said, "feeling sorry for myself when you've got more serious problems of your own. You've lost a job you loved, everybody suspects you of sabotage . . . and I bitch at you and let myself get jealous of that little—"

"Careful."

She snuggled closer. "Part of it is because living with Harry is becoming more intolerable all the time. And the other part is that I'm worried about what's going to happen to you if you keep breaking into buildings and computer files . . ."

"First of all, I don't intend to break into any more buildings," Llew assured her. "And second, everybody is *not* accusing me of sabotage—just Hess and his cronies. Including Harry. Hess is obviously trying to pressure me into quitting altogether, or looking for an excuse to fire me. He knows I'm on to something, so now I'm more of a threat than ever."

"I don't understand why he thought you were a threat to him in the first place. He never gave you a chance."

"I'm a threat because I'm honest. Remember my telling you that Mike Ebbsedik got an inquiry about me several weeks before this whole thing got started? I'm convinced that was Hess, checking up on my integrity . . . trying to find out how *reliable* I was.

"Hess had to have some motive for bringing in that computer and pretending it was to replace the old MAX. And if he had thought I would go along with it, I figure he would have offered to 'buy' my cooperation—he's Vice President for Financial Affairs, so he could have pulled that off easily enough.

"When Mike assured him I was virtually spotless, that sealed my fate right there. But he couldn't just fire me without a good reason, so he started casting doubts about my efficiency, and moved me to a menial position, hoping I would get mad and quit."

"Like Nina did."

"Exactly. But it didn't work, and now he's back looking for that 'good reason' to fire me. And he knows he's got to do it soon, before I blow the whistle on him."

"But you could still do that," Kay insisted. "And I don't understand what's stopping you from doing it right now."

"Because he's already damaged my credibility by linking me with the break-in. I still don't know what his game is—and unless I can prove some sinister motive, he's got the upper hand. And he knows it."

Llew drew a breath. "The other thing that slows me down is that tape output that came from the Sultan. Tully swears it's some kind of secret government code—which would seem to suggest that Hess and Slade might be involved in some sort of government security work. Much as I'd hate to believe that, it is a possibility."

"I don't see how," she replied. "If they worked for the government, why would Hess want to get rid of you? Especially after finding out you were honest, loyal, trustworthy and all those good things."

"It *doesn't* make a whole lot of sense," Llew admitted. "But I suspect there are a lot of unscrupulous people playing devious games in the name of national security."

Kay snickered. "Maybe Harry's one of them. My god, can't you just imagine Harry as a secret agent?"

"I can't imagine Harry as anything but a royal pain in the arse. Did you get him home okay after the party the other night?"

She nodded. "He calmed down a bit after that giant almost took him apart. He still thinks Byron was trying to seduce me, though."

"Wasn't he?"

"Of course. Boosted my ego a hundred percent, too. I denied it to Harry, naturally, but he doesn't believe me. So now I'm under strict orders to stay away from Byron Devilbiss. You too, I might add."

"Harry wants me to stay away from Byron?"

"No, silly—he wants me to stay away from you."

Llew took the half-smoked cigaret from Kay's fingers and leaned across her to deposit it in the ashtray. "Did he say for how long?"

Her arms encircled him. "Nope. Or how far."

The campus cafeteria was crowded. Llew filled a coffee cup from the dispenser, paid the cashier, and looked around for a table. All of them were occupied, so rather than stand and wait while his coffee got cold, he made his way over to a table with only two occupants.

Whom, he realized too late, were Stella Lukerella and Wally Webster.

"Well, if it isn't our resident troublemaker," Stella said in a contemptuous voice.

"Don't mind if I do," Llew said, drawing up a chair. "Hi, Wally."

"I never thought of you as particularly audacious, Llew," Stella said, "so I'm a little surprised to see you showing your face around campus these days."

"What part of my anatomy would you prefer me to show?"

"I can't think of any worthy of exhibition," she retorted. "I had rather supposed that all of it would have been sent packing by now."

"Really? By whom? And for what?"

"Don't play innocent, Llew. Everybody knows about the break-in at the Computer Center. And everybody knows who did it."

"And just how does everybody know that?"

Wally chortled. "Maybe the computer has a Llew detector."

Stella ignored him. "You're exhibiting the standard response to frustration—displacing aggressive action away from the actual cause. Your own behavior has brought these problems on you, but you can't accept this or adjust to it. The more you refuse to face reality, the more of an outcast you become."

"An outLlew, as it were," Wally said, and snickered.

Stella gave Wally an icy stare, then turned back to Llew. "So why don't you do yourself and the college a favor, Llew, and take your neuroses elsewhere?"

"Why should I do that, when I've got an expert like you here to exorcise my demons? And speaking of demons, how's your computer response these days, Stella?"

"Don't change the subject. That's just another symptomatic—"

"No, really. Since I left, and the new computer was installed, have you seen a significant improvement in efficiency, response time, storage capacity . . ."

She smiled demurely. "I know what you're getting at. And all that proves is that you were playing your little sabotage games well before the break-in."

This caught Llew by surprise. Oh, very clever, he had to admit—now Hess was blaming *him* for all the inadequacies of the "new" system. Now he had become a scapegoat for the growing number of complaints from users who had expected more from the Sultan. "Stella, if I really wanted to sabotage that system, there wouldn't be enough left of it to salvage."

Stella shook her head. "That's not your style, Llew. Your methods are more insidious—like interfering with people's files, making the system slow down, sending nasty messages to all the terminals—"

"Sending *what?*"

Stella sighed impatiently. "I'm referring to those childish attacks on the president's speeches. Like the one on there this morning. Really, Llew, that's carrying your spitefulness a little too—"

"So he's back," Llew grinned. "The Campus Curmudgeon has struck again."

"No use, Llew. You're the only one who knows enough about the computer to manage something like that."

"I'd like to think so," he said truthfully, finishing his coffee and getting up from the table. "But reluctantly, I have to plead innocent to this one."

"The defendent is granted a full McQuittal," Wally said, guffawing loudly.

"Shut up, Wally," Stella said.

Llew hastily logged onto his office computer and typed the dial-in number, hoping that the Campus Curmudgeon file would still be there. Fat chance.

The real question, he realized, is how did it get there in the first place? It would have to be done from a privileged account via the

Sultan, and it took *me* days to get around that . . . and even then it was Nina who figured out how.

Could it be Nina, then? No, I've already pondered that possibility, and rejected it on every count. No way she could write stuff like that.

Still no word from her. Where the hell could she be? I'm getting just a bit worried now. It isn't like her to just up and disappear, especially when we were finally getting somewhere with the Sultan.

A message appeared on the screen: NO CARRIER.

No carrier? What's going on? he fumed, checking to see if the modem switch was on. It was, and the unit was plugged in.

He tried it again, and the same message appeared.

He disconnected the phone from the modem and plugged it directly into the phone receptacle. Then he lifted the receiver.

Dead.

They've cut me off, he realized, not completely surprised. Now they're really getting serious.

He tried the second phone, and was relieved to hear a dial tone. He removed the jack from the wall, plugged it into the modem, and retyped the computer number.

This time the message said LINE BUSY.

Llew groaned, sat back and drummed his fingers together impatiently. Apparently they were not aware that he had a second line in his office, but they'd probably find out eventually. Might be a good idea to run in a third. If there are any other spares in the building. And with Paisley gone, he'd have a hard time managing this anyway.

He tried the line again. Still busy. Never saw this happen before, he thought. Must be a lot of people using the computer just now. Or maybe the system is down. Probably reached its capacity and blew a fuse.

After the third try, he turned off the modem and punched Gus Roddencroft's extension in the Music Department. Gus answered.

"This is Llew, Gus. Have you tried logging into the computer this morning?"

"Yeah," Gus replied. "I'm on now, in fact."

"Any trouble getting a line?"

"No . . . not after I remembered to go through the operator."

"To do *what*?"

"Didn't you get a copy of the new directive? All remotes have to go through the switchboard operator now—no direct connections. A real pisser, if you ask me."

Llew shuffled through his sparse stack of campus mail. "I don't seem to have gotten any such message."

"It says, 'until further notice'—which seems to imply that the arrangement is only temporary."

A cold feeling came over Llew, and he said, "I'll get back to you," and hung up. Then he punched "O".

"Operator," a voice said.

"Hi, Peggy. Extension 2701, please," Llew said, the feeling growing colder.

There was a pause. "Is this Mr McQuilla?" the operator asked.

"Yes . . ."

Another pause. "I'm sorry, Mr McQuilla. I have strict orders not to connect you to that number."

I knew it, Llew thought. "Whose orders?"

"I'm not at liberty to say."

"Peggy, it's *Llew*, for chrissake. What is all this?"

"I'm sorry, Llew—I'm only following orders. I don't want to lose my job. And I have other callers." She cut him off.

Llew slammed the phone back in the cradle and sat back. They're pushing me over a cliff, he thought, and there's not much left to hang onto.

So what are my options? I could use another terminal on campus, but it would only be able to access the MAX again, since Nina fixed it so only my own terminal could talk to the Sultan. And then I'd be back to square one.

The same goes for my terminal at home. It's this terminal or nothing. To make matters worse, the operator has obviously been instructed to check the source of any calls to the computer number. So now she'll be watching for any calls from this extension.

So let's try a different tack, he decided, rummaging through several stacks of papers on his shelves. They had never been sorted or filed because he had always considered this office—as well as this job—to be temporary at best. And now it looked like the end was fast approaching.

He found the folder he was looking for and opened it on his desk. Inside were the schematics and program listings for the computerized telephone system he had helped install on campus. He had remembered how to display the table of phone extensions in order to trace the new phone line from the Computer Center, but this was going to be a bit more involved.

He studied the extension assignment description for several minutes, then reconnected the modem and typed the instruction to autodial the telephone system computer, hoping it hadn't also been relegated to the no-no list.

It hadn't. The main menu was displayed, and he chose the appropriate option. Moments later, a table listing all the campus extensions appeared on the screen. Following the directions in the documentation, he substituted a different extension, not currently in use, for his own. Then he exited and disconnected the modem.

This will only work until someone tries to call me on the old extension and gets an out-of-service message, he reminded himself as he punched "O" again. But maybe by that time . . .

The operator answered, and in a disguised voice Llew requested the computer number. When the familiar response tone sounded, he breathed a sigh of relief and flipped on the modem switch. The computer displayed the Sultan log-in messages, and he was back in business.

Following the set of instructions Nina had written out for him, he reassigned his terminal to the MAX system and displayed the

Public Address file. As expected, it was now empty—Slade had already wiped out the Campus Curmudgeon's message.

Maybe someone had made a hard-copy printout of it—Gus had done so with the others. Llew logged off and punched Gus's number.

"Yeah, I printed it," Gus told him. "I'll send over a copy."

"Not through the campus mail," Llew said. "Nothing seems to reach me here any more."

"Right. By the way, I just had a call from Nina. She tried to call you, but said your phone was out of order or something."

"Nina? Where is she?"

"She called from Duffy's. She asked me to tell you, if I saw you, that she'd be there for a while."

"Good—thanks." Llew gave Gus his new extension, asked him not to mention the change to anyone, and hung up. Then he locked the office door and headed for Duffy's.

"Where the hell have you been?"

"Out of town," Nina said as Llew joined her at the table.

"I was worried. I thought you'd been kidnapped or something. Where out of town?"

"I'll tell you all about it. What's the matter with your phone?"

"It's a little complicated—I'll tell *you* all about it. But you first."

"I thought you might have been disconnected along with your phone," she grinned.

"Are you going to tell me where you've been?"

"Okay. I was with Hen3ry."

"Hen3ry? You mean with the '3'?"

"Right."

"But that's all the way over in New Jersey."

"That's not so far. Anyway, I thought it would be worth it. And it was."

"What was? I still don't get it."

"Look—when Hen3ry was here, we had a long talk, and he was real nice, and said if I ever got to New Jersey give him a call. I told him I had relatives there, and I might just take him up on that."

"Do you? Have relatives there?"

She sipped her beer. "I have relatives everywhere."

"That doesn't answer—"

"Anyway, after the night you and I broke into the Computer Center, I kinda got depressed about things, and I started getting mad again and thought about how unfair all this was—for both of us. So I left Calhoun with my landlady and caught a plane to New Jersey."

"Why didn't you let me know?"

"Because I was afraid you might try and talk me out of going. And I was determined to go *somewhere* and do *something.*"

"I'm still not sure I understand what you intended to do."

She shrugged. "I wasn't sure myself at first. I didn't even know if Hen3ry would be there, or would have other plans, or what. I just took a chance."

"So what happened?"

Her face brightened. "I had a great time. Hen3ry was delighted to see me, and took me to dinner and everything."

"That's great." Llew couldn't help feeling a little annoyed, thinking of Nina off enjoying herself while he felt the walls closing in around him. "Well, you don't sound mad or depressed anymore, so I guess the trip was worthwhile."

"Wait—that's only half of it. I didn't just go to have a good time. Hen3ry has worked under contract for Hess several times in the past few years, and he knows a lot about him. I was hoping to find out something that might be useful."

"And did you?"

"Wait'll you hear." She wiggled in her chair. "First off, Hess seems to spend very little time in any one job, and most of them are with small companies and rinky-dink colleges. Hen3ry said that every time Hess contracted him to do some consultant work, he was working for somebody else. He spouted off a whole ream of them."

"Can you remember any?"

"I wrote down a few." She rummaged through her handbag and produced a slip of paper. "Let's see . . . there's Meanwell Computer Company, Artifax Corp, Harvey Morris College . . ."

"Never heard of any of them."

"Most of them are in New Jersey, which seems to be his home base. But they're mostly small-time stuff."

"Then how the hell did—"

"—did he get to Wilbur Moody, right? Hold on, my friend—I'm about to tell you."

Llew leaned back and folded his arms. "So tell."

"Hess is a bachelor. Or has been for a while. Hen3ry says he's been married at least twice. Anyway, he says Hess has been keeping company with some woman for the past year or so. Somebody from out of town, he thinks. He saw them together at a company function once, and ran into them accidently in a restaurant a few months later."

"What's that got to do with—"

"Just hold on. Hen3ry described the woman as being big and sort of horsey, with a loud voice. And rich, judging from her clothes and jewels. And she wore these funny glasses with clusters of grapes along the frames."

Llew sat up straight in his chair. "Cushlamochree—*Roberta!*"

"It's got to be. Llew, I'd bet every cent I've got that that sonovabitch rode into the vice president's position here on her skirttails."

"But how on earth could he—"

"Listen, from what I've seen of Hess, he could do anything he puts his devious little mind to. He's a wheeler-dealer, Llew, and as unscrupulous as they come. When Wexler announced his retirement last year, Hess probably got wind of it and came up here on some pretext to do a little groundwork. Somewhere along the way, he made contact with Roberta—and the rest, as they say, is history."

"That explains why she's always hovering around him, and gushing like a schoolgirl," Llew said. "Unfortunately, there's no way to prove any of this, so it really doesn't do us all that much good."

"Maybe Hen3ry can find out some more things about him, stuff we can use."

"Would he do that?"

She rubbed her nose. "I don't know. I can't ask him to do anything more just yet—he'd think I was just using him."

"How much did you tell him? About what's going on here, I mean."

"Just as much as I needed to to get him to talk about Hess. But I made him think *I* didn't want to talk about it, so he wouldn't think I was pumping him for information. I sort of let him draw it out of me."

Llew grinned. "Talk about devious—you're as bad as Hess. Are you going to see him again?"

"Hen3ry? I hope so. He's supposed to call me in the next day or so. But when he does, I don't want to spend the whole time talking about Hess."

"Don't blame you. You, eh . . . sort of like this guy, don't you?"

She twisted one of the rings on her little finger. "Yeah, I do. I don't like to admit things like that to myself, because I've been burned a couple of times, so I end up just trying not to think about it. Until some wise-ass like you asks me flat-out, and then I *have* to think about it."

"Sorry."

"In this case, though, I really think he likes me too. He showed me around the place he works, and introduced me to everybody. *Introduced* me, for chrissake—most people don't even admit they *know* me."

Llew nodded. "That's why I hired you—because nobody was likely to steal you away."

"You're all heart, Llew."

"Anyway, I'm glad things are looking up for you. And the information about Hess just makes me all the more determined to get the goods on him before it's too late."

Nina rolled her eyes upwards. "Jeez—I've been babbling on about myself and what a great time I had while you've been trying to survive in this madhouse. Any progress?"

Llew brought her up to date on finding out that the equipment in the Computer Center was generating some sort of code, and that Hess and Slade were now apparently aware that their system had been infiltrated. "Now they're spreading the word that I'm to blame for all the system's ills, back to day one. Pretty soon people are going to start believing it."

"So there isn't much time left, is there?"

"Maybe none. In fact, I'd probably better get back there now and give it another crack." He tightened his mouth. "It would help if I knew what the hell to look for. I feel like I'm still groping in the dark, while the seconds are ticking away."

On the floor of his office, just inside the door, was a brown envelope. Llew opened it hesitantly, wondering whether to expect an eviction notice or perhaps a bomb.

It was a copy from Gus of the Campus Curmudgeon's latest stab at President Croup. Llew squeezed into his desk and read:

> Say—here's good news for all prospective students who worry that too much attention might be given to the academic side of the curriculum. Our illustrious president, Horace "Flag-On-The-Play" Croup, quoting the inspired words of Vince Lombardi—"A school without football is in danger of deteriorating into a medieval study hall"—has just assured a gathering of loyal

> alumni (read that "coffer-fillers") that the new stadium is nearing completion at a cost of six million dollars (hey, deterioration-proofing doesn't come cheap!).
>
> Refusing to knuckle under to the mystique of intellectualism that runs rampant even in some good colleges with very fine teams, our erstwhile president tells his audience, "Intramural sports are an indispensable part of our curriculum, and we intend to spare no expense to assure a football team that we can all be proud of".
>
> To point out that those other good colleges manage their fine teams without a megabuck stadium is begging the issue, of course, because as President Croup points out, "Sports builds character and encourages team spirit, and that's a very essential part of what we stand for here at the college". Right on—athletics, unlike such cold subjects as biology and computer science, teaches warm human values. You don't see physicists patting each others bottoms . . . and when was the last time you attended a microbiologists' awards banquet where they expressed their gratitude to all the wonderful people who have made it all possible.
>
> Besides, such studies do not tend to foster team-mindedness—there's something basically selfish and unsportsmanlike about learning such things as chemistry or French—they may be fine for the people who study them, but can you imagine what would happen to team spirit if all the players wanted to learn things only because of what was in it for them?

Llew nodded his approval, and hoped that the file had received wide circulation before being erased. It would probably be the last such installment, as Slade would doubtless now remove the Public Address facility altogether.

Well, more serious things beckoned at the moment. He was still determined to identify the nature of that equipment which now occupied his old office in the Computer Center. He had made several calls to electronics firms in hopes of tracing the serial number he had copied from the metal label on one of them, so far without success.

So he had to approach the problem through the existing software in the system. There had to be a set of command files to coordinate the functions of these units—maybe by examining them, he could glean some useful information.

Another thing, he decided as he punched the operator's number, was to see if he could somehow re-route the phone connections so anyone calling him on his old extension wouldn't find the phone out of service. Someone would eventually get suspicious . . .

When the operator answered, Llew requested the computer number. There was an uncomfortably long pause, then the operator said, "One moment, please," and put him on hold. Oh my god, he thought—I forgot to disguise my voice, and she probably recognized me. Now she'll check out this extension and find that it's not supposed to be in use.

He quickly hung up, reconnected the modem and logged back into the telephone network. The only thing to do, he decided, is to switch back to my old extension before she has a chance to check. This means I'll have to go through this whole exercise every time I want to get on the computer. At least anyone calling me won't get an out-of-service message . . .

He made the change, and was about to exit from the telephone network when he remembered the missing entry in the location code table. Maybe someone's filled it in by now, and I can find out who's on the other end of that new line to the Computer Center. He made the appropriate selections from the menu, and a moment later the table was displayed.

He found "99" in the location code column. The corresponding entry in the "name" column was still missing.

Apparently an entry here is optional, he concluded. Too bad it doesn't generate an error or warning condition so I could run diagnostics on it, which might show—

Wait a minute. You don't *have* to have errors to run diagnostics. And if I remember right, the on-line diagnostics package of the telephone system gives detailed information about all the components of the network. Maybe, just maybe . . .

He paged through the system manual until he found the section on running diagnostics, then typed a command to load the utility. When the confirmation code appeared at the top of the screen, he displayed the table of location codes and moved the cursor to the entry for "99", and hit the ENTER key. The line immediately changed to reverse video, and a table of detailed information appeared to the side of the entry.

His excitement mounting, Llew leaned forward to read the entries: date of installation, total hours/minutes/seconds of use from installation to the present, building corresponding to location code—unassigned, Llew noted with disappointment—and Sector, which was given as "11".

Sector? That rang a bell, and Llew looked again through the chaotic piles of manuals on the shelf until he found the schematics showing the proposed telephone network prior to its installation. Designated areas of the campus had been assigned "sector" numbers for the purpose of situating the signal boosters. Llew located Sector 11.

There were only two buildings in Sector 11—Dodgson House, which had burned down and therefore was unlikely to be the source of any current telephone transmissions . . .

And Higgens hall. Where the Post office was located.

And the government installation, in the basement.

Llew located his campus directory and turned to the section listing all the phone extensions for each building on campus. Several entries appeared under Higgens Hall, but—not unexpectedly—the one corresponding to the location code of "99" was not among them.

15

The afternoon of Byron's recital was unseasonably hot and humid. The more zealous of the attendees, who insisted on seats close to the piano, arrived early and suffered the discomforts of the un-airconditioned auditorium in sticky silence. The majority, however, collected outside, seeking shade wherever possible until a few minutes before the performance was scheduled to begin.

Llew stood with Gus Roddencroft under a large tree near the entrance. Gus was tugging nervously at his beard and glancing frequently at his watch.

Llew's car was parked in its usual place across the street, facing downhill, since he had still not found time to get the ignition problem fixed. He noticed that the vehicle parked just behind his was a service van with a stenciled sign advertising an auto repair shop.

"Know anything about 'Bob's Auto Service'?" he asked Gus.

"That's where I take my car," Gus replied, wiping his perspiring brow. "They do decent work, and don't charge an arm and a leg."

Llew pondered. "Maybe I'll take mine there after the recital. I've been putting it off for weeks. But I've had other things to worry about."

"Welcome to the club," Gus said sourly. "Byron has been threatening to cancel this whole program if we can't get that piano in shape. Opernocketti has done the best he can, but on a day like this . . . "

"What if he doesn't show?"

Gus hesitated. "Well, I'd like to say that I'd fire his ass for breach of contract—tenure or no. But he's enormously popular on campus, and always a big draw at concerts, so he knows he can get away with just about anything." His eyes narrowed. "One of these days, though . . ."

It was getting close to starting time. Gus left to check on matters backstage, so Llew joined the people who were beginning to file into the auditorium. Inside the lobby, those foolish enough to have worn coats were already removing them, and ties were being loosened. Otto, Byron's seven-foot valet, was silently passing out printed programs at the door to the auditorium, wearing the same tight-fitting tuxedo, and still minus shoes.

All the seats near windows had been taken, so Llew found one in the back of the auditorium near the entrance, hoping that someone would have the good sense to leave the doors open. With the kind of programs Byron played, hearing from this distance would be no problem.

As Llew sat waiting for the recital to begin, his mind returned to the phone lines he had traced to Higgens Hall. The whole business still puzzled him. Except for a few peripheral offices, the main floor of Higgens was occupied entirely by the campus post office—and it was hard to imagine any reason why Hess or Slade would need a direct line to the likes of Godfrey Daniels.

That left the government installation in the basement, about which no information whatever could be found. Nobody whom Llew had talked to seemed aware of its existence. He had checked all the transactional records, to which he had access as archivist, but there was no mention of the disposition of the facility or even its original purpose.

He had even called Paisley, in hopes of learning more over a few discreet drinks at Duffy's, but no one ever answered the phone. And a check of the tavern itself each night had brought no results.

Llew looked at his watch. Ten minutes late. Maybe Byron had copped out. It was unlike him, though—he needed his audience as much as they needed him. The auditorium droned with the murmur of conversation and rustle of printed programs, most of which were being used as fans.

Then, abruptly, the noise was replaced by applause as Byron strode out on stage, curtly acknowledged the audience, and seated himself at the piano.

As the applause died down, Byron gripped the knobs on the sides of the bench and gave several rapid turns. He stopped, then turned the knobs a few more revolutions in the same direction.

Again he stopped, a slight frown creasing his brow, and then resumed turning the knobs, somewhat more aggressively.

The auditorium was quiet now, except for a slight squeaking noise from the stage as Byron continued to twist the knobs. When it became obvious that the height of the bench had not changed, he began to turn the knobs rapidly in the other direction, with equally unsuccessful results. Finally, one of the knobs appeared to stick, and when Byron tried to twist it with both hands, it snapped off from the bench.

Byron cursed, stood up and motioned offstage. Seconds later, Giuseppe Oppernocketti appeared, rolling a swivel stool out to the piano. Byron looked in dismay at the stool, and said something to the piano tuner, pointing at the bench. Oppernocketti shook his head and shrugged.

As the bench was removed from the stage, Byron locked the wheels on the stool and swiveled the seat to the proper height.

Then he sat down cautiously, twisting experimentally in both directions, grimacing, and turned his attention back to the keyboard.

The first number was the Chopin *Scherzo in B Minor*, and Byron launched into the work at a breathtaking tempo, as if to make up for lost time. Things seemed under control again, and the audience began to relax and enjoy the performance.

Even Byron quickly regained his usual self-assurance, clearly relishing the wash of sound that filled the auditorium. He alternately leaned back, eyes closed, arms outstretched during the lusher passages, and hunched over the keyboard, steel fingers pounding out rapid chords during the fortissimos. Once again Byron was in his element, the audience in the palm of his hand, and all was right with the world.

Until the F Sharp key in the second octave began to stick.

Byron's eyes blinked rapidly several times, as if he had just been awakened from a trance. His hands did not falter, but he began to attack the offending key harder each time it occurred, as if in hopes of restoring it to life. His efforts, however, were to no avail.

As the note figured prominently in the middle section of the work, the problem became increasingly awkward. Byron played on doggedly, apparently determined to see the piece through to the end.

Only when the G in the octave below began to stick as well did his patience begin to wear noticeably thin.

The hall may have been old and uncomfortable, but the acoustics were excellent, and each note reached Llew's ears with great clarity. So did the stream of profanity from the performing artist as his efforts to cope with the keyboard were increasingly frustrated. Llew noticed some small children near the front covering their ears.

Matters were not helped by the stool on which Byron sat, which swiveled in all directions as Byron's agitation increased. At one point, as his hands swept up the keyboard, the momentum spun him completely around, so that his curses swept across the spun him completely around, so that his curses swept across the audience like a beacon.

Undaunted, he repositioned himself and immediately resumed where he had been interrupted. As the climactic section of the music approached, he hammered away aggressively at the keyboard, his feet kicking at the underside of the piano, as if in a last ditch effort to loosen the stuck keys, which were now steadily increasing in number.

The only thing to be loosened, however, was the right front leg of the piano, which suddenly buckled inward, causing the entire piano to tilt forward at approximately 35 degrees.

Byron sat frozen for several seconds, staring in disbelief at the careening keyboard. Then he rose slowly from the piano and walked unsteadily off the stage. The audience sat apprehensively, unsure whether the performance would continue with another piano, or whether Byron had given up altogether.

Several moments later, his reappearance on stage was greeted with scattered applause, until the audience saw that he was carrying a red-handled fire ax.

Byron moved quickly over to the piano and began chopping at the left leg, as if attempting to make it tilt at the same angle as the right. But when the weakened legs gave way completely, and the piano collapsed with a crash, Byron continued to chop. The children near the front, who had been holding their ears moments ago, now applauded wildly.

When Gus Roddencroft, Oppernocketti and the barefooted Otto rushed onto the stage and attempted to disarm the performer, it became clear to everyone in the audience that the recital was at an end. Most remained to watch the ensuing struggle on stage, doubtless intent on getting their money's worth one way or another.

Llew briefly considered giving Gus and his companions a hand, but then decided that he'd had enough artistic temperament for one day. As he left the auditorium, he could still hear the snapping of piano wires and the splintering of the sounding board inside.

At least now, he thought, Gus will *have* to get a new piano.

Hot as it was, the air outside was at least moving, and felt good. Llew glanced at his watch. Since the recital had ended prematurely, he had some time on his hands. Remembering what Gus had said about Bob's Auto Service, he decided to take his car into the shop and see what they could do about the ignition problem.

As he crossed the street, he saw that the van with the repair shop sign was gone, but there was a station wagon with "Custead's Floral Shop - Speedy Delivery"stenciled on the side double-parked next to his own car. Llew wondered briefly if it had been someone's intention to present Byron with a bouquet of flowers after his performance.

But as he approached the vehicle, a familiar face behind reflective sunglasses grinned out at him. "Howdy there, Mr Mac Willy. Ih, ih."

Oh my god, Llew thought—I never paid that ticket, and he's come to arrest me. No, that's ridiculous—they don't arrest people for that.

He walked over to the car. "What did I do now?" he asked.

"Nuthin' that I know of . . . at least yet," the patrolman replied. "I was just passin' by, goin' off duty, when I seed your car. I recognized the bumper sticker. You havin' problems with it?"

"The bumper sticker?"

The cop scowled. "Your car. They was a guy workin' on it when I come up."

Llew's first thought was that somebody was finally fixing the ignition switch. His second thought was that he hadn't called anyone, or even mentioned it to anyone.. "Working on my car? This one?"

"That'n's yours, ain't it? Said you had called, couldn't get it started."

"Who did?"

"Guy workin' on it."

Llew looked around. "Where is he?"

"Left, 'bout the time you all started comin' outa that there odditorium. Said he needed a part, he'd be right back." He looked at Llew suspiciously. "You sayin' you don't know nuthin' about this?"

Llew didn't have the vaguest idea what was going on, but he did know that the less the cop knew, the better. He forced a laugh, rubbing his chin. "Actually, yeah—it's just been a while since I called, and I kinda forgot about it. This, uh . . . guy, who was working on the car—what did he look like?"

"Tall and skinny. Had a teeny mustache, and chewin' on a matchstick."

For a few seconds Llew was speechless. Then when the cop started looking at him oddly again, he found his voice. "Yeah, okay," hoping the cop wouldn't pursue this. "Anyway, I appreciate you, uh . . . stopping to check."

A wide grin stretched across the cop's face. "Just lookin' after my faivert customers. Ih, ih."

Llew's knees felt weak. "Right. Well, I'll, uh . . . just wait for the guy to come back with the part. Thanks again."

"No trouble. See ya round." He gave a brief salute and drove slowly off down the hill. Llew waited till he was out of sight, then got into his car where he could think.

I don't believe this, he said to himself, his heart pounding. *Slade* was fooling around with my car. Pretending to be a repairman.

But doing what? Putting a bomb in the ignition? That's ridiculous. Stealing my radio? No, it's still there.

What, then? He couldn't have had time to do much—I wasn't in there much more than half an hour. The cop probably interrupted whatever he had in mind.

Leaving the car in gear, Llew inserted the key in the ignition to unlock the steering wheel and gave it a few turns in both directions. Doesn't feel any different. Then he pressed down on the brake, and his foot went to the floor.

Whoa, here. He pumped them several times, with the same results. Squish, squish.

I don't believe this, he said again, and pulled the hood release. He got out of the car, raised the hood, and found the brake fluid container. It was empty. There was a puddle of thick brown liquid under the car, oozing slowly down the steep incline of the hill.

"Lie down, Calhoun," Nina ordered, and the dog squeezed in between Llew's desk and the wall. "G-O-O-D lie down. Now stay."

"I had to use the hand brake to get the car to Bob's Auto Repair," Llew was saying, "Fortunately, Slade hadn't gotten around to sabotaging *it* yet.

"You were taking a risk doing it at all," Nina pointed out.

"I know. All the way over, I kept expecting that cop to show up again. Anyway, when I got there, I asked them if anyone fitting Slade's description worked for them, and they said no. And just then one of their mechanics came in and said they had found their missing service van, parked a couple blocks away. Someone had apparently stolen it earlier in the day."

"Did you tell them you had seen it?"

"I didn't see any reason to. I just left my own car there and told them to go over it with a fine tooth comb."

Nina wrapped her arms around her drawn-up knees. "This is getting scary, Llew. Maybe you should have told that cop the truth."

"Maybe. But then if it turned out that there was nothing wrong with the car, I would have just been complicating things by bringing the law in on it. And things are complicated enough as they are, especially since I can't prove anything."

Calhoun was trying desperately to reach an itch behind his ear with his short hind foot. Llew reached down and scratched. "I can always call the cop in to identify Slade as the person who was fooling around with my car, if and when I feel I've got something concrete against him and Hess."

"If you live long enough. They're beginning to play rough. I don't see why Hess doesn't just fire you and be done with it. It would get you off the computer and out of his hair."

Llew poured himself some coffee. "I've asked myself that a dozen times. I guess he thinks it would force my hand, and even if I came out on the losing end, it would make for a nasty scene and throw a lot of unpleasant suspicion on him. Besides, he still has no legal reason for firing me—*he* can't prove anything either.

"The Catch-22 is that since they won't let me access the computer, I can't even computerize the Archive files . . . which leaves me absolutely nothing to do except figure new and better ways of getting into their system. Not that I've learned a hell of a lot, but I've accumulated a lot of listings of whatever it is they're generating."

The phone rang, and Llew reached for it. "At least they haven't cut off my other phone," he grinned.

It was Mike Ebbsedik. "Llew? You still hanging in there?"

"Best I can. What's up?"

"Well, you got my curiosity up about all those goings-on at your shop, so I ran some diagnostics on that Slade guy."

"Let's hear it."

There was a rustle of paper over the phone. "Okay, he seems to do a lot of address swapping, but mainly works out of New Jersey . . ."

"Surprise, surprise."

"Some of the companies he's interfaced with . . . I don't know whether you're interested in this or not, but anyway . . . there's Wetwhistle Technology, Dobb's Software, Artifax Corporation, Hopper Business Systems—"

"Hold it—did you say Artifax Corporation?"

"Yeah. He was there just a couple of years ago."

Llew whispered to Nina, "Wasn't Artifax one of the companies your friend Hen3ry said Hess worked for?"

"Yes, it was."

"Mike, what kind of company is Artifax?"

"It isn't, anymore. Got absorbed by another company who eventually compiled into BrandeX—those nice people who sold you your Sultan."

"I'll be damned. Were you able to find out anything more about BrandeX—other than the fact that they seem to do all of their business through a telephone answering service?"

"Yeah, they seem to be legit enough. Deal exclusively in mainframes which have been configured for specialty applications. Got a no-questions-asked policy, which brings in business from a fair number of less-than-legitimate concerns. That's why it's a little tough peek-poking into their operation."

"Well, if Slade is any example of the people they use, I can see why they're so tight-lipped. I don't suppose you noticed, by any chance, whether Slade has any criminal record?"

"Mmm . . . not that I'm aware of. But he *was* aborted from a government job once."

"No kidding? What kind of government job?"

"No good feedback on that. Apparently some kind of communications network run by a government security agency."

Government security—Llew sat up in his chair, his mind racing. "A communications network . . . ?"

"Yeah. Like I say, the data is pretty full of noise, but seems the government sets up relay stations at sites all over the country. So in case of national emergencies, they have a way of keeping communications intact, using satellites and stuff."

Cushlamochree. "Mike, are any of these relay stations located on college campuses?"

"Couldn't say. But guess it would compute okay. Especially government land-grant colleges."

"One more thing. Do you happen to know *why* Slade was fired from this . . . government agency?"

"What else? Breach of security."

16

The following Monday, the beginning of spring holidays at Wilbur Moody College, Llew emerged from the library and trotted down the steps to the sidewalk leading to the Post Office. An hour's research on government communications systems had been informative but not particularly helpful.

Much of it, of course, was public knowledge. The government had established a world-wide network of communication stations, connected largely by satellites, for the rapid exchange of information, especially in times of emergency. These were mostly computer-controlled, and involved complex switching mechanisms to allow multipathing, so that if one node in the system were disabled, the information could be instantly rerouted.

A crucial component of this system was a series of relay stations, situated throughout the United States and abroad, to serve as intermediate nodes on the circuit. Like microwave relay towers, or electrical line amplifiers, they collected transmitted data, checked it for accuracy, amplified it if necessary, and sent it along to its destination.

All the classified information was transmitted in code, of course, and another function of the relay stations was to decode and sometimes *re*code the information between reception and transmission. It was this part that particularly interested Llew. Hess and Slade had been storing data onto tape which Tully Dunkle had insisted was sensitive government code. There was a classified government installation on campus which might very well be a communications relay station. And now, a telephone line connecting it to the Computer Center had been added. Q.E.D.

There was little doubt in Llew's mind that all these things were related, especially since Slade had been employed in such an installation before. And the fact that he had been fired for security reasons put an end to speculation that he and Hess might be working for this one.

It was nearly noon, when the Post Office was normally crowded with students checking their mail in the arrays of boxes in the walls. Now, during spring holidays, only a handful of individuals—the kind that haunt the campus year-round—were in sight. At one end of the hall were the windows where one could mail packages and buy stamps, and at the other end several offices and a set of elevator doors.

Llew walked over to the elevator and looked at the panel next to the doors. There was a single button, which contained a key slot, meaning only authorized persons could use it. There were no direction arrows, as this was a single-story building and the only direction was down.

The construction work which Godfrey Daniels had complained about had been completed some weeks ago. Llew remembered that Daniels had mentioned extensive rewiring and new cables being installed, and wondered whether any of that included telephone connections, since the line he had traced here from the Computer Center had been gone into operation at about the same time.

As he stood pondering, the light over the elevator doors suddenly blinked on, and a moment later the doors slid open. Llew quickly stepped over to a nearby bulletin board and pretended to be reading the posted notices.

Two men, each in coat and tie and carrying briefcases, emerged from the elevator and walked toward the exit. One of them had dark skin and a beard and wore a turban. He reminded Llew a little of Rama, except that he wore regular lace-up shoes on his feet instead of sandals.

The two men were halfway down the hall when the elevator doors began to close. Without stopping to think, Llew jumped inside. A second later the doors met with a soft "thunk" and the elevator started downward.

What am I *doing?* Llew asked himself. This is insane! There'll be other people down there, and what the hell am I supposed to say? I pushed the wrong button? There's only one. I thought it was the door to the men's room?

Only one chance—when the door opens, hope there's no one waiting, and get this thing back up . . . then hope no one sees me getting *off.*

There was no button inside the elevator, so he would have to be prepared to step outside and push the button on the wall, then hop back in. Good god, he thought—what if there *is* no button . . . only another key slot like the one upstairs?

He felt the elevator slowing, and readied himself, visions of a dozen stern faces waiting beyond the doors.

The motion stopped and the doors slid open. To his enormous relief, there was no one waiting. He hesitated a second, then stepped outside.

He was in a short narrow hallway with a door at each end. There was no one in sight, and he began to breathe a little easier.

On the masonry wall next to the elevator doors was a panel with a single brown button—and fortunately no key slot. He quickly reached for the button, but his finger hesitated.

He looked over at the door closest to the elevator. It was made of heavy metal and bore a sign which read "No Admittance—

Authorized Personnel Only", and in smaller print, "This Door Must Be Kept Locked At All Times." In spite of this warning, it seemed to be slightly ajar.

Against every instinct, Llew tiptoed over to the door and listened. No sound. He touched the doorknob. What if an alarm goes off? he wondered.

You're mad! a voice inside him yelled. Besides, you promised Kay you wouldn't go breaking into any more buildings. Quit while you're ahead.

But ignoring his own warning system, he carefully pulled the door toward him a few inches, then paused to listen again. A few inches more, until he could see inside.

What he saw was a fairly large windowless room, filled mostly with electronic gear. The walls were concrete, painted a light yellow, and covered with maps, some displaying large areas of the United States, punctuated by hundreds of clustered push pins of various colors, others displaying close-ups of smaller regions.

The lights in the ceiling were recessed fluorescent. There were several tables and chairs, a half dozen grey file cabinets, a desk with a computer terminal, and a rack stuffed with books and manuals. There was no sign of any occupants.

He pulled the door open further and looked around. A copy of the sports section of the local newspaper lay next to an ash tray filled with cigaret butts on the desk. A stack of opened envelopes bearing government logos and addressed to someone named Felix Donohue lay on the desk. There was a drip coffee maker on a fold-up table next to the desk, and beside it were two coffee cups and a paper plate with a half-eaten breakfast roll. The computer terminal displayed a static list of options.

A row of tape drives, two of them containing tapes which were rotating at a slow constant speed, stood along the far wall. At the end of the row stood a familiar-looking red and silver computer system.

A Sultan 6000.

My my, Llew thought, who'da thunk it? Any other coincidences around here?

Another item caught his eye—a tall metal cabinet, situated near the tape drives. It had been dark in the Computer Center when he and Nina had found the strange pieces of equipment in his old office, but this unit seemed very similar to the one from which they had copied the serial number.

He went over and examined it thoroughly. Yes, here was the tiny metal plate near the bottom with the number stamped in. *And*, he noted with enthusiasm, there was a manufacturer's name on the front of the cabinet—Logan Electronics. He hurriedly copied the number and name in his pocket notebook.

Enough—let's get out of here, he told himself. The two men he had seen leaving the elevator were doubtless at lunch, but there's no sense in taking any more chances. There could be others besides them.

He pulled the door nearly closed, as he had found it, and pushed the elevator button. For a moment, nothing happened, and he suddenly saw himself trapped down here until the two men with briefcases returned. He doubted that he could pull the same stunt of jumping on the elevator when their backs were turned.

Then the doors slid open, and he rushed in.

"Logan Electronics. Good morning," the pleasant voice announced.

"Uh, good morning," Llew replied. "I need some information about a product manufactured by your company. I don't have the name of the item, but the serial number is . . ." He glanced at the number he had copied . . ."2660671-D".

"All right sir. That would probably be in the communications department. I'll connect you with someone."

Llew waited. Communications department . . . sounds promising, he thought. I wasn't even sure the piece of equipment in that dungeon was the same as the one in the Computer Center.

"Sir, you were asking about one of the 'D' units? a voice inquired.

"Yes," Llew replied. "I need to know basically what it is and what it does . . . what kinds of applications it's used for."

"Well, it's basically a monitoring unit," Llew was told. "It can be hooked up to any transmission medium—like telephone lines—and provides means for analyzing, redirecting and storing the signal."

"You mean like a telephone tap?"

"Well, in its simplest form, yes. But it works for nearly all kinds of transmitted signals—satellite transmissions, fiber optics bundles. It's normally used in conjunction with some kind of interpreting device, so that the signals can be converted to some usable form."

Llew remembered the time when he was monitoring the Sultan, and this unit had suddenly gone active. All he got was garbage until he attached to a second active device, which was apparently converting the signals to readable form. "Can you send me some specs on this unit?"

"Sure. Are you with a branch of the government?"

"No. Do I have to be?"

"Not at all. It's just that most of these units seem to go to one government agency or another."

"Do you know offhand whether anyone *other* than the government has purchased one recently?"

"Mmm . . . seems like there was some company in New Jersey. But I'd have to check."

"Could you do that? It might facilitate our own installation procedure if we knew someone else who was using one. And the government applications might be classified or something."

"No problem. I'll send that information along with the specs."

Llew gave him his name and address, thanked him and hung up. So a company in New Jersey had purchased a signal monitoring unit like the one in the government relay station. Well, well.

More pieces were falling into place. All that construction work in the Post Office building—a way of tapping into the communications station in the basement. Llew remembered someone saying that an out-of-state contractor had been hired to do the work—he was willing to bet *which* state. And since Hess was using his own people, Paisley had to go.

The new telephone line between the two buildings—a means of transmitting the tapped information to Hess's own equipment. And Slade, of course, would know just what equipment was needed, having worked for a government communications station before.

The information itself—coded transmissions of a highly classified nature. And to break those codes, a Sultan 6000, because that's what the relay station was using to process them.

Cushlamochree.

So here are Hess and Slade, tapping into government security transmissions, and here am I tapping into their taps, and using their own computer to do it. The question is, where do I go from here?

I think it's time to bring it all out in the open. I've got copies of the coded transmissions for proof, and a witness that Slade was tampering with my car.

And if I wait any longer I may not be around to tell anyone.

Llew got up and went to the file cabinet where the copies were kept and dug the key out of his pocket. Even before he inserted the key in the lock, a sudden sinking feeling told him what he would see when the drawer was opened.

Seconds later, he slammed the drawer shut. You *idiot!* Why didn't you put them someplace *safer*? A safety deposit box or something, instead of leaving them in a flimsy cabinet that anyone could get into. He probably used his goddam matchstick to pick the lock.

Now what? Those were the only copies.

One possibility. Tully Dunkle worked on the listings I sent over to him, trying to break the code. He must still have them.

And if he doesn't, then the only thing I can do is get back into the system and hope to catch some more. God knows what barriers they will have put up by now to keep me out.

He grabbed the phone and punched Tully's number. The secretary answered after several rings. "I'm sorry, Dr Dunkle is out of town until tomorrow. Can I have him return your call?"

"Yes, this is Llew. Can you please tell him I—"

The phone went dead. Llew jiggled the buttons. Nothing.

He hung up, waited a few seconds and picked up the receiver again.

Dead.

So they've finally cut off my second phone. They must have spotted it when they broke in here. Now I have no way of getting into the system at all.

From here, anyway. I've got a terminal at home, but Nina set up my secret account to recognize only the terminal ID of this one here in my office.

So what I really need is a telephone that works. Which means taking this terminal home with me. It's college property, of course—I'm surprised they didn't confiscate it while they were stealing the listings.

On the other hand, it should be easier to get past the operator if I call in from an outside line—if I can just remember to disguise my voice.

I really don't have any choice, he concluded, unplugging the terminal and keyboard. I'm running out of options, and I don't think Hess is going to wait for me to come up with any new ones.

17

Lew switched off the terminal of his computer in frustration. The same damned message—SYSTEM UNAVAILABLE—had appeared on the screen every time he attempted to log in over the phone. He had tried last night till after midnight, and again since early this morning.

That could only mean one thing—user log-ins have been disabled, probably for the holiday week. Which gave them plenty of time to find and patch all the loopholes he had used to break in, and to add new security measures to discourage future attempts.

That cinched it. It was time to go public with everything he knew, for better or worse. There was nothing to be gained by delaying any longer, and a lot to lose. He would have to trust that he could get copies of the stolen listings from Tully as evidence.

But who would be the right person to go to? The police? This was hardly their kind of problem. Campus security? Likewise. President Croup? Wouldn't be surprised if he were in on the whole thing. FBI? CIA?

The answer popped into his head a second later. Of course—it was so obvious. If the government relay station in the basement of Higgens Hall was the target of all this clandestine monitoring, why not go there? Tell them what he had found out, and what he suspected, and let them take it from there. Even if he were wrong in his conclusions, they couldn't fault him for trying to help.

So now, how to contact them. Stop and think. He had seen several telephones in the place, but none of them had any numbers written on them. He had noticed some mail on the desk addressed to . . . what was the name? Donohue. Felix Donohue. And a post office box number that he didn't remember—if only he had thought to copy it down.

He paged through the city telephone directory, but there was no listing for anyone by that name.

The campus telephone computer system wouldn't be any help—it only listed extensions, and this place doubtless had a different exchange. And it was probably unlisted anyway.

That meant he'd have to go over there and do it in person. But the elevator he had used was operated by a key, so he'd have to stand around and wait till somebody came out. It had been around noon yesterday when he had seen the two men coming up, probably to go to lunch.

He looked at his watch. 11:00. That gave him plenty of time to get over there. On the other hand, they might get hungry early.

Let's hope they do, he thought, retrieving his jacket—the sooner I can unload all this, the better.

Llew's stomach growled. The digital clock on the dashboard of his car read 1:15. Why didn't I get a bite to eat before starting this surveillance? he muttered. Or at least bring a granola bar or something along, just in case.

He had been sitting in his car—conspicuously, he was sure—in the parking lot next to Higgens Hall since 11:30. There were only a couple of other cars in the lot, and he had a clear view of the entrance to the building.

The two men he had seen yesterday had neither left nor returned. Either they got hungry very early today, he concluded, or they're too busy to worry about such nonessentials. Or maybe they're being catered. Visions of a pizza-delivery boy with his own key to the elevator—"Let's see . . . that's two medium cheese and pepperoni pizzas, one with anchovies . . ."

His stomach interrupted again, more assertively this time. This isn't accomplishing anything, he thought. Only one thing to do, and that's leave a note.

It'll be right out there in plain sight, he realized. It's taking a chance . . . but then that's all I've been doing for the past several weeks anyway.

He found a piece of paper in the glove compartment and wrote, "Please call Llew McQuilla—*URGENT*", along with his phone number. He folded it, wrote Felix Donohue's name on the outside, and got out of the car.

The lobby of the Post Office section of Higgens Hall was empty, as it had been yesterday. Llew walked over to the elevator doors, just across from the entrance to the building, looking for a place to leave the note.

He saw right away that there was going to be a problem. The note wouldn't wedge in between the elevator doors, and there was nothing else that he could fasten it to. It had to be placed where it would be easily found when the doors opened, but no such location suggested itself.

He glanced over at the adjacent wall, matrixed with postal boxes. They probably get their mail in one of these, he thought. Maybe I ought to peek into each one and see if there's anything addressed to Felix Donohue. Only take me about a week. And I'd probably get arrested for commiting a federal offense or something.

I could tape the note to the elevator doors, except that I haven't got any tape. And the only place I'm likely to find any is the service window . . .

Unable to think of any alternative, Llew went over to the window, hoping that someone other than Godfrey Daniels would be minding the store.

No such luck. Godfrey was standing with his head back, his mouth open, his eyes closed, and a handkerchief poised in front of his twitching face. A moment later, he hunched over as a wet sneeze exploded into the handkerchief.

He took a deep breath and wiped his red, swollen nose. "Pardon the rude eructation," he implored. "Touch of the old respiratory infection."

"Sounds nasty," Llew observed. "Taking anything for it?"

Godfrey patted his coat pocket, from which protruded the neck of a flat bottle. "Indeed, I possess just such a tonic, and was counting the minutes until my next scheduled dose."

He thrust the handkerchief back into his pocket. "Now, Mr McQuilla—how might I be of service to you? Stamps, perhaps? New 'J' series, just in . . ." He rummaged in a wide drawer. "Still plenty of Christmas stamps left over . . . or how about some colorful commemorative issues—Azerbaijan Independence, Panama Invasion, Hubble Space Telescope . . ."

Llew was about to ask for a piece of tape from the dispenser, when a thought crossed his mind. Nothing ventured, nothing gained . . . "Well, some information, actually. I was looking over some blueprints among the archives the other day . . . part of my new responsibilities, you understand. And I noticed that the plans for this building show a sizeable basement. Do you happen to know what it's used for?"

"The basement, yes-s-s . . ." Godfrey squinted his beady eyes. "A veritable enigma, to be sure. Until a few years ago, it served quite handily as a storage chamber. Then someone, in his infinite wisdom, decreed that it would henceforth be put to other uses, which remained undisclosed. Subsequently, the elevator button was replaced with a key lock, and the existing locks on the stairway door reinforced."

"So there's another way down there? Besides the elevator, I mean."

"Required by law—Article IV, Section . . ." He was interrupted abruptly by a resumption of his sneezing fit. He groped the bottle out of his coat pocket and unscrewed the cap. "Apparently the last dose was insufficient to temper the affliction."

"Where is the staircase located?" Llew asked as Godfrey administered a greatly amplified second dose.

"Just inside the rear entrance to the building," Godfrey replied, replacing the cap on the bottle. "But to my knowledge it has never been used."

"So you don't know what's in the basement at the moment? Or who's using it?"

"I have on occasion observed a pair of well-attired gentlemen gain access to the elevator," Godfrey recalled. "But I have not had the opportunity to make their acquaintance."

"And you don't have any way of contacting them . . . in case it became necessary."

"One hopes, sir, that the need will not arise, as the means is less than immediately obvious."

Getting nowhere, Llew thought. But at least Godfrey seems clean. "Okay, well, the reason I ask is that my job as archivist requires that I trace the current as well as past allocation of building space, which means I need some up-to-date information on the basement complex. So I guess I need to talk to those persons you say you've seen. Would you object if I left a note for them?"

"I would be more than happy to deliver any message to the gentlemen the next time I encounter them," Godfrey offered.

Too risky. "Well, actually, to save time I thought I'd just leave a note taped to the elevator—if that's all right with you."

"As you wish. And if I should cross paths with the parties in question, I shall direct their attention to your message."

"Appreciate it. If you could just provide me with a piece of tape there . . ." indicating the dispenser on the shelf. "I'll try to stop back later this afternoon—maybe I'll be lucky enough to catch them."

As Godfrey was unrolling a strip of tape, Llew turned and glanced back at the elevator. It took him several seconds to realize that the doors were standing open . . . and now were beginning to close.

Cushlamochree! "Hey! Wait!" he shouted, and raced down the hall.

But it was too late—before he was halfway there, the elevator doors had closed.

Stupid, stupid *stupid.* How could I have been so *careless*?

Llew sat slumped in a chair in his apartment, cursing himself for the thousandth time for botching the perfect—and probably only—opportunity to contact Donohue first hand. If Godfrey hadn't been watching from the service window, he would have pounded on the elevator doors, hoping they would hear the noise and come back up. But such an outburst would have created too much suspicion.

So now his hopes rested in the note to Felix Donohue, which he had taped to one of the elevator doors so that half of it overlapped the other door. They couldn't miss it.

Neither could anyone else, unfortunately. And if Godfrey Daniels chanced to look at the name on the outside of the note, he'd realize that Llew knew more than he had let on.

None of this will matter, he told himself, when Donohue reads the note and follows through with it. And there's no reason why he shouldn't. How could anyone resist an "*URGENT*"?

At least the wheels had been set in motion, and there was no going back now. He felt a curious mixture of relief and apprehension. I could be making a serious mistake about this whole affair, he admitted, but I can't live in the dark like this any longer.

It was Slade and that business with the brakes in my car that did it. If he tried something like that once, he'll try again. And next time he'll make sure—

The thought sent a shudder up his spine. He got up from his chair and paced the floor, casting occasional glances at the phone on his desk. Surely they must have found the message by now, he thought. It's after five. And the longer that note sits there—

The phone rang abruptly, and he snatched up the receiver.

"Hello?"

"Mr McQuilla?"

"Yes, this is Llew McQuilla."

"This is Felix Donohue." The voice had a throaty, muffled quality.

"Yes—good," Llew said. "I apologize for the unorthodox means of contacting you, but I couldn't think of any other way to do it."

There was a brief hesitation. "I'm listening," the voice said, not unpleasantly.

"Okay." Llew took a deep breath. "A lot of this is based on assumption, so if I go off the deep end I'd appreciate your telling me before I hang myself."

In as concise a way as he could, without names and details, Llew described his discoveries and suspicions. If they proved rational, he reasoned, he could fill in the rest as it was warranted.

When he finished, the voice said, "All right, Mr McQuilla, I think we have a lot to talk about. Could you meet me in, say, an hour?"

"Sure. In Higgens?"

"Let's make it the Computer Center."

Llew went cold. "The Computer Center? But—"

"There's no one there. It's been shut down for the holidays."

"Are you sure? I mean, the persons I'm talking about—"

"Out of town. Both of them."

"Then that means you already know about—"

"We've known about this operation for some time, Mr McQuilla. But there's a lot *you* don't know, and I believe it would be a good idea to clear the air, as it were."

"I agree. Okay, I'll meet you there in an hour."

He hung up and looked at his watch. Grab a quick bite before going over to the Center. No telling how long this session might take.

He went into the kitchen and made himself a sandwich and poured a glass of jug white. Probably shouldn't eat, he told himself—my stomach is in knots as it is. But the last time I didn't I nearly starved to death.

When he finished the sandwich he returned to the living room and picked up the phone. Before I go anywhere, he thought, I should call Nina and let her know what's happening. At this stage of the game, it's better if someone else knows where I am and what I'm doing. I'm not out of the woods yet.

He punched Nina's number and waited while the phone rang. And rang.

Finally he hung up. Not good, he thought. I haven't got time to go looking for her. Winklejohn is out of town for a day or so, and Rama doesn't have a phone. Who else . . . ?

There was a gentle knock at the door. Llew hesitated, then opened it to find Dahnu standing in the hallway. "*Dahnu*," he said with relief. "You must have been reading my . . . well, never mind. Come on in."

"I was passing by," Dahnu said, gliding into the living room, "and thought I'd see if you were in. I need to ask you a question."

"I was on my way out, but I'm glad you stopped. What's up?"

"I won't keep you. I just wanted to know if you had any information on the status of the computer on campus. I had planned to make extensive use of it this week while everyone is away, but it's not responding to my attempts to log in."

"I know. It's been down since yesterday. I think that's dirty pool, because it's supposed to be available all the time, even during holidays. But I'm obviously not in a position to do anything about it."

"Most unfortunate," Dahnu sighed. "I believe I am on the verge of a breakthrough with the Zeta wave program, and hoped that the extra system resources available in the absence of other users would be sufficient to reach my goal."

"I know how you feel. Wish there were something I could do." Llew fetched his jacket from the rack next to the door. "Come on, you can walk me out to my car."

As he locked the front door, Llew had a thought. "Tell you what, Dahnu. I'm supposed to meet . . . some people at the Computer Center in a short while. If everything goes well, there's an off chance that you might get your time on the computer after all."

Dahnu's face brightened. "That would be wonderful, Llew."

"I can't promise anything. But try logging in tomorrow and see what happens. Oh—and if you should happen to run into Nina this evening, please tell her where I am."

"I'll see that she gets the message," Dahnu assured him.

"Don't go out of your way—just *if* you see her." He retrieved the keys and unlocked the car door. "I've got a few minutes before I have to be at the Center. Can I drop you someplace, Dahnu?"

He opened the car door and looked back around.

"Dahnu . . . ?"

18

Llew pulled his car into the nearly deserted lot near the rear of the Computer Center. The last time I parked here, he recalled, was when Nina and I broke into the Center. It was the middle of the night. At least this time it's still light. And I don't have to break in.

I still find it strange that Slade and Hess would leave town with me still at large, he mused. Must have been awfully important. But Donohue seemed confident that it was safe. At this point, I don't have any option but to trust him.

I'd feel better if Nina were here. Although I don't know how Donohue would feel about my bringing someone with me. He didn't ask how many people knew about this whole business, so I guess it wouldn't matter.

Llew got out of the car and headed over toward the rear entrance. The campus grounds were quiet, except for the faint sounds of a piano in the distance—Llew wondered if Byron was doggedly completing his short-lived recital program to an imaginary audience.

The entrance door to the Computer Center was closed but unlocked. He went in and stood in the hall for a few moments, hoping Donohue would appear to greet him. He tried the door to his old office, but it was locked, so he proceeded to the main computer room.

The door was open and the lights were on inside. Llew had an uneasy feeling as he entered.

There didn't seem to be anyone around. Across the room, the inside door to the office was closed. He could be in there, Llew supposed, wondering if he should call out or go over and knock.

Then he noticed something strange. The MAX computer, which had been relegated to the storeroom when he and Nina had broken in, was now standing alongside the Sultan. Why would they—?

The door behind him suddenly slammed shut, and Llew spun around to find Slade pulling up a chair in front of it and sitting down. A matchstick dangled from the corner of his mouth, which was angled up in either a grin or a sneer, it wasn't clear which. Llew's heart sank.

Then the office door opened and Hess came out, one hand in his coat pocket. In the other hand he carried a small valise, which he deposited on the desk.

I should have known, Llew told himself—any *fool* would have known.

He quickly considered his options, and, finding little to choose from, said, "Mr 'Donohue', I presume."

"Correct, Mr McQuilla. Thank you for coming—it will allow us to resolve a number of matters that have cost all of us valuable time and effort." Hess's face was somber, and the stubby fingers on his visible hand drummed on the edge of the desk.

"You found the note," Llew said unnecessarily. "How did you know it was from me? Or do you always go around opening other people's mail?"

"Mr Slade noticed your car sitting in the Post Office parking lot," Hess replied. "Which wasn't difficult, given that the campus is virtually empty this week. But then, to his credit, very little escapes Mr Slade's perceptive eye."

No end to his talents, Llew thought. Especially where my car is concerned.

"At any rate," Hess went on, "some discrete questions to Mr Daniels seemed to indicate that you were unaware of the true nature of the basement facility. However, when Mr Daniels pointed out the note you had left for Mr Donohue, a different picture emerged. And the course of action was clear."

That's a bit vague, Llew thought, but I don't think I want to pursue it for the moment. The usual procedure in situations like this is to stall for time . . . "Are you going to explain this whole thing to me? What you're doing with the Sultan, I mean."

"Dear me," Hess replied, rubbing his pug chin while keeping his other hand in his pocket, "I assumed you had figured everything out by now. However, I have no objection to answering any questions you may have."

The question uppermost in Llew's mind, of course, was what they intended to do with him. But at this point he wasn't sure he really wanted to know. "Well, we could start with why you're doing all this."

"That should be obvious—because someone is willing to pay for the information. And pay quite well, I should add."

"Who?"

Hess smiled and shook his head. "That part will have to go unanswered, I'm afraid. The name of the organization would be quite meaningless to you, in any case."

"And just how long do you think you can keep this up? Campus users are already getting impatient for all the improvements they were promised."

"That problem will be resolved very shortly, thanks to you."

"To me?"

Hess nodded. "Our original intention was to quietly install a second Sultan and gradually transfer the MAX functions over to it—as we tried to make everyone believe was being done with the first Sultan. To campus users, this would simply appear as a phasing out of the 'front end' used to make the Sultan behave like the MAX."

"Which, of course, never existed."

"Correct. As you have determined, it is the MAX which continues to serve the campus community, while the Sultan is dedicated entirely to its intended function."

"Tapping the government communication lines."

"A non-trivial exercise, I assure you. One which has required extensive planning, careful timing, great risks . . ."

"And a lot of wanton destruction—like burning down Dodgson House in order to justify rewiring Higgens Hall."

Slade smirked, removed the matchstick from his mouth, and popped the head with his thumbnail, causing a sulphurous flame to flare briefly. Then he snuffed out the flame with his fingers, crushing the charred head to powder.

"An unfortunate sacrifice," Hess admitted. "But it was the only way to gain access to the electrical and telephone circuitry in Higgens to attach the necessary monitoring devices."

"You had to have had help with all that activity."

"Oh, to be sure. But over the years I have made the acquaintance of a number of very capable—and discrete—individuals from whom I could elicit the required technical assistance. Mr Slade not least among them."

Hess moved around the desk. "However, since you have seen fit to involve yourself in these matters, which has disrupted our operations to an intolerable degree, we have had to revise our plans somewhat. Fortunately, another option conveniently suggests itself—one which should rid us of a number of problems."

There was unmistakable menace in Hess's tone of voice. Llew

looked over at Slade, who was staring coldly at him. He had replaced the matchstick, and was moving it slowly back and forth in his tight mouth.

"With a little help from us, Mr McQuilla," Hess went on, "you have acquired a reputation here on campus as a saboteur, out for revenge against those who relieved you of your comfortable position as Computer Services Director. Therefore, it will come as no surprise to anyone that, in desperation, you should take the logical next step, and try to destroy the Computer Center operations altogether."

Llew stared at Hess in disbelief. "Destroy . . . ? How?"

"By attempting to blow up the facilities," Hess replied, indicating the valise sitting on the desk. "During the holidays, of course, while no one is around."

Llew shook his head. "That's *insane.* No one would ever believe that."

"They'll be faced with irrefutable proof, I'm sorry to say. Because during your attempt, you became careless and ended up a victim of your own malicious efforts."

Llew's mind refused to comprehend what Hess had just said. "What . . . ?"

Slade leaned forward in his chair, grinning. "Your ass gets blown all to hell."

Hess placed a cautious hand on the handle of the valise. "Everyone will naturally assume that, as the bomb was being placed, it exploded prematurely. Of course, both computer systems will be destroyed, necessitating their replacement. The insurance will pay for a dual Sultan system, which should make all the users happy while allowing us to resume our own efforts unhindered."

I've got to get out of here, Llew thought desperately. But I'm not sure my legs will move.

"The amount of explosives has been carefully calculated to do minimum damage to the rest of the building. Thus, the monitoring equipment in the office will be spared, as well as the system and user backup files in the storeroom. This is, of course, why we moved the MAX system back in here—only the contents of this room will be damaged beyond repair. Along with the perpetrator, of course."

Llew wasn't listening. Got to stay rational, he told himself—there must be a way out of this. Hess has a gun in his pocket, and he's between me and the office door. Slade's guarding the only other exit, and he's probably got a switchblade or something. If I could just find something to use as a weapon . . .

As Llew glanced around the room, he suddenly noticed something peculiar—the door to the storeroom was slowly opening. At first he thought his panicked state of mind was causing his eyes to play tricks, but a moment later a short dark-skinned figure wearing a turban and carrying the biggest shotgun Llew had ever seen emerged and pointed the weapon at Hess.

"You will blease to raising hands up above your heads," Rama ordered, "bevore I am gounting to two. One . . ."

Hess's and Slade's hands shot up so fast the action was a blur.

The wave of relief nearly swept Llew off his feet. But he knew the danger was not over. "He's got a gun in his pocket, Rama," he said when he could find his voice.

"I thing it would be wise to relieve him of it," Rama suggested.

Llew made his way carefully around behind Hess and thrust his hand into his coat pocket. It was empty.

"Old trick," Llew muttered, backing out of the range of the ferocious weapon Rama held.

"How did you get here?" Llew asked him.

"I will exblain in due time. First, I thing you muzt gall the bolice," Rama replied. Llew completely agreed and picked up the receiver from the extension on the wall.

"You're making a serious mistake," Hess said coolly. "May I suggest an alternative?"

Llew's finger held down the receiver button. "What kind of alternative?"

"A person in my position of financial responsibility has the means to provide a substantial . . . let's say, compensation, for your cooperation. This would include, of course, the return of your administrative position, Mr McQuilla, and a sizeable amount of money for you, Mr Rama."

He's getting desperate now, Llew thought. Let's see just how far he'll go . . . "Sounds interesting. But what about him?" gesturing toward Slade.

Hess swallowed. "Under the circumstances, I believe Mr Slade's usefulness has been exhausted, and his continued presence is . . . well, let's say, counter-productive. If my proposal is satisfactory to you, I suggest we carry through with the plan I proposed, but substitute Mr Slade as the perpetrator . . . and unfortunate victim."

The matchstick fell from Slade's mouth. "Now wait just a goddam minute—"

"I have a better idea," Llew said to Hess. "Let's substitute *you* instead. Then we'll give Rama *my* old job, I'll take *yours*, and Slade can be Custodian of Institutional Archives." He glanced over at Slade. "Or how bout Disposer of Institutional Wastes?"

Hess began to lose his composure. "Look, I'm talking about a *great deal of money* here. I don't think you realize—"

"I am thinging it iz already too late," Rama interrupted.

Hess glared at him. "What is that supposed to mean?"

"The government iz already knowing that you are litzening to their tranzmissions and trying to zteal invormation."

"What is he talking about?" Hess demanded of Llew.

Rama turned to Llew. "When Mizter Roddengroft iz showing me the output from the tapes I zend him, I am regognizing the zecret godes and taking the tape to my brother. He iz axing me where I got it, and I am telling him—"

"Wait a minute," Llew interrupted. "How did you know those were secret government codes? And who is this brother you're talking about?"

Rama smiled. "My brother works in the gommunigation ztation that this one—" indicating Hess, who stood wide-eyed—"iz trying to litzen to each day. Many times I zee gomputer liztings with zymbols like the ones on the tape."

Llew remembered the two men who had come out of the elevator in Higgens Hall—and that one of them had reminded him of Rama. "So they've known what's going on around here all along—why haven't they done anything about it?"

Rama nodded. "Oh, they have done! They are making sure the invormation this one iz gedding iz not gorrect. It iz . . . how you say . . . garbidge?"

Hess paled and sank heavily into a chair, his arms dropping, his tiny mouth hanging open.

Rama grinned. "My brother iz veddy smart, izn't it?"

At that moment, the door behind Slade opened. All heads turned as Roberta Turnbuckle stalked in.

"Willard—what on earth is going on?" She demanded. "You were supposed to meet me—" Then she stopped, her eyes wide, as she saw the shotgun in Rama's hands. "My god—!"

A split second later, Slade was behind her, his arm around her thick neck, a gun in his other hand pointing at Rama. "Drop that thing," he hissed.

Rama hesitated, then lowered the shotgun carefully to the floor. Slade gestured with his gun. "All of you, over there together."

"*Willard—*" Roberta started, then gasped as the arm tightened around her neck.

"Okay, Hess," Slade ordered. "Lock the door to the office. Then toss me your keys."

"Listen, Slade—"

"*Do it!*"

Hess found his keys and locked the office door, then tossed the keys over to Slade. "What are you going to do?"

"Shut up and slide that bag over here," motioning to the valise on the desk top.

"Slade! You can't—"

"I said shut up! Let's have that bag."

We're right back where we started, Llew thought. "Don't give it to him, Hess. He can't shoot all of us."

"Maybe, maybe not," Slade said. "But I'll start with him if I don't get that bag in five seconds. Then you, big mouth."

Hess picked up the bag from the desk and slid it across the floor. It stopped a few feet short. Slade released Roberta and ordered her to push the bag toward him. "Then get over there with the others."

Trembling, she did as she was told, then backed away. Slade moved forward a few steps, grinning. "They'll have a great time figuring this one out. Mass suicide, maybe?" Keeping his eyes on Hess, he leaned down slowly, reaching out with his empty hand to retrieve the bag on the floor beside him.

But it wasn't there. Puzzled, he looked down, then sharply around to see a tall man in a dark suit standing behind him. He was holding the bag in one hand and a gun in the other, the muzzle only inches from Slade's head.

"If you bat an eye," he said to Slade in a slow drawl, "you're dead meat."

For the second time, Llew felt the weightlessness of relief. Cavalry to the rescue, by god—a CIA agent or . . .

But one look at the worried expression on Rama's face told him that once again his relief was premature.

"Thought I might find you two here," the man said, relieving Slade of his weapon. He set the valise down near the entrance, then shut the door. "You got a little explaining to do."

Slade and Hess both began talking at once, Slade pointing at Hess, and Hess pointing at Rama. The man waved his gun in the air. "Hey—one at a time," he ordered.

Slade and Hess both quieted. "That's better. Now, down to business. My client tells me the information you've been delivering is all phony, and he's not very happy."

"Look, everything was going along just fine," Hess insisted, a slight quaver in his voice, "then this operator person stole one of our tapes."

Rama looked over in surprise.

Llew said quickly, "He doesn't know anything—he doesn't even speak English."

"हाँ!" Rama concurred.

"And who are you?" the man asked Llew.

Llew's mind raced. "My name's Llew. Rama and I just work here. We heard Mr Hess and Mr Slade shouting at each other, and we came in to find out what was going on. Right, Rama?"

Rama nodded vigorously.

The man's eyes narrowed. "Shouting? About what?"

"He's lying!" Slade started, but the man shoved the gun in his face.

"Something about blowing up this place, and us with it, and skipping the country. Then Mr Slade said Mr Hess owed him money for passing fake information to somebody, and—"

Roberta turned to Hess, eyes full of anger and impatience. "Willard, what *is* he talking about? And who is this person?" indicating the man with the gun.

The man scowled at her. "Who the hell are you?"

She drew herself up stiffly. "I am Mrs Roberta Turnbuckle, Chairman of this college's Board of Trustees, and I *demand*—"

She was interrupted by a series of sharp sounds in the distance, like the popping of firecrackers. The man with the gun looked quickly around, frowning. "What was that?"

"Sounded like shots," Llew said.

The man look puzzled. "Somebody's going around shooting guns on a college campus? What kind of place is this?"

A split second later the door flew open and a small figure rushed in, tripping over the valise and sprawling onto the floor.

Oh my god, Llew thought—*Nina!*

As the valise tumbled over, Hess yelped and covered his head with his short arms. Slade backed up a few steps, his narrow eyes now open wide.

"Don't nobody move!" the gunman ordered, glancing back at the door to see if any other surprises were in store.

Nina scrambled to her feet, looking confused. Then she saw the gun in the man's hands and scampered quickly over next to Llew.

"Llew, what's going on? I heard shots . . ."

"I did too, but they didn't come from here. Not yet, anyway."

She looked back at the man with the gun, who was picking up the valise. "I should have listened to Dahnu—he said he had a premonition . . ."

"Where did you run into Dahnu?"

"I didn't. As usual, he just suddenly—"

"Knock it off, you two!" the gunman growled. "I still got unfinished business with these turkeys. You, kid—get over there and shut the door. And lock it."

As Nina moved across the room, Llew noticed that Slade had edged over to the wall, and now his hand was reaching up toward the light switch. Before Llew could react, the lights went out and a second later there was a flash of white as a gun went off.

Llew dove for the floor. He heard shouts and the sounds of scuffling across the room, but could see nothing but the hall light through the open door.

Then he heard Nina squeal and curse, and a rushing shadow blocked the entrance light for an instant. Keeping as close to the floor as possible, he crawled over toward the door.

Suddenly the lights came back on and the man with the gun moved over to the door, pushing it shut. "Everybody just stay where you are!" he ordered, blinking against the brightness of the lights.

Hess and Roberta had not moved, and it took Llew a few seconds to realize that there was no sign of Slade . . . *or Nina.* Then the barrel of Rama's shotgun poked up from behind the desk where the gunman stood. "Blease to dropping the gun or I muzz bull the trigger."

The gun clattered to the floor as the man's hands quickly rose. Llew scrambled over to retrieve it as Rama came around from behind the desk.

"Where's Nina?" Llew asked. "And what happened to Slade?"

"I am thinging Mr Zlade iz taking her off," Rama said, moving over toward the door.

As he reached out to open it, the door suddenly burst open and Byron Devilbiss dashed in, colliding with Rama and discharging the shotgun.

The blast rocked the room, and Llew hit the floor again, covering his head as papers and shotgun pellets rained down around him. Somewhere in the back of his mind was the nagging thought that he had taken this job because of the tranquillity of a college campus . . .

When he opened his eyes a few seconds later, the room was again in total darkness. My god, he thought, did the fuse box get hit? Or am I dead?

He heard a scuffling of feet, and a moment later the lights came back on. The first thing he saw was the gunman, standing next to the light switch looking bewildered.

But this time, there was no sign of Hess. The door to the office was standing open—obviously, Hess had not locked it as ordered—and Llew remembered that there was another light switch on that side of the room, near where Hess had been standing.

When the gunman saw the open door, he cursed and ran out into the hall. He looked around quickly, then disappeared toward the rear exit of the building.

Llew hurried over to where Rama was helping a stunned Byron Devilbiss to his feet. "You okay?" he asked.

Byron took a deep breath. "What the hell is going *on* in this zoo?"

"It's a little complicated," Llew admitted. "But I'm glad you could join us. What are you doing here, by the way?"

Byron shook his head, as if trying to remember. Then he said, "Oh my god—*Gross!*" He looked around wildly. "He must have heard the shot. How do I get out of here?"

"Gross? You mean Harry?"

Byron staggered back to the doorway. "He's gone *berserk*—chasing me all over campus with a gun! The sonovabitch is trying to *kill* me."

"Kill you? What for?"

"I don't know! He barged into my studio, waving a gun and yelling something incoherent. Something about his wife—"

Llew went cold. "Kay?"

"Yeah. I couldn't get it all. but I think he found out she's been having an affair with someone, and I guess he thinks it's me."

Oh my god, Llew thought. How did he . . . ?

"I've got to get out of here!" Byron insisted. "Where does that hall go?" Without waiting for an answer, he dashed out and down the hall to the stairs leading to the upper floors.

Rama was tugging at Llew's sleeve and pointing across the room. "I am thinging we have a broblem . . ."

A pair of legs extended out on the floor behind a table. Llew rushed over to find Roberta lying on her back, her eyes closed and her mouth open.

Llew leaned over her. There was no sign of blood, and she seemed to be breathing. "Mrs Turnbuckle?" He slapped her cheek lightly a few times. "Hello? Are you okay?"

When she didn't respond, he slapped a little harder, and her eyes opened with a start. "What—?"

"Are you all right?" Llew repeated, helping her to a sitting position.

Her eyes grew wide. "That man—he had a gun!"

"He's gone now," Llew assured her.

She struggled heavily to her feet. "And people kept running

in and out and turning the lights off and on and there was shooting . . ." She collapsed into a chair. "I've never in my life . . ."

She looked around. "Where's Willard?"

Before Llew could reply, a voice shouted from the doorway, "*Wherszh at slomovabltszh*!" Llew looked up to see Harry Gross standing there with a pistol in his hand.

"Oh my god—another one!" Roberta moaned.

Llew moved over toward Harry cautiously. Somewhere in the distance he could hear sirens. He desperately hoped that someone had called the police. "Harry . . . just calm down, now . . . okay?"

"Whizh way'd he glo?" Harry demanded. "Gollam summoblitszh!"

"Why, it's Mr Gross," Roberta exclaimed, blinking her eyes. "Harry—what on earth is going on?"

"Shlubbup, you fat szhlob!" Harry ordered, waving the gun at her. "Whereszh Dlevilblisztch?"

The sirens were growing louder, and Llew calculated that they were in the vicinity of the administration building, not far away. He pointed in that direction—"If you're looking for Byron, I think he went that way."

Harry turned and disappeared out the door, yelling hoarsely. Llew thought of Kay, and hoped Harry hadn't taken his wrath out on her.

Rama wiped his brow. "I am never zeeing zo many guns in one blace in all my life!"

Roberta staggered to the door. "I'm getting out of this madhouse. I don't think my nerves can take much—" Then she shrieked.

Looming in the doorway, a huge razor-sharp scimitar in his hand and eyes full of fire, was Otto, Byron's giant valet. He bared his gleaming teeth, and Roberta slumped again to the floor.

He glared momentarily at the other occupants of the room, and a second later he was gone.

Llew started toward Roberta, then suddenly remembered Nina.

Slade had taken her with him when he ran out. "I've got to find Nina," he told Rama. "Stay here with Roberta. The police will probably be here as soon as they pick up Harry."

"What muzt I tell them?"

The thought of Rama trying to explain matters to the police was beyond Llew's powers of imagination. "Tell them Slade has kidnapped Nina, and I've gone after them. Maybe they can alert the State Police or something." He rushed out the door.

What am I going to do? he asked himself as he ran toward his car in the parking lot. I haven't the faintest idea where Slade is headed. I don't even know what his car looks like, for Pete's sake. Which way is New Jersey from here?

He jumped into his car and started the motor, grateful that he didn't have to worry about the ignition problem anymore. It isn't likely that Slade would head back into town with a hostage, he figured, and there's only one highway *out* of town from the college. So let's try that.

He raced down the narrow driveway to the college entrance and turned onto the main highway. The rush hour traffic was still heavy and it was getting dark. This is hopeless, he groaned—I don't even know if I'm going in the right direction.

As he sped along the road, he glanced into each car that he passed and watched the sides of the road in case Slade stopped for any reason. Poor Nina, he thought—I should have left her out of this. I should have stayed out of it *myself.* Just gone to the police or—

He suddenly caught sight of a dog running alongside the road as fast as its legs would carry it. A big dog with tiny legs. My god, Llew thought as he passed it—it's *Calhoun.*

He pulled off the side of the road ahead of the dog and jumped out of the car. "Calhoun!" he shouted. "Come!"

The dog recognized Llew and veered off the road toward him, panting and wheezing. "G-O-O-D come, Calhoun!"

He hustled the dog inside the car, pulled back out onto the road and stepped on the gas. At least now he knew he was going in the right direction.

But it was growing even darker, and most of the other cars had their lights on. The only hope now was that Rama could convince the local police to—

Up ahead, there were flashing lights in the road. Llew slowed down as he approached.

An accident of some sort. There were skid marks on the pavement and marker flares spaced at intervals. An ambulance was on the scene, and a policeman was waving traffic around a pair of vehicles. From the looks of things, a sports car had run into a Tastykake delivery truck.

Llew edged around the commotion, and was considering stopping to ask the police if they had seen a car containing a skinny guy and a tiny girl when he heard a voice shouting his name. Calhoun barked and scrabbled at the door. Llew looked over toward the ambulance and saw Nina standing beside it and waving her arms at him.

He pulled quickly over to the side of the road and got out, followed by a frantic Calhoun. Nina ran over to them and wrapped her arms around Llew as Calhoun danced around them both, barking excitedly.

"Are you okay, Nina?" Llew asked. "What happened?"

She ran a hand through her disheveled hair. "I'm fine. I think Slade broke something, though, when we hit the truck. Serves him right, that son of a—"

"Where is he?"

"In the ambulance, along with the cop he hit."

"Cop? He ran into a *cop*?"

"Yeah—would you believe there was a *cop* driving that Tastykake truck? Some old geezer who cruises in unmarked cars."

"I'll be damned. Is he okay?"

"I think so. But you never heard so much cussing in your life when he hauled Slade out of the wreckage. If another police car hadn't showed up about then, I think he would have finished the job."

Llew drove back to campus, Calhoun in tow, while Nina accompanied the police back to town to file charges. Llew had informed them that there would be plenty of additional charges, and the police assured him Slade would not be going anywhere.

He parked beside the tree next to the Computer Center and went inside. Rama was cleaning up the damage done by the shotgun blast. He was relieved to hear that Nina was unharmed.

"What happened after I left?" Llew asked him. "Did the police catch up with Harry before he caught up with Byron?"

"Yes, and they are taking him away. He iz screaming and gursing, but no one iz undersdanding him. Then the bolice are goming here and talking with the Turnbuggle lady, and she iz telling them about Mizter Hezz and the man with the gun. She says she hopes they will gatch him."

"The police or the man with the gun?"

"I thing maybe both. She iz galling him many names. And alzo Mizter Grozz." He grinned. "I thing they are both in zerious trouble, izn't it?"

"Looks that way. Hell hath no fury . . ." And Roberta is not a woman to trifle with, he thought. It'll be interesting to see what form her retribution takes . . . "What about Byron? Is he okay?"

Rama shrugged. "I thing no one iz finding him yet."

Probably still running, Llew thought. "Say, you never did tell me what you were doing here tonight."

"My brother iz axing me to make gopies of all Mizter Zlade's tapes for evidenze. And while I am doing this, Mizter Zlade and Mizter Hezz are goming in. So I hide in the ztoreroom."

"Where did you get the gun?"

"My brother iz telling me to geep a weapon, in case they are gatching me."

"Your brother thinks of everything," Llew observed. "And I need to talk to him soon—or else the real Donohue. I'm sure they'll be very interested in all that's happened."

"I am already telling him tonight on the phone. He axed if you will see him tomorrow."

"Good." It'll be a relief to get this all resolved, he thought. Now, one last item . . .

He picked up the phone and punched Kay's number, figuring there wasn't much chance of Harry being there under the circumstances. The phone rang a dozen times before he concluded that she wasn't either.

It's probably just as well, he decided as he hung up. I need some time to think this whole thing out. She probably does, too.

He left Rama and walked back out to his car. There was a full moon out and the night was clear, the air crisp. He took a deep breath and began to relax for the first time in a very long evening.

He had left Calhoun in the car, but when he got there he saw that the car was empty. Cursing himself for leaving the window open, he started down the campus walk, calling the dog's name.

Moments later, he heard a familiar barking nearby. "Calhoun?" Where are you, boy? Come to Llew!"

The dog came running to him from the direction of a large tree off to the side of the walkway. Just making a quick bathroom stop, Llew figured. "Atta boy . . . G-O-O-D come to Llew!"

Then the dog turned and ran back to the tree and stood barking into the branches overhead. Llew went over and looked up, shading his eyes against the harsh walkway lights.

At first he couldn't see anything. Then he grinned, and reached down to quiet the barking dog.

"Good, Calhoun. G-O-O-D find Byron . . ."

19

"I think Harry has suspected for some time now that I've been seeing someone," Kay said, cradling her coffee cup in her hands. The campus coffee shop was empty except for a few faculty members who had reason to be on campus during the spring break. "Every time the subject of his own little escapades came up, he would mutter something about the pot calling the kettle black."

"And it's only natural that he'd suspect Byron," Llew said, "especially after that scene at his party."

"At least it kept *you* out of the picture," she reminded him. "Not that Harry would have ever suspected you in the first place."

"Thanks a lot."

Kay smiled. "Consider the source. Anyway, Harry came to my office yesterday after I had gone out, and found a note from Byron on my desk. It made some reference to a recent treatment, and naturally Harry, with his one-track mind, took it another way."

She sipped her coffee. "So he went gunning for Byron, but couldn't find him. And he couldn't find me either, which of course only made him more suspicious. So he got drunk and then went back after Byron again. This time he found him. Fortunately, someone heard the commotion and called the police."

"Good thing they got here before he caught up with Byron. Or before Otto caught up with *him.*"

"Probably would have been better for Harry if he had. He's in a pot of trouble now. By the time I got down to the police station, he was still racking up charges—resisting arrest, verbal abuse, assaulting an officer . . . They'll throw the book at him."

"And then there's Roberta," Llew added. "I hear she was in Croup's office for two hours this morning, demanding Harry's head. And Hess's, of course."

"She's welcome to it. After our lawyer salvages what's left of Harry, I have another little matter for him to handle."

"You're really going to go through with it this time?"

"Yes I am. I'll stick around for the rest of the term, until this mess is straightened out—Harry's got enough problems at the moment—then I'm off."

"Off?"

She drew a breath. "Off. And alone. Somewhere away from here where I can think. About you, and myself . . . everything."

"Oh."

She smiled. "Don't look so glum. It'll only be for a while. And you need to do some thinking, too, now that everything is in such a turmoil. I have a feeling that the next few months are going to be very busy ones for you."

Kay left to return to the infirmiry, and Llew walked back toward the Computer Center. Off to the left, the charred remains of Dodgson House still seemed to smoulder. With a shudder, he realized again how close the Computer Center had come to looking like that. With him inside it.

He felt tired and achey. A long morning at the police station, answering questions, filing charges and filling out forms, had been followed by an early afternoon session with Rama's brother, who confirmed Llew's assumptions about the communication relay station.

Yes, he was told, they had been onto Hess's scheme since Rama had recognized the coded information on Slade's tape. They had quickly traced the monitoring line Hess had had installed during the rewiring of Higgens Hall, and had taken great delight in inventing phony information to pass along to the unsuspecting Hess.

Llew couldn't help feeling a little depressed as he pondered Kay's decision to leave Harry and town, in that order, but decided that she was right. A lot had happened in a very short period of time—things would be different now, including their own relationship, and they both needed time to think and plan.

She was right about another thing too. The next few months were going to be busy ones, starting next week when classes resumed. By that time, the whole scandal would be public knowledge, and the college would have its hands full trying to get back on track. He wasn't sure just how he would be involved, but with Hess gone and Harry sinking fast, the prospects didn't seem so bad.

Inside the Center, Nina and Winklejohn had just finished checking out the Sultan system to determine the extent of damage from the assault the previous night. One badly damaged tape drive, which had taken the force of the shotgun blast, had been removed, and Nina said everything else seemed okay. Both the MAX and the Sultan were back up and running.

"We marked the bullet holes in the walls and ceiling," she pointed out. "We decided to just leave them there to remind us that things aren't always dull around a Computer Center."

"Once again it has been my misfortune to be elsewhere when all the fun is taking place," Winklejohn lamented. "Not unlike Clark Kent, I suppose."

"Getting sprayed with shotgun pellets isn't my idea of fun," Llew said. "And a person of your size would be hard to miss."

"True," Winklejohn agreed. "In fact, I am considering having my crutches outfitted with appropriate defensive missiles, so that the next time we come under seige—" The phone rang, and Winklejohn picked up the receiver. "Desert Storm Headquarters . . ."

"Any word yet on Hess?" Nina asked Llew.

"Not that I know of," he replied. "He apparently threw everything he had into a couple of suitcases and beat it. Unless that thug caught up with him first."

"What about Slade?"

"He's in the hospital with a concussion. It's not clear whether he got it in the accident or from the cop trying to bludgeon him to death."

Nina waved a tiny fist. "If I could have found something to bludgeon with, I would have given the cop a hand."

Winklejohn had hung up the phone, a worried look on his face. "That was Dahnu. He seemed quite excited—as far as one of his reticent temperament can generate emotions of that nature."

"Excited about what?" Llew asked.

"He says that the program he's been using to isolate the Zeta waves is apparently working much better—doubtless because he currently has the whole system essentially to himself. He's about to run a test on himself, using a bio-feedback system, to see if he can control or even boost his own Zeta state."

"So what's wrong with that?"

Winklejohn frowned. "Perhaps nothing . . . except that it's not clear what kind of effect such an action will have on the mind or body."

"Is he in the lab now?"

"He just called from there."

"Well, I'll drop by and check on him. I've got a couple things to do yet anyway."

Winklejohn transfered his weight onto the crutches and made his way to the door. "I'll be in my office if anyone needs me."

When he was out of the room, Nina went over and shut the door, then motioned Llew over to one of the console terminals.

"Want to show you something."

She typed a command, and a page of text appeared on the screen. Llew leaned over for a closer look.

"'Out of the mouths of boobs oft come such swill as to cause cramps and vertigo and defy rational commentary. Here's the latest entry in that category, from a speech by President Croup to the Board of Trustees last week—another masterpiece of mangled metaphors, slaughtered syntax and garbled grammar . . .'" He looked back up at Nina. "Where did this come from?"

"Do you recognize it?"

"It looks like Campus Curmudgeon stuff . . . but not one I've read before."

"It was in Winklejohn's files . . . along with all the others."

"*Winklejohn's* files?"

Nina nodded. "Cleverly disguised with system program names. I was going through all the accounts, and printed this out, thinking it was a system utility program."

Llew stared at her. "You mean . . . Winklejohn is the Campus Curmudgeon?"

"He tried to insist that he had just copied them from the Public Address file each time they appeared, for safe keeping. But this one was only half written, about a speech Croup made just last week."

"I don't believe this," Llew said. "I mean, I always knew Wink was bright, but . . . where did he learn to do this sort of thing?"

"He was an English major or something before he came to work here."

Llew shook his head. "Okay, I can see how he could manage this on the MAX—he had a privileged account and access to all the system files, including the Public Address file. But how the hell did he get on the *Sultan*? You had to show *me* how to do that."

"He was with me when I discovered how to break into the Sultan system. It just never occurred to me that he would have any reason to try it himself."

"And another thing—Winklejohn couldn't have attended all the functions where Croup gave those speeches. How did he know what Croup said?"

"Apparently Croup's secretary used the word processor on the MAX to type the speeches. They were all in the computer in the administrative account. Anybody with a privileged account could access them."

"Cushlamochree."

"Now, Winklejohn made me promise I wouldn't tell you. But I just had to. So don't let on you know."

"I won't. I still can't—"

He was interrupted as Rama opened the door and announced that Nina had a call on her office phone. "I thing it iz that Hen3ry berson."

"Oh, good—be right there." She turned to Llew. "Stop by later and we'll all go to dinner. And remember—not a word to Wink."

Llew left the Center and walked leisurely over to the lab where Dahnu's bio-feedback equipment was situated. One thing's for sure, he thought—nothing around this place is ever going to be the same again. Kay is going off somewhere, Harry has fallen through the cracks, Nina is getting involved with Hen3ry, and a whole new facet of Winklejohn's personality has emerged. And I'm still in limbo. Life used to be so comfortably predictable . . .

As he entered the lab, he looked around for Dahnu. Several pieces of electronic equipment were turned on, including a remote computer terminal and an on-line feedback unit. A pair of electrodes stretched over to an empty couch, and the lines on the terminal screen labelled "brain waves" registered flat. A continuous stream of graph paper was still inching through the electroencephalograph, but the pens which recorded the various brain waves traced only straight lines.

Odd that Dahnu would go off and leave all this equipment

running, Llew thought. The door had been closed but not locked, a violation of standard campus policy for all scientific labs.

He gathered up a bundle of graph paper which had collected on the floor, and observed that earlier traces had recorded an increasing amount of activity. One line in particular seemed almost chaotic at one point—just before the lines abruptly flattened out. Llew wondered if this line had anything to do with the Zeta wave business Dahnu was experimenting with.

Well, he thought, I can't wait around forever. I'll lock the door, just in case—Dahnu obviously has his own key.

All things considered, however, I'm not convinced he really needs one . . .

Epilog

Glass of Chardonnay in hand, Llew followed Van Ruedge through the trellised rows of vines, now heavy with dense green foliage. From each shoot hung fist-sized clusters of still-unripe fruit—it would be another month before the berries began to show the first blush of color which signalled approaching maturity. The hot noon sun overhead had burned away an early morning fog, and the sky was now clear and blue. Van stopped to tie a sagging shoot back onto the supporting wire. The leaves exhibited a faint powdery residue from a recent spraying. "Things look good," Llew observed, sipping from the glass.

"So far," Van replied. "It's been a pretty dry summer, so there hasn't been much fungus problem—that's always the biggest worry. But now it's getting on into Japanese beetle season."

"Always something, eh?"

"Seems that way. And what about you? You seem in better spirits these days."

"No complaints. Except for losing Nina."

"That's right—off to New Jersey, wasn't she?"

"Yeah. Her friend there got her a job with his company. I'm still not sure whether it was him or the job she went for. Both, I guess. Can't blame her."

"Got anyone to take her place?"

"Not yet. But at least I had no trouble getting approval to hire some new people—President Croup is too busy trying to replace Hess to worry about the Computer Center, so he's leaving it all up to me."

Van traced a lengthy bull cane to its source and snipped it off. "I hear rumors that Croup may be on his way out, too."

"If Roberta has anything to say about it, which she usually does, he will. Croup is trying desperately to appease her—like firing Harry Gross and giving me his job. Which means that I've got to hire a new Computer Services Director as well as a new systems programmer."

"What about the new computer—are you going to replace it too?"

"The Sultan? No, I've kind of gotten used to it now. It's basically a good machine, and it's paid for, so we'll use the MAX strictly for administrative functions, and reserve the Sultan for academic use. The new systems programmer will have to reconfigure it to get rid of all the extra monitoring stuff Hess was using."

They reached the end of the row, and Van pulled a checkered handkerchief from his hip pocket and wiped his brow. "Speaking of Hess, did they ever find him?"

"Not yet. Nor any of the valuables that were missing from the college house he was living in. He probably sold them to pay for a ticket to South America. Or else that gunman caught up with him first."

"What about his henchman—Slade, wasn't it?"

Llew nodded. "The government has brought charges against him for illegal phone tapping, espionage, arson and attempted murder. His trial comes up next month."

Van tied the scarf around his neck. "Sounds like enough to put him away for a while."

"No doubt—although the attempted murder charges will probably be dropped. The only witness to him tampering with my car was that traffic cop . . . and he apparently had a nervous breakdown or something after Slade ran into him. I understand he's in the care of relatives on a farm around here somewhere, and isn't well enough to testify."

Van chuckled. "So that's why I haven't seen him. Well, at least we won't have to worry about getting stopped for speeding by some nut in a pickup truck anymore."

"That's a relief. Well, I've got some job candidates coming in for an interview, so I'd better get back to the office. Thanks for the wine. By the way, who's doing the program at our next club tasting?"

"I thought you were."

"Cushlamochree, that's right! I've been so busy I forgot all about it. What kind of wines should we have?"

Van scowled. "I don't care as long as it's something decent. I haven't yet recovered from those rotgut imports that Bosley featured a few months ago."

"I'll see what I can come up with. See you later."

As he drove back toward town, Llew pondered the year ahead. Kay had been right—it would be an unusually busy one. He was now responsible for both Information Services—Harry's old job—and the Computer Center. The sooner he could find a new director for the computer facilities, the better.

At least Winklejohn was staying on part time, while finishing up his degree in English. If Croup would bend far enough, the next order of business after the new systems programmer would be another applications programmer to take some of the load off Winklejohn.

He thought about Kay and wondered how she was getting along. She had left Harry, and was spending the entire summer with friends, someplace in Maine. She had told Llew she needed the time to get her life back in shape, and to think things out where he was concerned. He felt the same way, and hoped that their eventual decisions would be mutually compatible.

It was close to one o'clock, and he still had to grab a bite to eat before the first interviewee showed up. He turned the radio up a notch and stepped on the gas.

Just up ahead, on an intersecting farm road, stood a battered farm wagon, hitched to an ungainly-looking horse. The stocky man sitting in the driver's seat wore overalls and a wide straw hat. Beneath the hat were a pair of reflective sunglasses, and behind those were a pair of glazed, bloodshot eyes.

As Llew's car zipped past, the man made a sound like "Ih, ih" as a wide grin spread across his stubbled face. Then he lifted the reins, gave them a snap, and shouted:

"Giddap!"